THE MYTH OF

DR. KUGELMAN

The Myth of Dr. Kugelman
Copyright © 2015 by David Margolis

Cover by Kristina Blank Makansi

ISBN: 978-0-9912154-2-3

Printed in U.S.A

THE MYTH OF DR. KUGELMAN

BY DAVID MARGOLIS, MD

I would like to dedicate this book to my wife Laura who endured my single-minded obsession while writing this novel.

CHAPTER ONE

Zeus was in agony, and if gods could die he would have considered suicide. He had been awakened before sunrise by cramps shooting through his belly like the thunderbolts that he had once used, and his abdomen seemed ready to explode. Yet he was not surprised that his intestines were acting unruly, for he had partied into the wee hours, gorging and boozing, trying to relieve his mind of the depressing thoughts that constantly haunted him. Sadly, the physician god Asclepius and his four physician daughters had been unable to quell his gastrointestinal upheavals, while the great healer, Hippocrates, a mere mortal, had left the world of the living in 370 B.C. The man's soul now resided in the Elysian Fields, the mythological counterpart to heaven, and Zeus soon realized, like many earthlings, that a good family physician was hard to replace.

As he lay on the divine bed, curled up in the fetal position, his thoughts returned to the source of his despondence. It had been thousands of years since anyone had worshiped him or his pantheon of gods. With the start of the new millennium, he had hoped that conditions would improve, yet neither a prayer nor a blessing had come his way; even a curse would have been welcomed, but to no avail. Most of the Olympians had gone into semi-retirement or had suffered eternal burnout, and revenue to support the pagan theology had completely dried up, causing his palace to experience poorly flushing toilets and a leaking roof. To his mortification, cheap Formica had replaced many of the beautiful marble accoutrements, and there was no heat or electricity in the building for days at a time. As another excruciating spasm ripped through his gut, Zeus called for his slave, the eunuch Castro, to bring him a laxative tea made from Senna leaves. Finally, after a productive sojourn on the celestial commode, he fell into a fitful sleep.

Zeus, despite being a god, had an unusual family tree. His father Cronus (yes, Father Time was really a father), married his sister Rhea, who was Zeus's mother as well as his aunt. Cronus had become king of the gods when he deposed his father, the sky god Uranus, by castrating him with a sickle, and throwing his testicles into the sea. However, before he died, Uranus informed Cronus that he in turn would be eliminated by one of his children. This put the crafty Cronus in a bind, because for reasons unknown, he kept having children with his sister, a total of five, and in order to thwart this prophecy, he decided to swallow them whole like a python ingesting an unsuspecting rodent. To his dismay, these empyreal godlets weren't digestible, and they languished in his stomach without ever exiting his anus.

Rhea became fed up after five children had been transferred from her uterus to her husband's gut, so she developed a plan. When Zeus was born, she filled the infant's swaddling blanket with rocks, deceiving the unsuspecting Cronus into thinking he was swallowing a child, when in reality he was ingesting a pile of rubble. After that, she inveigled her husband to drink some nectar mixed with mustard. This potion must have been plenty hot, for soon afterwards Cronus vomited the limestone and granite composite followed by the five children who had reached adolescence while in his stomach. They instantly elected Zeus as their leader even though he was still a young child, and an epic war commenced between Zeus and his father.

Zeus rounded up several Cyclops deep in the marrow of the earth, grotesque beings with just one eye and one bushy eyebrow. Nonetheless, despite their monocular vision, these fellows were terrific fighters. They were joined by the Giants known as Hundred-handed Ones. These beings could deliver some punches with their left, left, left etc., right, right, right etc., combinations. Still, Cronus had his own cronies, the Titans. They were enormous creatures, over seven feet tall and colossally muscular. A great battle ensued. For the first time, Zeus unleashed his thunderbolts which were exceedingly effective. Cronus and the Titans were defeated and Zeus took over as king of the Olympian gods.

Zeus was not an exemplary god. In fact, he had many failings, possibly the result of a turbulent upbringing without parental guidance, because for reasons not entirely clear, his mother Rhea disappeared from sight. The burdens of a widow with six kids may have unnerved her, but we will never know. Depending on the version of the myth that one reads, Zeus was raised by: a) his grandmother, b) a goat, c) a nymph, d) a different nymph, e) a third nymph named Mellissa who fed him goat's milk, or f) by a shepherd who raised goats. Regardless of these ambiguities, it's clear that nymphs and goats were primary players in the rearing of young Zeus.

At an early age, he wedded his older sister Hera-- you would think these deities might have learned--one of the gods who had marinated in the enteric juices of Cronus. That acerbic ordeal may have imbedded a bilious personality, for Hera was a scheming and mendacious goddess who was prone to jealousy, but she had some justification, for to put it simply, Zeus was an unscrupulous philanderer. Moreover, there was no such thing as a condom in those times because this immortal had a plethora of illegitimate offspring, for while he had three children with Hera (some say six), he had over one hundred children with goddesses, princesses, queens, maidens, another sister, and his own daughter Persephone. Then there was the damsel Io, whom Zeus turned into a cow to prevent Hera from discovering his infidelity. Even so, this was polytheism, and many gods were needed to supply subjects for the temples and shrines that the ancient Greeks liked to build. But this adultery had transpired eons ago, and maybe it was his depression, or just his age, estimated between five thousand and ten million years old, but Zeus had lost his mojo. The scantily clad nymphs, fairies, sylphs and naiads that paraded by his throne no longer stirred a carnal yearning in him, and of late, he had become cognizant that he needed to produce more substance than a licentious liturgy to entice the mortals on Earth to worship him again.

He had been spiteful and vindictive, devising punishments for his subjects which, if not ungodly, were significantly inhumane. In his heyday, he had an absence of remorse, which is less noticeable, although still present in the deities of the modern era: the likes of Yahweh, Allah, The Father who Art in Heaven, and a Hindu god or two. Take for example Prometheus. He was a member of the defeated Titans, but became a turncoat and went over to Zeus's side. In appreciation, The Supreme One gave him the job of creating man. Prometheus started by making clay models of wormlike animals and frogs, then bringing them to life. Soon he had a fairly serviceable monkey. He cut off the tail, moved the thumbs around, set the creature upright, and presto, humans were born. Prometheus became concerned that mankind did not know fire. When he broached the subject with the top-god one day, Zeus had a callous explanation, don't give man too much knowledge, keep him in the dark and demand obedience; not much empathy for a divinity. But Prometheus wasn't satisfied with that explanation as he witnessed the stringy mortals trying to chow down the stringy morsels of raw meat while huddling in their huts on frigid nights. One morning at sunrise, he took a reed and held it to the sun, then brought the burning stalk down the mountain while all the inhabitants intoned in unison, *come on Promy, start my fire.* After that, man was able to heat and illuminate his dwelling, cook his food, and forge utensils. In spite of that, Zeus was angered when he observed the happiness of his subjects, for Prometheus had disobeyed his orders. He chained the luckless Titan to a rock and had an eagle eat at his liver until he was finally rescued by Hercules, but that's another story.

When Zeus awoke late in the afternoon, he was determined to find a solution to the declining fortunes of his religion. He decided to seek out his illegitimate son Apollo, the god of truth, prophecy, music and poetry. Apollo kept an oracle at Delphi and relayed his predictions through a bevy of priestesses. Men and gods came to hear the pronouncements from the women as they sat on a three-legged stool, but sorrowfully, Apollo hadn't produced a correct prediction in ages, while the temple had become more of a tourist attraction in modern times. He tried his hand at sports betting, learning the hard way that it was more difficult to make money on NFL contests than the pentathlon winner at the Pythian Games. Apollo had stopped strumming his melodious lyre a long time ago and was currently listening to Bruce Springsteen's *Thunder Road* on his iPod. He reluctantly removed his headphones when he saw his father approach. "Son, I've got a job for you, something that's very important to me and to the survival of our creed. You may have noticed that things are a bit shabby around here, the mattresses are lumpy, the power keeps going out and the toilet keeps plugging from those rusty pipes and--"

"Dad, just get to the point."

Zeus was about to unload a little thunder himself on his insolent son, but instead he pleaded. "I need the oracle's help, some advice on how to bring back the old time religion."

"You call this place a religion, this den of debauchery, this home of the hedonist, this lair of lustfulness?"

"Oh, I plan to eliminate all that, then start again with a clean slate."

"Dad, I'm busy. There's no hope. Forget about it."

At that point Zeus grabbed the iPod, yanked out the earphones and was about to throw the entire contraption into the Aegean Sea when Apollo stopped him. "O.K, O.K. put that down, let me talk to my people and come up with something." He consulted with a somewhat frumpy priestess, Virginia, and the next day returned to Zeus with his counsel. "Dad, here's the plan. You need to send one of the gods back to Earth to perform great deeds and gain publicity for you and your religion. Personally, I think it's a longshot, but I guess you have nothing to lose at this point."

"That's it!" cried Zeus. "I need a promotional god, but whom?" He spent the next few days pondering this strategy. Aphrodite came to mind, the goddess of love and beauty, whom he had not seen in years. *She's a gorgeous babe, a real show stopper, and she can start a line of perfumes like Elizabeth Taylor or an exercise video a la Jane Fonda.* He summoned her to Mt Olympus, but to his dismay, she had put on some weight and was carrying a muffin top around the waist, and her recent plastic surgery--yes, even Gods need a tuck in a place or two--had been of questionable benefit. He knew immediately that she would not fill the bill. He took Hermes out of consideration, deducing that moderns had no need for messengers with the advent of social media, and he rejected Dionysus--the Romans called him Bacchus--believing that wine drinking and lecherous orgies were unlikely to sanctify the old beliefs.

Then Hades recused himself, preferring to live in Hell rather than as an earthling in the twenty-first century. Zeus' musings were interrupted by a loud crash. Another son, Hercules, had arrived at the palace inebriated. In his stupor, the pickled god had knocked over a priceless vase that had been passed down from Granddaddy Uranus.

Hercules was begat from a Zeusian relationship with Alcmena, a mortal woman. He was conceived when Zeus took the form of her husband and seduced her on the couple's wedding night. Naturally, Hera was angry with Zeus over yet another adulterous affair, so she sent two serpents to the crib to kill Hercules and his twin brother. To everyone's astonishment, the infant grabbed both snakes by the neck and strangled them. The resentful Hera didn't give up that easily, and she bided her time. When Hercules married, she cast a spell that caused him to go mad and kill his wife and three children. In order to redeem himself, he was forced to execute twelve incredibly difficult labors which were devised by the cowardly King Eurystheus. Among others, he had to eliminate a lion; kill a hydra monster with nine heads; flush out feces from a sovereign's stable; round up ferocious cattle while subduing a two-headed dog; gather golden apples while assisting Atlas in scaffolding the sky; and deliver the three-headed dog Cerberus to the craven king. Eurystheus was terrified by the vicious tricranial canine and sent him back to Hades posthaste. Initially, Hercules was only required to complete ten tasks but two of them were disallowed because of outside assistance-- today we would put an asterisk beside them. After that, the he-man was the star performer in a war between the gods and a residual group of obstreperous Titans. These behemoths were soundly routed by the strapping hero and his minions. Zeus made Hercules a deity after he was immolated by a flammable robe given to him by his petulant second wife.

Many eons passed. In that time Hercules grew lazy and succumbed to wantonness. He ceased working out and his enormous strength dissipated. His large pectoral muscles morphed into man boobs, while his six-pack transformed into an unsightly paunch. He palled around with his half-brother, Dionysus--another illegitimate son--drinking a daily cask of wine, and roaming the environs of Mt. Olympus propositioning sensuous damsels and maidens. In a drunken stupor, he stole the chariot from Helios and crashed it into an asteroid. Hera constantly kvetched to Zeus about the misdeeds of his wayward son. Finally, she gave him an ultimatum: *corral Hercules or find another queen.* Her husband agreed that the situation was becoming intolerable, but what could be done? That evening while Zeus was imbibing a good bottle of wine with a fine-looking man named Ganymede--yes, Zeus was bisexual--the priestess Virginia arrived from Delphi to visit the deity in person.

"I'm sorry to inconvenience your highness at this inappropriate time, but I merely want to refine my prediction about your promotional project." She said this as Zeus was arranging to have her removed from his presence by the palace guards; yet this topic greatly interested him, so he paused to hear her out. "I suggest that you send your son Hercules back to Earth to perform a modern set of labors and thus restore the ancient Greek religion."

The Preeminent Being jumped from his royal

recliner and exclaimed, "By Jove, what a sockdolager! I'll reincarnate my illegitimate son. He'll generate pagan publicity and I can remove the indolent lout from the mountain. Hercules, born of the inappropriate conception, can Jesus top that? Now if I could only find a doctor who could cure my belly aches, I'd be in heaven. I can't wait to tell Hera the news. Maybe I'll get lucky tonight." And poor Ganymede was ushered out through the servant's exit.

CHAPTER TWO

Dr. Norman Kugelman was not a handsome man, not by a longshot. His hair was flecked with gray and an embarrassing shiny bit of scalp had revealed itself at the apex of his skull and was slowly expanding, at the same pace that the arctic ice cap was slowly receding. His eyes were dark and deep in their sockets, well protected from the sun and the rain which they seldom encountered. A pair of gold rimmed bifocals perched themselves on both flanks of his out-sized nose. The nasal bone itself was reasonably straight, but the cartilaginous component took a large bend downward forming a major hook, so that the tip wasn't far from a luxuriant mustache. Kugelman had contemplated shaving it off, except this would have required extra time in the morning to scrape his upper lip with a razor, time that Kugelman didn't have in his haste to get to his work. His sallow jowls had started their descent from the mandible into the upper reaches of his neck, while his ears had found ways to grow hair that they had not known about when he was a younger man. In short, when he put on a white lab coat and placed a stethoscope around his collar, Norman Kugelman had the appearance of a middle-aged Jewish doctor, which in fact he was.

Kugelman had a successful gastroenterology practice in New Jersey where he lived with his wife, Selma, and their nine year old son, Adam. Over the years, his workload of the sick, and the fearful of being sick, had multiplied, but because of diminished reimbursement from the insurance carriers, and a rising clientele of poorer black and Latino patients, his longer hours at the job had not resulted in a commensurate increase in the revenue of the practice. There had been white flight from the location of his office in Paterson to more affluent neighborhoods. Indeed, the Kugelmans themselves had moved several years ago to a large two story brick dwelling with white Doric columns in the prosperous town of Ridgewood, even though this required a twenty minute commute to his work. Nonetheless, he had always had concern for the less fortunate, and would often treat patients for free if they lacked health coverage. Lately, in an attempt to decrease his time at work and appease his wife, Kugelman had brought other MD's into the practice, allowing the couple to enjoy idyllic vacations in Hawaii or exclusive cruises to the Caribbean and Europe. The doctor dutifully attended religious services at the synagogue, and had served a term on the governing board of the congregation. A generous fellow, he gave a sizeable portion of his salary to several charities. He even volunteered to build a house with Habitat for Humanity, though his skill as a carpenter, like most Jewish men, was minimal.

He had a wry sense of humor about his choice of such an unpleasant career, and joked that if the heart surgeon was the CEO of the human body, then the gastroenterologist was the janitor who cleaned the toilet. Because of the incongruousness of belonging to such an indecorous profession, he deflected questions as to the reason for his selection of this specialty with awkward attempts at comedy. *I wanted to be a plumber and couldn't get into plumbing school* was his stock answer for a while, or he'd reply, *I finished last in my class in medical school and this was the best job I could find.* He quickly learned never to use that one with a patient. Then he tried, *It was a process of elimination*, but of late, he had employed a more philosophical aphorism. *Most people look ahead in life. I look behind.* When he needed to pick a name for the corporation that would own the building housing his office and outpatient colonoscopy center, he came up with "Uranus Land Company."

Norman met his wife Selma at SUNY on Long Island. She was from an orthodox Jewish family of very modest means. Her father owned a struggling tailor shop in Brooklyn, and her mother supplemented the family's income by babysitting for wealthy Wall Street folks. The socially awkward Kugelman couldn't believe his luck when he stole Selma away from his best friend, five foot three inch Howard Fishman, at the fraternity Hanukkah bash. Kugelman and Fishman had grown up together in Great Neck, and Howard hoped to have a career directing movies in Hollywood. He had met Selma in an acting class and asked her to the party. Kugelman was attracted by her intelligence and wit, and he was smitten by her inquisitive brown eyes and jet black hair complemented by a pimple-free alabaster complexion. Selma, in turn, was impressed with his brilliant academic record (he was Phi Beta Kappa) and his burning desire to become a doctor. And she couldn't stop laughing at his silly jokes. Kugelman asked his friend if he could escort her home, and the hapless Fishman nodded his assent. Thus, the romance began. In her senior year, Selma was selected for the role of Ophelia in Shakespeare's Hamlet, put on by the drama department and directed by Howard. Norman attended every performance. The couple spent evenings together reading the great bard's sonnets and attending Woody Allen movies, and their sex life was new and exciting. Until they met, both of them had been virgins.

When Norman was accepted to medical school at Washington University in St. Louis, he asked Selma to marry him. She had planned to move to Manhattan to fulfill her dream as a Broadway actress, but her mother convinced her that being married to a doctor would eliminate her financial worries forever. Howard was the best man at the wedding, and soon after, he moved to Los Angeles to pursue an uncertain film career. In St. Louis, Selma sold women's apparel to help pay the bills, but she did manage to land a few parts in the local theater. After Norman graduated from medical school, the couple moved back East. Norman completed his training at Rutgers, while Selma continued to work in retail and perform with an amateur Shakespearean company.

Selma had difficulty conceiving, and the couple was considering in-vitro fertilization, when out of the blue she became pregnant at age thirty-five. The mama-to-be was a bit prickly as some pregnant women can be after the initial excitement of the fecundity wanes. Her midnight yen for pickles was only a minor craving compared to her passion to chastise her sleepy husband for not getting out of bed to buy a jar of gherkins at the all night grocery across town. In spite of that, it was all worth it in the end when eight pound nine ounce Adam came into the world. Norman took the morning off and cancelled his office hours for that day, although the compulsive physician did make hospital rounds in the evening to the annoyance of the new mother. After Adam was born, Selma quit her job at Macy's, and her modest acting career came to an end.

Unfortunately, the years took a toll on the marriage as Kugelman matriculated from a self-centered medical student to a workaholic doctor. Selma was no longer a lively, amusing university student and an aspiring actress. Her raven hair required a significant injection of color on a monthly basis, and the constant battle with her weight had been lost after her son was born. She had become, some might say, a nagging wife, constantly nitpicking at him about little things: leaving his dirty underwear in the middle of the bedroom floor, forgetting to take out the garbage on the appropriate day, or intermittently leaving the toilet seat up. Over the years, as he became busier in the practice and worked more hours even with additional associates, her displeasure proportionally increased for reasons that weren't entirely clear; at least they weren't clear to Norman. She purposely filled the little free time that he had with a multitude of humdrum tasks such as cleaning out the garage, weeding the garden, or checking the amount of chlorine in the swimming pool, when her unenthusiastic husband only wished to read a book, take a nap, or golf at the country club, trying to lower his handicap. Nevertheless, he was resigned to her complaining and the endless assignments of petty jobs, and being the upright man that he was, he endured her fits of anger and occasional despondency as best he could. He had never been unfaithful.

Kugelman's existence would have been tolerable if he hadn't been plagued by a dilemma which in due time took on a central role in his life. That problem was his constant craving for pork which of course was against Jewish dietary laws. Norman had a legacy of eating the forbidden flesh. His grandfather had emigrated from Russia and found a job in a meat packing plant scraping together enough money to open his own butcher shop. To the surprise of his relatives, he started selling non-kosher meat to gentiles, becoming an expert in the production of pork sausages. Norman had witnessed him noshing on these wursts, away from his grandmother's watchful eye, when he had visited the store as a youngster. His father, an otolaryngologist, also had a love affair with hog victuals and had eaten two strips of bacon for breakfast almost every day of his life, although he did draw the line at ham, and patently eschewed the chewing of pork on the Jewish high holidays. When Norman and Selma were married, she insisted that they keep a kosher home. Regrettably, he became more obsessive as the years wore on, such that his pig eating eventually caused him indescribable anguish.

He would sneak out in the noon hour and visit the Rib Shack, a small restaurant that was known for its pork ribs. There, he could polish off two or three hickory smoked slabs, then hastily return to his office before his afternoon appointments commenced. On Sundays, he went to the synagogue for the weekly men's club breakfast of lox and bagels, but often left early to visit the local pancake house for some Belgian waffles with extra sausage and bacon piled high on his plate. Every Christmas, he received a large ham from one of his patients who was unaware of his religion--even if she didn't know that Kugelman was a Jewish name, his large Semitic nose should have been a giveaway. He would put the Hillshire Farm product in the break room refrigerator, and in the evening when all the employees had left, he would slice off a big hunk and ruefully devour it before heading home to Selma. Norman attended medical conventions out of town and was invited to upscale restaurants, ingesting a mammoth pork chop while listening to some expert physician extol the newest product for intestinal gas.

After his pork pig outs, Norman had sleepless nights dreading that his friends at the synagogue might find out about his salacious desire for *the other white meat.* He was tempted to make an appointment with the rabbi to discuss his compulsion, but was afraid that the holy man would never hold him in high regard again. He had performed a colonoscopy on the senior rabbi, Herschel Horowitz, removing two pre-cancerous polyps, and last year he had cured the rabbi's diarrhea, which seemed to worsen before important sermons to the congregation. At the Yom Kippur service, when it came time to atone for the sin of gluttony, Kugelman clenched his prayer book and prayed that his addiction might somehow be alleviated. He couldn't confide in Selma, for he feared that her dissatisfaction with him would only worsen, knowing that she came from an orthodox upbringing. Once he had not eaten pork for three weeks, but the next day one of his patients developed a major complication during a procedure. After work Kugelman had wolfed down some baby back beauties before arriving home, where upon he told his wife that he was too distraught to eat dinner.

One day, on his way back from the Rib Shack, the guilt ridden gastroenterologist failed to see a vehicle turning into the intersection. In retrospect he had probably gone through a red light, except there were no witnesses to corroborate this fact. Norman's small BMW T-boned a delivery truck, and though he was wearing a seat belt, he suffered a concussion, several cracked ribs, a punctured lung, as well as a fractured femur. He was rushed to the hospital unconscious, and placed on a respirator. While Kugelman was in his obtunded state he experienced a flash of light, then a grey figure appeared, almost like a man, but he couldn't see his face.

"Who are you?" inquired the gastroenterologist.

"My name is Morris, I'm an angel sent from Yahweh."

"As a matter of fact, I don't recall any angels in the Old Testament by that name."

"No, I'm not a famous cherub like Gabriel or Raphael. I'm an underangel just like the Undersecretary of the Treasury, a lifelong civil servant that nobody has ever heard of. I was once the Norse god of silence, Hoenir, when Odin ruled. Remember him, up there in Norway? But as you know Odin became obsolete, and there wasn't much of a market for a god who kept quiet most of the time. I had to accept this humdrum position working for the God of the Chosen People and He changed my name to Morris as Moses was already taken. He calls me Moe which I despise. But I've already talked too much. You've been in a very serious but nonfatal accident so you won't need our full service for now. Just let me complete some paperwork and I'll be on my way. You can't believe the forms we have to fill out nowadays."

"Well, that's good news, but can I ask you a question about something that's been bothering me for a while?"

"Sure."

"I've got this embarrassing desire for pork. Will that prevent me from entering heaven when the day comes, if you know what I mean?"

"No I wouldn't worry too much about it. In fact Yahweh sort of regrets making that regulation for the Jews. God knows there are enough rules for you fellows, 613 commandments the last time I checked. This interdiction seemed important in the biblical epoch when pigs harbored tapeworms and roundworms, but more lethal substances such as cigarettes, booze, and drugs have become the scourges of mankind. You might not believe this, but in the past millennium the Almighty himself has developed a taste for pickled pig's feet." And with that the angel vanished.

When he awoke from the coma, his nurse, a sweet bodacious lass by the name of Polly Polk was the first person that he recognized. A few years previously, she had assisted him with his colonoscopies, before taking a job in the Intensive Care Unit. Norman slowly recovered and was transferred to the medical floor, and then to the rehab hospital. Polly came to visit him daily, even when he was no longer critical. She had that reassuring smile and innate cheeriness that most nurses radiate. When she bent over him to take out his thermometer, he couldn't ignore the scent of her lavender perfume or the glimpse of the cleavage that was formed by her ample breasts. He spent many afternoons chatting with Polly, and maybe it was the morphine, but he even talked about his out of body encounter and his humiliating addiction to pork. She listened intently with a concerned expression, her lustrous blue eyes exuding sympathy and her luscious lips emitting words of encouragement. Selma visited daily, and of course she never nagged him while he was recovering, but even so, she did make a nuisance of herself to the hospital personnel with her constant carping about the lack of nursing attention for her important husband who was on the medical staff of the hospital.

Three months later, Norman returned to his practice. At first part time, but soon he was carrying a full load. After a while, he noticed that he had lost his hankering for hog flesh. The angel had assuaged his anxiety, and despite the fact that he could eat all the bacon, ham, and ribs that he wished, the Jewish man had totally lost his craving. He was on top of the world; his greatest burden had been lifted; he was a free man. When Norman ran into Polly at the hospital, he could hardly contain himself, bursting with news about his good fortune. She was happy for him, and gave him a hug. Alarmingly, this innocuous gesture stirred a ribald sensation in his groin which greatly embarrassed him. He hurriedly turned away and left the ICU, horrified at the erotic desire that had possessed him. He lay awake in bed that night as his mind kept wandering back to the voluptuous Polly, while at the same time fearful that his wife, friends, and rabbi would think him a slimeball if they discovered his lascivious fantasies. The hours ticked by as Norman stared into the blackness of his bedroom ceiling wearing his guilt like a shroud. He had exchanged his compulsion for pork to a compulsion for Polly Polk.

CHAPTER THREE

Zeus summoned his off-the-wagon offspring to inform him of the oracle's pronouncement. At first the Hellenic hunk merely harrumphed and held his hungover head in his hands, but as he sobered up, he began to contemplate his father's proposition. He wanted to know who would select his new tasks now that King Eurystheus was no longer in the land of the living. Zeus had a ready reply. "I have already consulted with Descendants.com and have found a relative of the king who now lives in Brooklyn, New York, a hot dog vendor with the name of Demetrius Georgopoulos. His friends just call him George. Soon I will send you to the United States to meet with George and receive your assignments, so it will be necessary for you to improve your physical conditioning as your new contests will require phenomenal strength."

Hercules was apprehensive about the undertaking before him, yet he knew it was futile to oppose the wishes of his father, and besides, he was tired of his decadent life which had gone on for an eternity. He initiated a diet of arugula, fennel, and olives while disdaining the wine and baklava. He started pumping iron and felt his vitality returning. Even so, he quickly recognized that he could never recapture his strength or physique of five thousand years ago. Obviously, holding up the heavens is not something that can be done on a whim, even if he was temporarily sitting in for Atlas. On the appointed day, he hitched a ride with Helios, and with good bye huzzahs from the other gods (even Hera was there to bid him farewell), he made his way down to Earth. He was deposited in Brooklyn near the Barclays Center just before sunrise, when the inhabitants of the brick and brownstone dwellings were mostly asleep. He wandered down Flatbush Avenue toward Seventh, searching for Mr. Georgopoulos' residence. Sergeant Walter O'Malley was walking the beat that early morning and was about to interrogate the large man clad only in sandals and a loin cloth, noting that his attire was somewhat odd even for New York City, but then he recalled that the Gay Pride Parade had taken place the previous day, so he continued on his rounds. Just then, Hercules found the apartment's address, located above a laundromat, and rang the buzzer. "I am the god Hercules. I'm here to see a Mr. Demetrius Georgopoulos," he announced in a stentorian tone.

"Come on up, pal" a gravelly voice replied, as he remotely unlocked the outside door. Hercules bounded up the two flights of stairs. A corpulent, fifty-something man was waiting for him at the entrance to the flat. His frizzled mane was arranged in a small ponytail, and a bulbous nose protruded above his three-day-old beard which was most noticeable on the first roll of his double chin. He was wearing a sleeveless New York Mets t-shirt with *STRAWBERRY* on the back, purchased years ago when he had been much thinner. Thick, heavy arms hung out of both sides of the jersey and a protuberant hairy belly extruded between the shirt and his faded tartan pajama bottoms. Hercules detected a remote resemblance to someone in his past. All at once it struck him that the fellow looked like the old monarch who had given him those impossible tasks in antiquity.

George came right to the point. "I've been expecting you. I began having visions in my sleep about three weeks ago where a holy being named Virginia appeared. This apparition informed me that she worked for the god Apollo, and announced that you would be coming to Brooklyn. As a relative of the primordial king, I would be assigning your new labors. At first, I didn't believe these dreams. I assumed they were flashbacks from the hallucinogens that I used in my youth, but last night she indicated that you would be arriving today and here you are. Let's first get you out of this archaic underwear."

After breakfasting on slices of Grecian sheep cheese wedged between toasted sesame seed bagels, they proceeded to the nearest used clothing store where Hercules picked out a track suit, sneakers and some boxer shorts with red hearts on them. He started toward the door when the manager stopped him. "Yuh fohgot to pay, bustah." Hercules was about to tell him that Immortals don't pay for anything, but George quickly intervened and gave the man his credit card. Back at the apartment, he was shown the tiny bedroom where he would be residing for the next several weeks. Hercules emitted a prodigious yawn; he had slept poorly in the sparsely padded seats of the Sun God's conveyance. Soon he was fast asleep, his large body overhanging the small mattress. When he awoke, George had beef gyros delivered which Hercules swore were as tasty as any banquet that Dionysus had ever prepared.

That night, Virginia came to George with the first assignment. When Hercules awoke, he found the royal descendant already in the kitchen with a cup of coffee in his hand and an earnest expression on his face. "O.K. pal, your first task is to capture a lion that just escaped from the Bronx Zoo. I need to pick up some spicy mustard in that area. I'll give you a lift in my car but then you will be on your own." When they reached the Bronx, Hercules exited George's Mercury Marquis and set off in the direction of the zoo, eventually arriving at a small park swarming with police cars. A large crowd had gathered, and the area had been cordoned off by ropes. The lion was surrounded by cops and zoo personnel. Hercules broke through the barrier and charged toward the beast with a phalanx of authorities running after him. His plan was to strangle the enormous cat with the same technique that he had used against the ancient lion. To his chagrin, one of the zoo employees shot the brute with a tranquilizer gun before he got near the animal. Hercules saw the lion collapse in a stupor. The next moment he was shoved to the ground, slapped in hand cuffs and foot shackles, and thrown in a paddy wagon on the way to the precinct jail. When he arrived at the police station the officer asked him his name. "Hercules," he replied.

"Hercules, is that a first or a last name?"

"My full name, thrust on me by mother and the supreme god Zeus, is Hercules from Thebes," answered the deity.

"OK, Hercules Frum-Thebes. Are you related to the Frums who own the bakery in Brooklyn Heights? They make a wonderful rye bread with caraway seeds."

"No, my esteemed family is not in the bagel business, more like the fable business," answered the Greek truthfully. The officer led Hercules into a cell, and later that evening George paid the bail and the Powerful One was free on bond. He took to his bed, exhausted from his failed endeavor.

Hercules awoke the next morning stiff and sore. George was already dressed. "I know the first labor was a debacle but I've got good news, bud. Last night, Ginny, that's what I call her, came to me with a new assignment. If you remember, your second task in antiquity was to exterminate the nine-headed hydra, but Apollo and his think tank couldn't find a serpent with that many heads, so they substituted a hydrant. Your job today is to remove an SUV that has crashed into one. The spewing water has trapped some children in a nearby day care center. Go get 'em, pal."

Hercules mulled this over and thought to himself. "Killing monsters is one thing, but emergency plumbing feats are not in my divine repertoire." Nevertheless, after consulting George's Garmin, he located the accident site. The brawny divinity pushed with his mighty strength against the front end of the truck, trying to extricate it from its perch on top of the hydrant, but it wouldn't budge. He lost his balance, hit his head on the fender, and fell backwards into the small lake that had formed around the wreck. After that, all he remembered was an emergency medical technician pulling him from the water. In the meantime, the firemen arrived, shut off the water main, extricated the vehicle, and carried the toddlers through the flooded street to their anxious parents. Hercules, wrapped in a flannel blanket, sat shivering on the curb with a doleful look on his face. The EMT who had rescued him came over and patted him on the back. "Next time let the professionals handle it and stay out of our way." That was the ultimate humiliation for the Super-hero, and he dejectedly trudged back to the apartment.

George was sympathetic as Hercules related this shameful misadventure. "O.K. bud, you've had a little bad luck, but I still have faith in the Olympian brain trust. I'll have a new assignment for you tomorrow." Hercules slept fitfully. He had aspirated some water which resulted in paroxysms of coughing. Despite his discomfort, he stumbled out of bed the next day and received his third task from George. "There's a rumor that you're skillful at taming ferocious dogs. A savage canine attacked a kid in Queens today, took a bite of his leg. The Animal Control was called and they found the mutt in an abandoned dwelling. Your task is to break into the house and butcher the dog."

Hercules put on his track suit, placed a small knife in his pocket, grabbed a hunk of feta cheese should he become hungry, then set off to complete the task. He started jogging and eventually came upon a group of people and a police van in front of a shabby house with an absent window pane. He approached the officer and politely inquired if he could be of help in subduing the animal. The cop questioned him, "Do you have any experience with vicious dogs?" Hercules replied. "As the great gods on Mt. Olympus will attest, I have vanquished a two headed dog and ensnared a three headed dog." The officer was caught off guard by this assertion. Before he could answer, Hercules had entered the vacant dwelling.

In the late afternoon, the interior of the house was dark, and at first, Hercules could only make out shapes in the living room: a beat up sofa, a shabby armchair with some springs exposed, and a couple of crack pipes on the floor. He heard a low-pitched growl, and when he looked in the direction of the sound he could barely distinguish the form of a cur with a thick body, short legs and an outsized head. The growling became an aggressive bark, as the animal bounded toward him bearing his fangs. Hercules tensed. He aligned himself in a crouch and prepared for the dog to strike at the same time reaching into his pocket for the weapon. Instead, his hand encountered the lump of cheese that he had brought with him. Hercules pulled it out and placed it in his other hand to better find the blade hidden away in his pants. Straightaway the dog quit snarling, tilted his head to one side, and started sniffing, as he caught the scent of the goat curds. The canine trotted up to him, then sat with his tongue hanging out. Hercules offered a morsel to the dog who ravenously devoured it. After eating all of the cheese, he lay down at the brawny man's feet, and looked at him with admiring eyes as if to communicate *that's the best meal I've ever eaten!* The small assemblage broke into a cheer as Hercules exited with his new companion.

At that moment a small boy ran up to the Immortal.

"That's my dog, Bernie!" shouted the little fellow. "We were at the park when some kids from school started to really pick on me. They called me a sissy. Then they kicked dirt on my shoes and they like pushed me down. I kind a scraped my knee." He pointed to a small abrasion. "Anyway, Bernie took out after one of them and bit him on the leg. Then they chased after him. He like jumped through the broken window into the house."

The lad's mother broke through the crowd, and addressed the deity. "I can't thank you enough. I just talked to the bully's mother. She says her boy only had a superficial wound, and maybe that was coming to him for what he did."

"I appreciate your thankfulness. My name is Hercules, Hercules from Thebes."

"Nice to meet you Mr. Frum. My name is Alice Kapusta and that's my son Jimmy. We live just a few streets over. Why don't you come by and I'll reward you with my blueberry muffins." He accepted her offer and the three of them walked to the house with Bernie in tow on his leash.

Their modest frame home was a short distance away. From the outside it was a bit rundown and needed a coat of paint, but inside, it was well kept. Alice went into the kitchen while Hercules and Jimmy sat out in the living room. Bernie, who was exhausted from his exertions, promptly fell asleep on the rug. The muscular god broke the silence by asking, "Young man, do you live here with your Mother and Father?"

"No, just my Mom. You see, my Dad lives in Jersey. I'm in the fifth grade and like my best friend is Bernie."

Just then, Alice entered the room with the delicacies.

For the first time Hercules noticed her perfectly sculptured attributes wedged into a gauzy tank top and a pair of extremely short shorts. "Mr. Frum, tell me what brought you to this part of Queens today?"

Hercules decided to bend the truth a smidgen. "Mrs. Kapusta, I've recently immigrated to America from Greece. I'm staying with my honorable and generous cousin Demetrius Georgopoulos, who lives in Brooklyn, New York. A few years ago my wife and three children were unfortunately killed in a vehicular accident. I've decided to make a fresh start in this great country in order to ease my grief. I run several miles a day to keep my sanity, and I just happened by the house where your canine was imprisoned so ruthlessly."

A saddened expression clouded her demeanor, "I'm terribly sorry to hear that. That's an awful thing to have happened to anyone. What was your occupation in Greece?"

Hercules countered off handedly, "I was a theologian in the old country. I hope to enter into a commercial enterprise in the United States of America. I'm looking into the restaurant business. James informs me that your husband lives in the state of New Jersey."

"Boris Kapusta is my ex-husband. In Polish, Kapusta means cabbage. After the divorce, we had to sell our home. Jimmy and I moved to this dump to be nearer my family. In New Jersey, I was a receptionist in a doctor's office. Now I'm working as a waitress until I can find a job in the medical field. Please stay for dinner. I've got a pot roast in the oven. It's more than Jimmy and I can eat tonight."

Hercules was taken aback by her boldness. He had

an overwhelming desire to accept the invitation but instead he answered, "Thank you for your hospitality Alice Kapusta, but I need to be taking my leave of you and your noble son. I told my cousin I was going out for a small quantity of exercise, and I've been absent over three hours."

At the apartment, George was waiting for him with a wide smile on his visage. "Nice going pal. You really tamed that blood-thirsty pooch. I just got word from Ginny."

Hercules was about to reply that the dog was quite harmless but he elected to change the subject. "I'm starting to like it here in the magnificent country of America. I think I'll take up residence for a while. Do you desire an extra employee in the hot dog emporium?"

George gave him an astonished look. "You've got to be kidding me, right? You're a god, what do you want with my schlock enterprise?"

"I believe I would desire to learn about your operation. At the present time, the frankfurter occupation seems more attractive than the god profession."

"Well, if you're interested, I could use some help until the big boys think up another task for you."

George's food cart was situated in downtown Brooklyn. He taught the Greek divinity the technique of grilling wieners and imbedding them in buns with gobs of greasy onions and mustard. Soon he had him working the cash register and swiping the credit cards.

A few days later, Hercules ran into George as he was exiting the solitary bathroom--his prostatitis was acting up again. The king's kin had a worried look on his face. "I had the dream last night," George remarked in his raspy voice. "Zeus was disappointed that you didn't kill the mutt. He's getting annoyed. You know, everyone knows your strength. Heck, you held the world on your shoulders once upon a time. There's been a construction accident. You need to get over there pal, and free a poor guy who has been trapped under a girder."

Sergeant O'Malley recognized the Immortal when he showed up at the site. "The last time I saw you I thought you were auditioning for a Charlton Heston movie" he quipped. "There was an equipment malfunction. A large steel beam fell on the unlucky fellow and pinned him to the ground. We're waiting for another crane to arrive." Hercules approached the victim. "My leg has been crushed. I can't take the pain!" the fellow croaked in an anguished tone.

Hercules took charge. "I'm going to lift the beam about a foot and when I do, move your leg away as fast as possible." The hero grasped the bar in his two large hands. With a mighty thrust from his powerful legs, he raised the piece of steel just enough for the man to pull his limb free. The small gathering gasped at this manifestation of superhuman strength while the unfortunate chap was immediately placed in an ambulance for a trip to the nearest trauma hospital. A news reporter tried to interview him, but Hercules brushed him off. He was disillusioned with these contemporary contests. The rush of excitement that he had experienced in ancient times was no longer present. His mind kept drifting to Alice.

George was ecstatic. "Way to go bud. You know, I can hardly wait to go to bed tonight so I can find out about your next assignment."

Hercules stared at him with a phlegmatic expression.

"My lumbago has reactivated from the heavy exertion. I'll be retiring to my bed, George."

At six a.m., the regal relative shook Hercules awake. "You won't believe the new job. Ginny came to me last night with a doozy. The oracle remembered your skill in cleaning the dung in the king's stables. She told me the crap had been there for thirty years. Well, there's been a backup of one of the municipal sewers on Long Island. Your task is to go down a manhole and get that sucker unblocked."

Hercules remained silent as George left for work. He had no intention of travelling to Long Island. That afternoon, he took the subway to Alice's house and knocked on the door. Jimmy answered with Bernie close behind. "I've come by to say hello, James. Is your mother home?"

"No, but you know, she should here soon. Like she gets off work right about now. Do you want to play some catch? I have an extra glove."

"I would be pleased to throw the ball with you. In fact, I was a champion in the shot put at the games of ancient Corinth. I always competed completely naked, but I'm sure your mother would not approve of that." They went into the tiny back yard and started tossing the ball to each other. Shortly Alice appeared from inside the house. She was obviously pleased to see the big fellow.

"Mr. Frum, it's good to see you again."

"I am here to honor your dinner invitation, Alice Kapusta."

"That'd be great. I'll put some steaks on the grill and mash some potatoes. We have some left over chocolate cake." Alice was an excellent cook. Hercules asked for second helpings and then a third. After putting Jimmy to bed they sat on the sofa and watched an old western on TV. He worked up the courage to hold her hand and was surprised that she didn't resist. Before long it was ten o'clock and Alice had to get up early the next morning. As they rose from the sofa, Hercules unexpectedly embraced her; their lips touched in a brief kiss, then a longer one as he felt the softness of her tongue. She pulled away, and Hercules, his heart pounding with excitement, headed toward the front door.

"When will you be coming back, Mr. Frum, or can I call you Herky?"

"Tomorrow," answered Hercules "I'll return tomorrow, and I would be privileged to accept the appellation of Herky."

When he returned to the flat, George was waiting for him. "I watched the evening news, pal. When the obstructed sewer story came up, all I saw was a large Roto Rooter truck. You weren't anywhere in sight. What happened?"

"I spent the day with Alice and young James."

"You've got to be kidding me? Are you nuts?"

"I wasn't in the mood for shoveling the waste of humans and beasts. Inform the priestess that I refuse to perform any more of her distasteful tasks."

The next day the door buzzer buzzed and George heard O'Malley's voice on the intercom. "I found this transvestite on the sidewalk dressed in a bird costume. He says he's looking for his brother Hercules." When the hot dog proprietor opened the door, he saw a man wearing a porkpie hat with little wings, a turquoise tunic, a gold earring, and a silk ascot secured impeccably around his neck. He had appendages growing from his Achilles tendons which looked like flippers on backwards except they were covered with feathers. "Sir, I've got a message for my brother."

At that moment Hercules came to the door with a smile on his face. "Ah Hermes, come on in and share some divine baklava, then take a box for your divine comrades."

Hermes ignored the attempt at humor. "Zeus is displeased with your pathetic performance. He orders you out of the mortal world and back to Olympus."

The face of the preternatural Popeye turned scarlet and his giant muscles started to tense. "Inform my esteemed father that I have tired of being a deity. For the first time in a millennium, I've found love with the beautiful Alice Kapusta, and I want to spend a human life with her. As they say in America, tell Papa to go have intercourse with himself!"

Hermes was stupefied at the intensity of his diatribe. He hadn't seen Hercules like this since the battles with the Titans. "If I come back without you, Zeus will go ballistic. I fear the retribution that he will exact from your hide."

"I am willing to accept the consequences of my actions, dear brother." Then he picked up Hermes in his burly arms, deposited him on the stairs, and slammed the door.

When the messenger returned to Olympus, Zeus was finishing a five course meal with a large helping of ambrosia, the nourishment of deities, smothered in whipping cream from the finest goats on the mountain. He went into a frenzy when informed that Hercules had disobeyed his orders, and stormed around the palace cursing his insubordinate offspring. Soon his gut started to rumble uncontrollably. Paroxysms of pain radiated from the left side of his abdomen down to his rectum, and despite superhuman effort, a good passage of wind was not forthcoming. "Not only has my son flubbed his new labors, that macho miscreant of mythology has decided to stay on the planet as an average Joe," he fumed. "By Jove, I'll show that upstart who's boss in this universe! Can someone fetch me a doctor?"

Shortly thereafter, Hercules announced to George that he was moving in with Alice. George shrugged his shoulders and fingered the hairs inside his nose but didn't attempt to dissuade him. He was relieved that he would no longer need to share the toilet, particularly during the prostate flare-ups. Hercules continued to work part time at the hot dog stand while helping Alice around the house. She taught him to vacuum and dust, a bit mundane for a former god, but he took satisfaction in earning his keep, and he rapidly discovered that having sex with fetching Alice was infinitely more enjoyable than any mountain nymph or aquatic naiad. Jimmy looked to Hercules as a father figure, replacing the erratic Kapusta. He listened intently as Hercules regaled him with stories of his feats of strength. The kid began to brag to his classmates that his mom's boyfriend was the most powerful man in the universe. Alice became unsettled, hearing these amazing tales, and she wondered about the true identity of this immigrant who had come into her life. When she questioned the inscrutable hulk, he just laughed, saying "Children will be children." Hercules repeated the story that he had been a body builder in Greece, and had won several contests of strength when he wasn't doing god's work, though Alice had never seen him reading the Bible or attending any house of worship.

George was disappointed by the setbacks that the Olympian had encountered with his twenty-first century tasks. Yet they remained friends, and Hercules continued to work at the hot dog stand. One muggy August evening, George treated them all to a ballgame of the fifth-place Mets, where the low flying jets were noisier than the small crowd. Alice remembered going to games with her father and brother when there were only twelve thousand fans in attendance, and who could forget the 1993 season when they lost 103 games? Of course, little Jimmy was a huge fan. He dreamed, like every other red blooded American kid, that his favorite team would someday win another World Series. He would be their star pitcher, forgetting for the moment that he currently played right field and batted last on his Little League baseball team. During the seventh inning stretch, Herky took Jimmy to the concession stand for a bathroom visitation and some ice cream. Alice was alone with George as he wiped mustard from his face, missing a few fragments that clinged to his stubbly beard.

"I want to thank you for inviting us to the game. Jimmy couldn't sleep the last few days. He was so excited about tonight."

"It's my pleasure. I've been a Mets fan all my life, ma'am. I went to high school with the original Mr. Met. He was recently elected to the Mascot Hall of Fame. I always hated the Yankees." George took a large bite of the frankfurter with a pensive look on his countenance. He slowly chewed the large mouthful. "These hot dogs can't compare to my creations. The buns are a bit stale, plus, they don't use Hebrew Nationals like I do. The Jews know how to make a wiener. And if they only sautéed the onions in some olive oil…." Alice interrupted his ruminations on the competition. She had something else to discuss before her boys came back with their food.

"So Mr. Georgopoulos, tell me about your cousin, I'd like to know more about his past."

"George, ma'am, just call me George, or Demetrius except only my dear deceased mother, may she rest her soul, ever called me that. I have lots of cousins. The Georgopoulos' are numerous in this part of the country. Which one do you have in mind?"

"You know who I'm talking about, my Herky honey."

"Oh, he's not exactly my cousin. Did he tell you that? No, he's sort of a religious fellow, almost like a holy man. You know from ancient Greece, up there on Mt. Olympus. Because I was a distant relative of King Eurystheus, Zeus sent him to visit me and perform some tasks. That's how he found your dog. He was supposed to kill him but he didn't. Now Zeus is angry and god knows what he will do." As he went along, George seemed relieved to get this secret off his chest. Anyhow, if this woman was living with Hercules, maybe she better know at least some of the facts.

"You're not making any sense, I don't understand. Don't jack me around, George. Ask my ex, Boris. You don't want to mess with me when I'm angry. What's this Zeus crap and these jobs he was sent to do? King who? From where?"

"He's the god Hercules ma'am. There, now you know. He's come back to Earth to complete more labors and promote the Greek religion, but now all he wants to do is sell my wieners and be with you and Jimmy." Just then, Hercules and Jimmy returned with their ice cream. The kid had two scoops of chocolate on a sugar cone. Some of the contents had already melted and were dripping on his pants. Alice turned beet red after her conversation with George but she kept silent for the rest of the game. The Mets blew a five run lead and lost to the Cardinals in ten innings, but by then most of the patrons had left so as to beat the freeway traffic and the subway congestion.

After Jimmy was put to bed, poor Hercules caught hell from Alice. He would rather have been fighting the Titans down in Tartarus than tangling with Ms. Kapusta when she was pissed, and so it all came out. He described the unusual circumstances of his birth, his twelve ancient labors, his decadent existence on the mountain, and his reincarnation to perform new duties which included slaying a vicious dog. Then he begged her forgiveness for even contemplating the evisceration of Bernie. The big fellow talked of his desire to live as a simple human being, and naturally, he expressed his eternal love for her.

Alice didn't say anything except to tell Hercules to get some blankets from the closet and sleep in the living room. Hercules just nodded, but Alice could see his eyes moistening. Little did she realize how rare it was for a god or a former god to cry, and although she was nonplussed by this recitation, her generous nature did not allow her to be angry for long. Her judgment may have been clouded by her attraction to the strong man, but all the same, she decided to take the gentle yet powerful Hercules at his word, notwithstanding that his explanation seemed out of this world.

Zeus consulted with the other gods about the cruelties he could mete out to his rebellious son. He had hoped to send a pack of savage, mythical dogs to attack Hercules, but his brother Hades, boss of the underworld, told him that Cerberus now suffered from cataracts in five out of six eyes and deafness in four of his six ears, while Orthos, the two -headed dog, had developed dementia in both brains following repeated blows to his heads administered by the Greek gods and heroes. He then contacted Poseidon in the hope of finding a sea monster, only to find out that they had gone extinct except for Puff the Magic Dragon.

The Supreme One finally came up with a plan. He would use the weapons that had made him the most feared immortal in mythology: thunderbolts. Still, there was a cause for concern. He had not used them since antiquity and these projectiles could only be made by a Cyclops. Hermes was sent to bring such a being named Brontes to the royal residence. Zeus could hardly recognize the one-eyed troglodyte as he shuffled up the stairs of the palace, using a walker with two old tennis balls anchoring the front legs.

"Good to see you, my good man, you're looking great," Zeus lied. In reality he was distressed by the ghoul's appearance. He was almost bald; the shock of black hair that he remembered had long ago vanished. His former bronze facies, a result of many hours playing in the heavens with his father, the sky-god Uranus, had resulted in a large profusion of liver spots, while his oversized globulous nose was a fiery red and pockmarked as a result of untreated rosacea. The one big eye in the center of his forehead was now covered by a large monocle with a very thick lens.

"Why have you brought me here, sire?"

"I have a special job for you. Remember those thunderbolts that you made for me so many eons ago? It was those armaments that defeated the Titans and brought me to where I am today. Hercules has angered me and I am once again in need of some bolts to fire at this disobedient son of mine. I'm ordering you to produce more of those weapons for my employment."

"Me? I haven't made one those missiles since about 800 B.C., and my two brothers have long since retired."

"I'll reward you handsomely. I'll send a voluptuous concubine to your home. I'll supply you with all the sheep mutton you can eat. By Jove, I'll even make you an appointment with a dermatologist to look at your skin."

"Oh, what use would an ancient creature like me have for any of those gifts? These days I just sit and meditate. Worldly passions and possessions are no longer paramount as I search for Zen. No, I will do it for you in gratitude for freeing me from the evil Cronus eons ago, but I must tell you this project might take a while. I'll need to locate all my former suppliers, and with my decreased vision and impaired memory I work very slowly, and I couldn't guarantee their quality. But give me three or four weeks and I'll see what I can do." Despite these disclaimers, Zeus was thrilled with the prospect of using his old armaments again, so he waited patiently for the flame throwers to be delivered.

As promised, the old ogre eventually revisited the regal residence with the thunderbolts wrapped in parchment. Zeus excitedly opened the packages like a child at Christmas. The next day he took his new toys to the edge of Mt. Olympus and hurled the first one towards the Kapusta residence. He was out of practice and the missile bounced off the ionosphere and into outer space. Zeus was undeterred, and he threw the second one with more force. It was a bit of a dud, landing in Kansas where the inhabitants passed it off as the usual sudden thunder storm that can occur in that part of the country. Encouraged by his improvement, he launched the third projectile. This one was successful and it scored a direct hit on the dwelling in Queens, but Hercules was prepared for this onslaught. He had constructed a lightning rod on the roof so that the electricity was directed harmlessly into the ground. Alice and Jimmy were shaken by the enormous flash of light and the force of the concussive sound, but Hercules just smiled and reassured them that this was Zeus playing games in the heavens. Alice suddenly felt sheepish about doubting her boyfriend's past.

Zeus was dejected by the failure of his weaponry. Moreover, his attempt to bring back Greek mythology to its previous glory had been a complete bust. He lapsed into a lugubrious funk, suffered from crying fits, and his abdominal maladies were worse than ever. He retired to the royal bedroom with a pillow over his head, refusing to talk to anyone. Finally, Hera had had enough of his self-pity. She pointed out that there had been no drinking parties, sexual harassment, or chariot accidents since Hercules had left and she was much happier without the muscled misfit. Zeus had to admit that things were more harmonious at the palace; nonetheless, he was humiliated by the unpredictable predictions of Apollo and the virginal Virginia. He summoned them to his throne and gave them the tongue lashing that he had been reserving for Hercules, and his digestion and disposition improved temporarily.

The following day, Hercules, Alice and Jimmy were eating breakfast when the doorbell rang.

"What do you want this time, brother Hermes?" groused the erstwhile hero, when he opened the door.

"It's not what you think, Hercules. I have a message from Zeus. He's still furious but he now understands that in the contemporary world there is nothing he can do about it. I'm here to announce that he grants permission for you to live as a mortal, except never again will you be allowed on Mt. Olympus."

A satisfied smile manifested the face of Hercules. Alice hugged him tight. Jimmy pumped his fist in the air and even Bernie commenced to wag his stub of a tail like a Sikorsky helicopter.

Sometime later, Hercules was at work when he was approached by an immaculately attired individual who was walking with a pronounced limp.

"My name is Donald Rich and I'm looking for a fellow by the name of Frum."

"I am that man."

"I want to thank you for saving my leg in the building accident. I was supervising the construction of my new apartment complex when the steel girder came loose. I've come to give you a ten thousand dollar reward for your services." He was hesitant about taking the money but the man insisted, and Hercules really needed the cash.

He and Alice were married on a cold November day. The former god signed the marriage document with his new moniker "Herky Frum" and listed his religion as "pagan," still respecting the ancient ways, although recently he had started attending Christian services with Alice. With the money that he received from Mr. Rich, he was able to buy his own food cart and soon began producing *Herky's Jerky Turkey*. Hercules was more content as a man than he ever had been as a god. He now understood that the inevitability of death was much superior to the lassitude of eternity, and while most humans desire to live forever in some form or another-- hence the need for gods--he resented his father for ever making him immortal.

CHAPTER FOUR

It was four a.m. when the phone rang, waking Kugelman from a deep slumber. He had been on call for the entire weekend which didn't end until seven a.m. Monday morning, so he was still on duty for a few more hours. After his guilt-producing encounter with Polly Polk six weeks previously, he attempted to eradicate the prurient hunger for her from his mind, or at least place his lust as far back in the corner of his cerebrum as he could without forgetting about her altogether, which of course the human brain under normal circumstances is unable to do. The only decent sleep that he seemed to enjoy was just before sunrise, but even this transient respite was not to be. As he fumbled at the night stand to pick up the receiver, an image of Polly crept into his consciousness, and he wished for the days when the only loins that anguished him came from a pig.

Lamentably, the phone call from the intensive care unit was the harbinger of bad news. He had been consulted to see a sixty-year-old man, Elvin Thomas, who was hemorrhaging blood from his stomach. Kugelman had no choice but to drag his tired body out of bed, shower, put on a suit and a tie, and take the lonely drive from his cushy home to the hospital in Paterson. At four-thirty a.m., there isn't much traffic on the roads, mostly hulking produce trucks delivering fruit and vegetables to the grocery stores, or fast food workers and security guards driving their beat up jalopies to their employment. The movers and shakers of the world are rarely up that early. So as the first pink sky of dawn tinted the opaque darkness, Kugelman eased his new Lexus (the BMW had been totaled in the accident) into the lot reserved for physicians, parking it next to an Infinity and two forlorn Mercedes that were already present and had probably spent the night.

When he arrived at the patient's room, he noted that a tube had been inserted through Mr. Thomas' nose, and was draining blood from his stomach into a plastic canister attached to the wall. Intensive care units--ICUs--are somewhat intimidating for gastroenterologists. These places are the happy hunting grounds of cardiologists, pulmonologists, intensivists (a new specialty), and surgeons who deal with acute medical problems on a daily basis. These chaps are experts in regard to life-saving drugs and monitoring devices, relishing the rush of adrenaline that accrues from making split second life and death decisions for these desperately ill patients. The gastroenterologist, on the other hand, is more of a laid back fellow, dealing most often with slow moving chronic diseases such as irritable bowel syndrome, colitis, Crohn's disease or hepatitis. The high stress level of the ICU had always made Kugelman a bit nervous. Had he been keen on this atmosphere, he might have become a heart specialist, or a neurosurgeon, but it was the anxiety, regardless of his joking, that was the true reason why he had not chosen a specialty with a more prestigious calling. Kugelman reviewed the patient's chart, then telephoned the gastroenterology nurse on call who was fast asleep in her bed. After hearing the doctor's voice, she immediately understood that she was to come into work, retrieve the scope from the area of the hospital where it normally resided for routine examinations, and cart it over to the ICU for an emergency procedure.

In the late 1960's, engineers invented gastroentero-logical instruments that were flexible, allowing them to be easily passed into the esophagus, stomach or colon. Fiber optic bundles were employed to bend natural light, and a small camera was placed at the tip of the device to produce an image that could be visualized on a television screen. Over the years, accessories were developed for the endoscope (also known as the gastroscope) and the colo-noscope, enabling the operator to obtain biopsies, remove polyps, cauterize bleeding arteries, or occasionally extract the wayward hunk of meat that might catch in a person's esophagus. Before long, Kugelman found himself per-forming emergency examinations at all times of the day or night. As he became older, he relished these procedures even less, although if the truth be told, he had spared many patients from extensive surgery, and as a consequence had saved many lives, but Kugelman wasn't thinking these thoughts at five am. He was already tired, and the day had barely begun.

He quickly obtained a history from Mr. Thomas, soon recognizing that he had seen this fellow about eight years previously for the very same problem, a bleeding ulcer. For anyone who has vomited blood, this is an exceptionally frightening event in their lives. After that episode, Elvin Thomas had stopped drinking alcohol and ingesting the large amount of Alka Seltzer for the ensuing hangover. A few months ago, the electrician had hurt his knee at work. He started taking ibuprofen over the counter, not comprehending that this medication was an NSAID--non-steroidal anti-inflammatory drug--similar to the aspirin in the Alka Seltzer, which had corroded his gastrointestinal tract in the first place. So there he was with his old buddy Dr. Kugelman in the ICU at five a.m.

"How ya doing doc. Sorry I interrupted your sleep," the fellow offered with a wan smile on his face.

This guy is uncommonly stoic mulled Kugelman. "Do you remember me from the last time you were here? I just reviewed your old records. As a matter of fact, it looks to be the same problem. According to the ICU doctor, you started taking those pain killers again."

"Yeah, I didn't realize that the ibuprofen was just as bad as the Alka Seltzer, pretty stupid of me."

"Yes, STUPID is the correct word" ruminated Kugelman," and if you hadn't been so unbelievably stupid I would be in a warm bed enjoying a night's sleep." Of course he didn't say anything of the sort, and in fact confusion about NSAIDS was a common mistake made by many people. Still, at the crack of dawn he was in no mood for *stupid*. But instead of excoriating Mr. Thomas, he glanced up from the computerized chart and quizzed the nurse about the vital signs, number of units of blood transfused and the medications administered.

"In just a few minutes my nurse will arrive and we'll put you to sleep. I'll pass the black snake down into the stomach to see what's going on, if you know what I mean. You will need to sign the consent form but it's the same procedure that you've had in the past." Kugelman sounded like a matter-of-fact auto mechanic, but in reality this type of skill is very similar to a plumber or a grease monkey, one just needs six years of training after four years of medical school, most of which is completely unnecessary to the job of manipulating the instrument. However, the gastroenterologist wasn't thinking about the vagaries of life at this point in time when the sun had yet to penetrate the horizon.

Kugelman started to concentrate on the job at hand and soon he had directed the scope through the esophagus and into the stomach. Then a funny thing transpired as it most often did. He forgot about his lack of sleep, Selma, Polly Polk, and the dumb mistake of Mr. Thomas. He became engrossed in the search for the bleeding blood vessel as he expertly twisted and turned through the interstices of the stomach, searching for his quarry while washing away the blood with a specialized water jet that he operated with a foot pedal. Finally, he found the culprit in the center of a whitish cavity that represented the ulcer. Kugelman was relieved that the artery was small. He injected a few milliliters of epinephrine to constrict the vessel, then cooked the artery with a heated probe placed through the channel of the endoscope. Like Zeusian magic, the bleeding stopped. The dedicated medical personnel present at that ungodly hour watched on the overhead screen, and they nodded their approval at the skill of Kugelman. For a few minutes the gastroenterologist reveled in the satisfaction of a job well done.

He removed the scope, wrote his report in the computer, and thanked the nurse who had trekked in from home to assist him at that early hour. As he was leaving the intensive care area for his car and some breakfast, he encountered Polly just arriving for her day shift at the hospital. She smiled seductively--or so he thought--and gave him a little wave. Kugelman's heart jumped to his throat upon seeing the beguiling woman, but he masked his excitement by averting his gaze and uttering the asinine phrase that has taken over our society, *have a great day*. Is there something wrong with just plain *hi* or *hello* or s*ee you later* or *good-bye*? Nowadays we feel the compunction to invoke a *great day* for everyone we meet. But Kugelman wasn't contemplating the relative goodness or badness of Polly's day. No, he was reflecting more on Polly's attributes hidden under her nurse's uniform. Even so, as he left the hospital, he tried to concentrate on his own day ahead, and he wasn't at all convinced that it would be great, which regrettably it wasn't.

When Kugelman arrived at the endoscopy center owned by the Uranus Land Company LLC, he poured himself a large cup of coffee, added a package of sweetener and ersatz milk, then smeared some low fat cream cheese on a stale bagel that had been left over from the Friday before. He perused his appointment schedule. He had ten colonoscopies and two upper endoscopies that morning, followed by fourteen office patients in the afternoon; the same schedule that he had previewed day after day for the last fifteen years. Yet unlike the Intensive Care Unit, this was his bailiwick. Most of the work had become fairly routine, and although he hated to admit it, there was a considerable ego boost from knowing that he had started from nothing, and now he was the boss of twenty-five individuals.

When he began his fellowship in gastroenterology, the scopes were in their infancy as a diagnostic tool, but colonoscopy became much more popular after Ronald Regan developed colon cancer and Katy Couric had her colonoscopy televised. In 2000, it was established that regular colonoscopies could prevent colon cancer. Soon, Kugelman was performing twenty-five colonoscopies per week. After about one thousand of these procedures, most doctors are fairly proficient, and Kugelman had performed more than fifteen thousand. His first colonoscopy that morning was uneventful. The gastroenterologist easily snaked the colonoscope, a longer version of the gastroscope, into the cecum which is the end of the line after traversing the twists and turns of the rectum, sigmoid, descending, transverse, and ascending part of the colon, in that order. Basically, the colon is a four-foot hose coiled up on itself.

When things are proceeding smoothly and the patient is asleep, the conversation turns to the personal lives of the people in the room just like the passengers riding in a car. His anesthesiologist that day was in the midst of a divorce, and Norman had to hear all the boring details of that failed relationship for the umpteenth time. The assisting nurse offered a tale about a black bear that had tipped over the garbage cans at their lake house, while the tech bragged about her brilliant granddaughter who had obtained straight A's on her report card. Kugelman, battling his emotional and physical fatigue, was surprisingly quiet. Notwithstanding, he couldn't resist identifying the names of the classical music pieces piped into the room, while his employees faked enthusiasm of his knowledge as employees tend to do of their superiors. The third patient had to tell him the funny anecdote about one asshole looking up another, a joke that Kugleman had encountered a hundred times. Despite that, he laughed as if he had never heard it before. He was about to suffer through another stale yarn, when the patient suddenly succumbed to the anesthesia, sparing Kugelman the trouble. This man had a fairly large pre-malignant growth, also known as a polyp, which he removed easily by placing a snare around it and then cutting through the lesion with an electrical current. The remainder of the morning passed uneventfully as the gastroenterologist extirpated several more polyps. The hospital called to inform him that Mr. Thomas was doing well enough to be transferred out of the ICU. Eventually, Kugelman headed to the lunch room for a repast supplied by a new drug rep. His partners were already there, visiting with the well-endowed young lady, ogling her name tag perched precariously on her low cut sweater as they introduced themselves.

The afternoon was taken up with his office patients. Kugelman enjoyed this part of the day because many of these people had been patients for years, and had become like old friends. Ms. Joyce Rogers was a single mother with chronic abdominal pain who struggled to raise a child with cerebral palsy. She possessed an underlying fear that she would die of cancer and her disabled son would have no one to care for him. Over the years, he had done numerous evaluations to find the cause of her symptoms. When he reviewed her old records, he counted two upper endoscopies and three colonoscopies. All these examinations had been negative. After each test, he would reassure her that nothing serious had been found, but within a year, she would inevitably return with the same worried countenance. She usually complained of pain in various quadrants of the abdomen, sometimes sharp, sometimes dull and sometimes cramping, yet not infrequently there would be new symptoms such as diarrhea, constipation, vomiting, or a slight passage of blood, obligating Kugelman to repeat the tests on the small chance that something sinister might have reared its ugly head. In the litigious world that Kugelman lived in, he could be sued if he was wrong even one time in a hundred, while Ms. Rogers was in the subset of patients that exist in this country where no amount of testing ever completely satisfied them. Nevertheless, he was fond of Ms. Rogers and appreciated her intelligent conversation. She was a high school history teacher, and Kugleman loved reading the works of William Manchester, Doris Kearns Goodwin, and Robert Caro which read more like fiction than fact. On this occasion, he informed her that no further tests were indicated. He prescribed one of the antis: antibiotics, antacids, antispasmodics, anti-gas or antiemetics. Antipasto would have been offered, if he thought it could cure her ailments. She left the office somewhat downcast that no procedures had been scheduled, but Kugelman told her to come back in three months if she was not improved, fully expecting to see her at that time.

The next patient was a young man, Daniel Stewart, who was afflicted with ulcerative colitis. He was a relatively new patient who had recently experienced a flare-up of this disease which causes multiple microscopic sores or ulcers to form in the colon. The twenty-five year old had responded well to an anti-inflammatory medication known as sulfasalazine- Kugelman had spent his entire three year fellowship in gastroenterology trying to spell the name. This drug had been available for years and could be obtained as an inexpensive generic. Daniel informed him that he had stopped the drug due to headaches which he presumed were related to the pills. He no longer had a job and therefore no health insurance, consequently, he could not afford the newer more costly agents. Kugelman advised him to call if his symptoms resurfaced, but he worried that without maintenance medication the disease would exacerbate again. The last recurrence had been severe enough to require a hospital admission, and unfortunately, the next time the disease flared, he could still be without medical coverage. The gastroenterologist recoiled at this possibility. Then he remembered that the rep at lunch had dropped off some samples of an exorbitantly costly drug which might not provoke the headaches. He gave Daniel some free samples, hoping that he could enroll him in a compassionate program if the medication was effective. He wished that practicing medicine was not quite so difficult particularly as the afternoon wore on and the sleepless fatigue started to encroach upon his mental alertness. Abruptly, he had an urgent need to sleep.

Kugleman dragged himself into his office, a small space with the walls plastered with his accomplishments: medical degree, national board and internal medicine diplomate, residency and fellowship certificates. On the bookcase were pictures of him in group golf photos at physician tournaments where he had participated with mediocre abandon. On his mahogany desk sat a statue of a monkey wearing a doctor's lab coat given to him by a grateful patient so long ago that he couldn't remember the woman's name. There was a framed photograph of Selma taken when they had first married, and another one of his son's baseball team that he had helped coach the year before, where dealing with all the type A parents was more difficult than instructing the kids. He told the office manager not to let any calls through, turned off his cell phone, took off his glasses, and folded his arms on the desk to cradle his head. Instantly, he was peacefully snoozing while those patients not yet evaluated waited impatiently in the waiting room. After thirty minutes, he awoke feeling remarkably refreshed. He began to see the remaining individuals who by this time had repeatedly inquired at the front desk, or emerged half-naked from the exam rooms wondering what had happened to their doctor. Kugelman methodically proceeded at the same pace as before his nap, spending as much time as needed with each person. He tried not to appear rushed, as he listened to all their complaints with a sympathetic nod of his head, occasionally cracked a joke, or inquired about their families and their pets. Then he made a diagnosis or reassured them about their afflictions before prescribing a medication or ordering a test. Most of the people left satisfied, not remembering how long they had sat in the waiting area or on the exam tables.

The next to last patient on the list had recently been hospitalized with an attack of idiopathic pancreatitis. *Idiopathic* is a cryptic medical term for *we have no idea what is causing your problem.* This fellow was somewhat disingenuous, a bit of a wise guy, and Kugelman had suspected in the hospital that his problem might be related to excessive intake of alcohol, which is the commonest cause of pancreatic inflammation. Mr. Johnny Franklin had been evasive on this topic, claiming that he never missed a day of work from drinking, and only occasionally visited a bar for *just a few*. This denial resulted in the diagnosis of idiopathic, except that Kugelman had seen it all in his career, and multiplied the patient's recall of his libations by a factor of five. Before discharge he sternly warned Franklin to stay away from the hootch. As he opened the door, the fellow greeted him like an old friend "Hi Norman. I sat out in your waiting room quite a while. Guess you got tied up on the golf course," and Franklin tittered at his foolish witticism.

Kugelman was about to answer. "No, I was busy examining a lot of assholes today but I left the biggest one to the end, you," a variation of the joke that he had endured earlier in the day. Instead, he replied "I'm sorry I'm so far behind. As a matter of fact, it's been a very busy day." As he started his examination, Kugelman's sensitive proboscis detected the faintest odor of alcohol on the man's breath--another skill that he had picked up over the years, like a bloodhound learning to sniff for drugs. "Been doing any drinking lately, Mr. Franklin?" he asked in an off-hand manner.

"No, not much Doc. I learned my lesson in the hospital and you told me no more booze. I try to stick to that."

"Well how about if we draw a blood alcohol level in the office today just to confirm that you haven't been sipping on the bourbon, if you know what I mean. Then we can document that in your record."

Franklin's visage reddened and he started to back track. "Let me tell you something in the strictest confidence. I've been laid off for the past few weeks, and with this weather, car sales have been pretty slow. The manager of the used car lot told me that I wouldn't be called back in until the fall. We're expecting our third child, and the missus is all over me for not looking for another line of work. You know, my buddy recently lost his mother. We went out for a few beers today, but honestly no, I'm really not drinking the hard stuff."

Kugelman looked at the man plaintively, repeating his warning about alcohol. He offered Franklin an opportunity to obtain counseling and warned of the risk of another attack. He typed in his laptop *still drinking despite being advised to abstain.* There was no point in obtaining the alcohol level to prove the obvious.

The last patient was new to his practice. She was a fifty-five year old woman by the name of Bertha Tootle. He noted she had been referred by Dr. Leonard Zuckerman, an internist who sent most of his patients to his competitor, Bruce Katz, a medical school classmate. They had been assigned to dissect the same cadaver in the first year anatomy course (four students to a body) as their last names started with the letter K. Kugelman had always disliked the slippery Katz with his greasy hair and his sleazy smile. He never forgot that Katz pounced on him that first week in medical school and snatched the scalpel from Kugelman's hand when he botched the dissection of the right arm, as their classmates Kang and Kilduff worked smoothly as a team on the left limb. For unknown reasons, both men had pursued gastroenterology as a career, and Katz had an office twenty miles away in a more northerly suburb, cherry-picking the affluent patients, while leaving the Medicaid clientele to Kugelman.

The gastroenterologist quickly recognized that this

woman might be a problem, for why would Zuckerman not refer this delightful lady to Katz instead of himself? It didn't take long for his suspicions to bear fruit. For fifteen years, Mrs. Tootle had suffered from episodes of severe abdominal distress. Her gut would inflate like a hot air balloon, accompanied by a sensation that a baby elephant was stomping around in her bowel. Sometimes the discomfort could be alleviated by placing a ten pound Buddha on her abdomen, on other days she would obtain relief by drinking a kudzu tea followed by the ingestion of twelve pitted prunes which then produced an explosive bowel movement. She was currently on a strict diet of rice, onion soup and numerous garlic tablets.

At first, Kugelman tried to make eye contact but as her endless recitation continued, he instinctively gazed down at his polished wing tips, absorbing the punishment of her discourse with an impassive expression. He began to feel slightly nauseated as the fatigue crept back into his system, while he silently cursed Zuckerman for referring the gaseous Tootle. The good doctor wanted to charge out of the exam room and instantaneously fire his receptionist for scheduling this patient, particularly in the last time slot of the day, but he sat stoically, as she continued to ramble on. He was hesitant to pose any questions for fear it would prolong his ordeal. Finally, he screwed up the courage to ask her if she had tried any medications for her problem, whereupon which she bent down and hoisted a large brown shopping bag which must have contained about a third of the entire supply of a Walgreen's pharmacy. She proceeded to describe the efficacy of each medication and each gastroenterologist that had prescribed each drug going back to Dr. Isadore Sokolov who had been dead for over ten years. Naturally, she had seen Katz as well. He hadn't helped her and had been quite dismissive of her complaints. At that point Kugelman could sympathize even with the despised Katz, and he understood why Zuckerman, who sent him one patient a year, had dropped the untreatable Mrs. Tootle into his unsuspecting lap, only she wasn't through. The woman pulled out records from Johns Hopkins, the Cleveland Clinic, and the Mayo Clinic which documented a voluminous number of tests with the final diagnosis of Irritable Bowel Syndrome. This diagnosis is simply another way of stating: we really don't know why you have these symptoms so we are pinning this diagnosis on you for lack of an alternative and more specific disease, except as one would suspect, physicians never say that. Kugelman had made this diagnosis after the first few sentences had been uttered by Mrs. Tootle, for if these pains had been the harbinger of a more serious disease, she would have been dead years ago. To be truthful, these complaints were common to many individuals in his practice and indeed throughout the world, causing frustration to both patients and their doctors. On a better day, Kugelman might have been more receptive to her condition.

Then his cell phone went off. He had the phone on vibrate, so when he felt a throb in his left thigh, he pulled out the device. It was Selma. The sound of her voice immediately caused him to regret that he had taken her call. This was the evening that she had selected for their subscription tickets to the live theater; no, not on the weekend, but on a Monday when Kugelman was his busiest, for Cynthia and Max Levy, their companions at the concerts, could not attend any other night. Levy worked in his father-in-law's scrap metal business. He usually rolled in at four p.m. and took a nap before dinner. Norman appreciated that he was in some trouble when he heard the angry words, "Where are you?"

He looked at his watch. It was already 5:45. He had promised to be home by six so they could have dinner with the Levys which obviously he would be unable to accomplish. But if he backed out of attending the production all together, he would receive the wrath of Chief Selma on the war path. Instead he replied, "I'm just on my way," which of course was a complete lie. Yet this doctor who had saved a patient's life early that morning, removed polyps preventing colon cancer in five people, reassured an anxious woman who feared a terminal illness, worried about obtaining medicine for a young fellow with a difficult disease, and was perplexed by someone he could never cure in a million years, was afraid to tell his spouse the honest truth: that he wouldn't be home for another hour and they might be late for the play. Yes, he feared the fury of his wife more than the challenge of any patient or any ulcer that was bleeding from any god damn blood vessel in the human body.

He fumbled through the rest of his visit with Mrs. Tootle, racking his brain for some remedy, some hope, even if only a placebo, some Hippocratic balm, so she would be on her way and he could rush home to face the lacerations of Selma's razor sharp tongue slicing into his tired and worn psyche. He pulled out his ace in the hole: yogurt. Yogurt with special bacteria imbedded in that wonderful, soft, creamy-white, gooey substance. Yes, these microorganisms would crowd out other bad bacteria in the gut which were producing the gas. These good little varmints would work wonders for her bloating. This had been proven in a scientific study, never mind that it barely reached statistical significance which of course he didn't mention. He had some coupons to get her a dollar off on each pint that she purchased. He would be delighted to see her in three weeks to ascertain if she had made any progress. Kugleman had learned long ago that patients had to exit the office with something, anything. That's the reason that homeopaths and chiropractors do a booming business for even the most untrustworthy remedy, and why the eighteen year old salesperson at the vitamin shop can offer some worthless capsules for a patient with some disease that even Dr. House couldn't diagnose. Furthermore, yogurt couldn't harm anybody, akin to chicken soup, only he didn't have a coupon for the Jewish penicillin.

As Kugelman pulled into his driveway, he could see Selma looking though the kitchen window. The look on her face would have frightened a ghost. He hunkered down in his shell like a Galapagos tortoise under threat, and walked through the door. There was no shouting and screaming, only an icy silence, which in his experience was more ominous for it lasted longer. He could expect that his dog house visitation would be extended with possibly a night or two sleeping on the couch in the den. He gulped down the cold congealed meat loaf that had been served to his kid about one hour previously, changed his shirt, applied some fresh deodorant and soon they were on the way to the play. The only word that Selma had spoken was good-bye to their son Adam and the baby-sitter.

When they reached their seats, his wife's stony silence abruptly ended. She bubbled on and on to Cynthia about her day volunteering at the kid's school, buying a coat on sale at Neiman Marcus which might be the wrong color, describing the ensuing anguish over whether to return it or not, and waiting for her husband to come home. You know Norman's *so* busy these days. As Kugelman studied his program, he suddenly realized that the evening's production was Hamlet. He recalled Selma's marvelous portrayal of Ophelia, and his enthralled attendance at every performance. He vaguely remembered that she had mentioned this to him several weeks ago, and he became awash with guilt. How could he have forgotten? Unfortunately, in his exhausted state, the play had a potent soporific effect. Despite his efforts to keep his eyes open, he fell into a deep stupor midway through the first act. His sleep was intermittently interrupted by Selma's sharp elbow applied to his rib cage which repeatedly jerked him awake. This was a signal to him that if he wasn't to arrive home at the proper hour and share her favorite play, he certainly wasn't about to enjoy a satisfying sleep.

CHAPTER FIVE

Zeus strove to put his eternal life in order after the Hercules catastrophe. He had no further kerfuffles with Hera. Still, their love life had not improved, and the lack of intercourse with his wife for over three thousand years must have qualified as some sort of record. To put a better face on his religion, he tried to curtail his extramarital affairs, but his libido reasserted itself, resulting in a dalliance with a mermaid which necessitated a transsexual transformation to a dolphin to consummate the relationship. He forgave Apollo, who picked up the lyre again, and his beautiful playing softened the old god's heart, although his son's penchant for gambling had not subsided. He abandoned the football wagering, but more than once he visited Earth to bet on the ponies or frequent the dog track. His worst compulsion was playing poker on the internet. But then unexpectedly, he had a pretty good run. Zeus became enamored by Apollo's profitable venture and started playing himself. However, after a short period of time, the small stakes Hold'em began to bore him, and like many bettors, he wanted to play with the big boys. As previously mentioned, the resources were seriously depleted on Mt. Olympus, so Zeus was desperate to find a partner with deeper pockets. He took an even larger gamble and decided to look up King Midas, who had been ensconced in Hades for twenty-seven hundred years, ignoring the former sovereign's unsavory reputation as evidenced by his residence in the underworld.

In the eight century B.C., Midas became king of Phrygia (or three other municipalities depending on the version that one reads). He was a simple peasant, but one day as he rode into the town of Gordium towing a vegetable wagon, an eagle landed on the vehicle, causing the gullible townspeople to assume that a predatory bird perched on a produce truck confirmed a prophecy that the man driving the cart would be a king. Shortly thereafter, they made the rustic lad a royal. As a response to this very good fortune, Midas tied the hallowed dray to a post to honor the gods, and this knot was only untangled four hundred and fifty years later when Alexander the Great sliced through it with his sword. One wonders why four centuries had to pass before this rather simple solution was devised, nonetheless, to this day an insolvable problem has been referred to as a Gordian knot.

Midas married and produced a brood. It didn't take long for him to realize that this nondescript kingdom could not deliver the goods that he needed to be a well-heeled monarch. Like many others in the crown crowd, he greedily hankered for fine trappings, particularly gold, to enhance the majestic existence. By a chance encounter, he gave assistance to a needy colleague of the god Dionysus, and this friend of a friend--helpful in any walk of life, even a mythical king--was so grateful that he granted Midas one wish. As legend has it, the avaricious ruler had the chutzpah to request that everything he fingered would turn to gold, the so-called Midas touch.

At first, Midas was thrilled with his power. He caressed an oak twig and a stone; they precipitously transformed into the auriferous substance. Next, he encountered his daughter, frolicking in the garden, and while describing his good fortune, the regal gave her a perfunctory hug. Sadly, this was enough to turn her into a solid gold statue, which appalled even the materialistic Midas. Subsequently, he put some iced tea to his lips, but it became iced metal and the poor rich king soon became very thirsty while the gold chips lodged in his esophagus. He contacted Dionysus and begged him to reverse his wish. The god told him to jump in the lake which he did and the dunk in the pond caused the spell to be broken. He could eat and drink again, but his gold making habit was severely attenuated. The shards of gold scarred his gullet forever. From then on, Midas needed to chew very carefully to prevent food from lodging in his esophagus on its way to his stomach.

Later in life, Midas angered Apollo, when as a contest judge he chose the goat-god Pan's pipe playing over Apollo's lyre performance. In a malicious streak of petulance, a trait he inherited from his father Zeus, Apollo transformed the face of the grasping king by protruding his teeth, broadening his nostrils, and enlarging his external ears to those possessed of a donkey. Midas wore an oversized crown to cover them up, so that only his barber knew that this ass had ass ears. In due course, Phrygia was defeated by another dreadful king, causing Midas to commit suicide by drinking ox blood (the original Red Bull). The disgraced monarch was transported to Hades, not in the deepest section known as Tartarus where the bad fellows resided, but not in the Elysian Fields either.

Zeus made the trip to the underworld to search for the mercenary monarch. He crossed the river Styx on a boat ferried by a ferocious fellow named Charon, and paid the lonely attendant a shekel--O.K., it was like a shekel- -to row him across the waterway to his destination. Cerberus was still guarding the entrance but spent most of his day napping. Zeus gave him three ox bones, one for each mouth, then patted him on all of his skulls. He passed by Sisyphus who was still serving his punishment by being forced to push a rock up a hill. As it neared the top, the boulder rolled back down, necessitating the ex-king to repeat the exact maneuver. These days he chanted *I can't get no satisfaction* made famous by the Rolling Stones. When Sisyphus asked Zeus how his appeal was progressing, the Supreme One mordaciously answered that he was contemplating clemency and would have an answer for him in the next century. Finally, Zeus reached the elaborate castle of his brother Hades, who had the same name as the infernal region that he ruled. The two embraced each other and reminisced about all the battles with the Titans. Old Brontes soon joined them with a few of his other Cyclops buddies. They opened a barrel of the finest wine and went on a hellish binge, such that even the one-eyed creatures were seeing double. Hades pointed out the whereabouts of the long dead king and granted permission for Zeus to take him back to Mt. Olympus, but cautioned his brother that the Midas touch had become a bit calloused.

The following day, Zeus approached the exiled regal. He was puttering around outside the Elysian Fields, rattling some gold in his pocket, hoping to gain entrance into this paradise which was analogous to the Garden of Eden without the serpent. His ears were still long and covered with dark grey fur, and along with his prominent nose and severe overbite, he had a striking likeness to a burro. The top-god couldn't stifle a snigger when he laid eyes on this odd looking royal.

"By Jove, you still look like the donkey I remember from years ago."

"Yeah, that's me. It's quite a comedown from the time when I could produce instant treasure. Let me be honest. I'm remorseful that I turned my daughter into a sculpture, but what the heck, she's got all the wealth she'll ever need. I'm trying to find religion so I can frolic in that beautiful meadow over yonder and take a swim in the Oceanus River which meanders through that paradise. Hades tells me that I'm still as rapacious as ever, and I should worship the gods with more reverence. But let me tell you one thing. It's tough to venerate a god like you knowing all about your vices, even a greedy bastard such as myself."

Zeus was shocked by his insolence, but he subdued his mercurial temper and responded. "Those things are behind me, my good man. I have reformed, and I want to improve our religion to make it more attractive to the humans of today. I sent Hercules back to earth to reacquaint the moderns with our beliefs, but that knucklehead has found love and is never coming back. I'm here to ask you a favor. Even with your diminished talent for procuring gold and even though you're a sordid prick, I thought you might want to give me a hand to improve the finances of our creed."

"You mean, you'll take me out of this no man's land?"

"You betcha," enthused Zeus, "and if you do your job correctly, you might have a shot at mowing the grass in the Elysian Fields. I'll even buy you a Toro to do the job right!" and he roared at his stupid joke.

"What the heck, count me in. I'll pack my bag and meet you at the Styx in twenty minutes."

The following day, Zeus brought his new companion to meet Hera and the other gods. Even Dionysus showed up to see if his former acquaintance still possessed his old bag of tricks. Zeus presented the erstwhile king with a couple of large pebbles. First Midas put the objects in his mouth, and several hours later he spit them out. Then he began to rub them while meditating, rocking back and forth like a religious Jew reading the Torah. After a few days, the stones turned into spheres that contained some gold but also other elements such as silver, zinc and copper. Clearly, his capacity for creating the precious metal had diminished since ancient times. In spite of that, Zeus was delighted that he was producing some capital. The coffers of the Olympian treasury started to grow, allowing Zeus and Apollo to increase their bets. At the same time, the Preeminent Being was careful to hide his infidelities and petulant peccadillos from the skeptical monarch. Midas, for his part, was flattered by the attention paid to him by

Zeus, and began to consider the old mythology in a more favorable light. He re-read the poet Homer, his Iliad and Odyssey, while continuing to crank out the golden stones in a steady, albeit slow fashion.

All was well until the gods had a persistent losing streak with their poker playing--there's nothing worse than a hard luck god. In a very short time, their savings vanished precipitately as did their stash of gold. Apollo needed a scapegoat, and it was convenient to impugn the ill-reputed king. The musical god still held a deep seated animosity to the sovereign, remembering his second place finish to another goat centuries ago. Apollo demanded that Midas relocate to the underworld. Zeus was hesitant to oppose his son, even though he didn't share Apollo's explanation for the monetary reverses, but then he had an idea and summoned Midas to his presence.

"We have a problem here, King. Our recent losses at the virtual poker table have been substantial. My son Apollo, who has a reputation for being smart, has looked pretty stupid. He's blaming you for our reverses and insisting that you return to Hades for good. That means no Elysian Fields. But I have another plan. I'm sending you back to Earth to produce some gold and popularize our religion. Who knows? If you do well down there and avoid any hanky-panky, you may one day be catching fish in the celestial river! Ha-ha!"

"I guess I don't have much of a choice eh?" answered the regal," But I have one request. Could you change my appearance for my trip back to the living? To be honest with you, I don't believe I can help paganism with this pair of donkey ears. I'll look like an ass down there."

"I think that can be arranged, my good man."

Hermes guided the former monarch back to Brooklyn where Demetrius Georgopoulos was waiting. The sovereign was wearing the kingly robes that he had last donned before drinking the bull's blood, while the faintest coating of gold dust still clung to his sandals. His ears were prominent but no longer furry, and his teeth protruded less than before his makeover. After a shower, and a change into blue jeans and an old New York Rangers hockey sweater borrowed from George, Midas was directed to the kitchen table to begin orientation.

"O.K. pal, here me out. I have a complete set of fake credentials including a driver's license and a green card. Your new name is Kevin Midas. I felt that "King" was just a bit pretentious. My first idea was employment at a muffler outlet, but greasing your hands might not befit a retrofitted royal, so I asked Hercules if he would take you on in his turkey factory. I'm proud to say that *Herky's Jerky Turkey* has been a success. He's refurbished a warehouse in Jersey City to process the birds. He and Alice are living nearby in Hoboken. Once you get your bearings you can start fabricating some gold, and pushing the old Greek myths. With the help of the good priestess, I've prepared some pamphlets. You can pass these out to people walking by. Hey, most folks in this country are used to oddballs handing out all sorts of crap."

The following day, George drove Kevin to Hoboken to visit with the Frum's.

"It's good to see you ancient king, welcome to America," announced Hercules.

"Yeah, The last time I was here there were only savages in this part of the world, but let me be honest, I'd rather be in the blissful fields of Elysium."

"Oh, it's quit blissful here without a doubt." And he put his arm around Alice.

"I have greetings from your dad. He wants you to know that all is forgiven, and the bills for the wine and chariot repairs have greatly diminished," snickered the onetime ruler.

"That sounds like the humor of my not so honorable parent. Still, I find it difficult to absolve him and that harridan of a stepmother. But all that's behind me. I'm a happy man as an Earth dweller. I have a caring wife and son, and we've another little fellow 'in the oven' as they say in America. George tells me you need some employment. We can get you started tomorrow. Only tell me why have you come back after all these years?"

"To be honest, it's a long story, but Zeus has persuaded me of the worthiness of the Greek myths, and after rereading the classics, I've decided to beat the sacred drums for paganism, and make some gold along the way. Let me show you some of the literature that I've brought with me."

"No thank you, King. I must admit that I'm pessimistic about your prospects. I think you'll have an arduous time convincing anyone that polytheism is superior to the one god belief, particularly when you are dealing with that pantheon of malcontents. I'm sorry to say it, but Zeus is a poor excuse for a supreme leader."

"Let me tell you one thing. Your dad has been a different deity in the last few years. He was chaste all the time I was with him."

"I won't stand in your way, but I should tell you that I've been attending church services with Alice. I'm considering becoming a Christian. The compassionate

Jesus is pointing me in the right direction, but in the end, it's what you are on the inside that counts," and he pointed to his muscular chest with a muscular finger. "Since I've been down here, I've quit the alcohol and the philandering, and settled down with the best woman in any world. But tell me your Majesty, are you still able to produce gold? We would welcome some additional remuneration with the new baby soon to be born."

"Yeah, I still can. Bring me a pebble." Jimmy went out to the yard and retrieved a smooth stone which Kevin put in his mouth. "It'll take me about three or four days after I spit it out," replied the king, his speech muffled by the object in his cheeks.

Shortly afterward, Kevin started work in the turkey plant. Herky gave him the task of plucking the unlucky birds after the slaughter. The job reminded Kevin of his peasant days when he killed chickens on his small farm near Gordium, only in those times the conveyer belt had not yet been invented. He lived in a spare room in the Frum household, manufacturing two or three golden stones per month. The former ruler grew his hair over his outsized ears, 1970's style, and whitened his teeth which had become discolored from sucking the rocks. Kevin gave one gold ball to Herky every thirty days to cover room and board, and with his salary at the factory, he was able to buy a suit at the Men's Warehouse, so when he looked in the mirror *he liked the way he looked.*

After several months, Kevin had saved enough money to purchase a small table and display case for his precious orbs. He rented space at the flea market in the Meadowlands near the football stadium, where he exhibited his merchandise and distributed the literature regarding the ancient myths and their relevance to modern man. The stories had been somewhat bowdlerized to put the Greek deities in the best light possible. He had about ten small golden spheres to sell, which he advertised as pure gold, only Kevin had no way of polishing or shaping them, so their nondescript appearance didn't attract much attention. His flyers on the Trojan horse and the great battle between Achilles and Hector seemed to elicit no more than a yawn from the few customers that wandered by. He noted that one woman had used his hand-outs to wrap some green onions purchased at the farmer's market nearby, while several others found their way to the trash bin not far from his stand.

As he wandered around the market visiting the other vendors, he befriended a woman named Sally Simpson who was selling silver and pewter jewelry. She was in her mid-forties, admittedly past her prime, but at one time she must have been quite a looker. Now she needed some foundation to cover the web of tiny wrinkles that had started to form around her mouth and neck. She had intelligent hazel eyes and strawberry blond hair cut in a pageboy. Her figure was full although over the years her hips had enlarged somewhat more prominently than she might have wished.

She was born into a working class family. Somehow all seven kids and her parents crammed into the small frame house packed together with all the other small frame houses on their block. Sally and her siblings attended Catholic parochial schools where the nuns inculcated a strong work ethic as well as compassion for the disadvantaged. Just out of high school, she got a job as a medical technician assisting in outpatient procedures at the nearby hospital in Paterson, earning enough money to obtain her RN. She worked her way up, eventually becoming the head nurse in the Intensive Care Unit of the hospital. Sally met a dark, good looking fellow at the community college, an immigrant named Achilles Papadopoulos, who had come to this country to obtain a business degree. The loquacious fellow talked her into a precipitous marriage and obtained his green card just before he was to be sent back to Greece. The union lasted ten years. She bore one child, a girl that they named Amy who was now in college on a soccer scholarship. Achilles flitted from one business startup to another, and Sally tired of loaning him money for his failed ventures, which led to numerous arguments. Eventually he left her, striking up a relationship with a bodacious bartender half his age. She filed for divorce and reclaimed her maiden name but despite that, the couple remained friends. Sally started making jewelry after attending a class with her co-worker and friend, Polly Polk. She quickly discovered that not only did she enjoy the craft, but she had considerable talent as well. Unfortunately, she couldn't make a living designing and producing bracelets and necklaces so she only sold her trinkets on weekends.

When Kevin introduced himself, she saw not a handsome individual, but a man with charisma and an unusual majestic bearing, and he was another talker and a charmer. Moreover, they had something in common when Sally revealed that Achilles was a cousin of Demetrius Georgopoulos. Maybe she was eager, too eager, to befriend Kevin. All the same, she had no men in her life at the time. She invited him into her well-kept and fully paid for house in Bergenfield and showed Kevin her jewelry studio in the basement. The former monarch marveled at her skill. He claimed that the beautiful rings and bracelets reminded him of the jewelry that Helen of Troy had worn to bewitch Paris, and start the Trojan War. She offered to produce some creations from his golden stones, and they agreed to merge their operations and split the profits. She was quite puzzled as to how her new partner had acquired all this gold, selling at twelve hundred dollars an ounce, so he showed her some fake invoices indicating that he had bought the raw nuggets wholesale at a dealer in Manhattan. He failed to mention that the objects were nowhere near twenty-four carat purity.

A few weeks later, Sally fashioned some exquisite pieces from Kevin's gold, which were much more popular than her silver creations. They decided to take a gamble. Both of them quit their day jobs and went into the jewelry business full time. They opened a small store in a strip mall near her home and of course their union became more than a business partnership.

After hearing this news, Hermes became anxious that this relationship might once again release Zeus's awful temper, and he persuaded George to meet with Kevin for a man to king chat. At their rendezvous, George expressed doubts that Kevin could promote the Greek religion if he was involved romantically with a Christian, even though the hot dog entrepreneur had known Sally for years and admitted that she was a "good woman" to use his words. Midas seemed oblivious to future problems. He couldn't stop chattering about Sally and her stunning talent. George went back to Brooklyn fearing the worst, not knowing that the worst was worse than he imagined.

At first, their cohabitation was blissful. Sally was in love and excited about the business venture. As for Kevin, intercourse was verboten in Hades unless you were a god, so the former sovereign hadn't been with a woman since 724 BC. Yet like all relationships, the initial sexual attraction diminished, and Sally began to ask questions about his previous life including his infatuation with Greek mythology. She wanted to know if Kevin was in the country illegally, thinking back to her marriage with Achilles. He convinced her that he had been persecuted in Greece for his ancient beliefs, and he pulled out his forged green card as proof. Sally was taken in by this bit of master salesmanship so she put her doubts aside. She had fallen for the slick shtick of Kevin Midas.

Kevin wandered about their neighborhood searching for pebbles and stones. After Sally was asleep, he discreetly fished in his pants for these orbs, as they needed time in his mouth and then constant caressing in his pajama pockets in order for the gold to form. Thus, Kevin went from fondling Sally's breasts to fondling his little rocks all in the same evening. Late one Saturday night, he was sitting in the living room half asleep with a pebble in his mouth, when without warning there was a monstrous clap of thunder, not quite as potent as Zeus's thunderbolt several months earlier, but still plenty strong. Sally's poodle, Elmo, was skittish like many of his breed. In his anxiety, he jumped into Kevin's lap. The unsuspecting gold producer was jolted awake when the dog landed on him, swallowing the stone that had been soaking in his mouth. It caught in the bottom of his esophagus, stuck

DAVID MARGOLIS

on the scar tissue that had formed when he had ingested the gold shards eons ago. Attempting to dislodge the sphere, Midas immediately drank a glass of water, but to his dismay, the liquid came right back up and the gold ball remained impacted. He went to bed and laid there wide awake, constantly spitting his saliva in a cup, but even his buccal secretions could not pass the obstruction. Finally after a completely sleepless night, he woke Sally early Sunday morning to tell her that while snacking the night before, a piece of leftover steak had stuck in his gullet.

Sally, from her experience working in outpatient procedures, knew that Kevin would need a specialist to remove the obstruction and she drove him to her former place of employment in Paterson. After explaining the problem in the Emergency Room, a gastroenterologist was called in to extirpate the putative piece of beef. They wheeled him into a procedure room where the doctor put him in twilight with intravenous midazolam and fentanyl, then passed the scope into his esophagus. He visualized the foreign body wedged into the bottom end of the Midas gullet. A sheathed basket was passed through a channel in the scope. The assisting nurse then opened the basket as the scope approached the foreign object. After a few minutes of jockeying the controls and repositioning the instrument, the doctor was able to entrap the item in the retriever, then pulled the scope and the basket with its cargo out through Midas' mouth. When Kevin awoke, the gastroenterologist brought the swallowed item to show to the couple—Sally was now at the bedside. He recognized Sally and gave her a warm hello, but he commented that he had expected to remove a piece of meat. In its place, the doctor handed Sally a medium-sized pebble which of course looked very much like a prototype of the raw gold that she had used to make her jewelry. After leaving the hospital, they stopped at a Bob Evans where Kevin ate a large breakfast of bacon, eggs and pancakes. They both remained silent. It was only when they arrived home that Sally accosted him in the bedroom where he was changing into his pajamas to catch up on his sleep.

"Kevin, what in heaven's name caused you to put that golden stone into your mouth?"

"I don't know, I just like the taste of a well-aged juicy rock," replied the former monarch with a sardonic grin, but he was silly to think that the savvy Sally would fall for such foolishness. A few minutes later, Sally took his suitcase from the closet and began to pack his things, throwing his work clothes and his precious suit from the Men's Warehouse willy-nilly into the satchel.

"What the heck, here's the real story." Sally stopped packing and stared at him expectantly. "I didn't tell you the entire truth about why I came to this country. Zeus sent me."

"Zeus?"

"Yeah Zeus, the ancient god of the Greeks. He wanted me to produce some gold for him but I got on the wrong side of Apollo, remember him? Zeus sent me to earth again to try to rejuvenate Greek mythology and maybe sell a little gold along the way."

"You've been here before? Who are you?"

"King Midas."

"King Midas?" responded Sally incredulously. "I don't believe it. You must be psychotic with delusions of grandeur."

"Bring me a stone from the garden and I'll demonstrate." And Kevin proceeded to carefully put the pebble in his mouth. In a few minutes he took it out and showed the astounded Sally that the piece of granite was already beginning to turn a golden color.

"I don't know what to say, but I'll tell you this. Don't ever perform these magical tricks again. It's either me or your King Midas act," and as she said this, she began to unpack Kevin's duds and put them back in the drawers. She didn't really want him to leave.

"I agree to that. And I'll be honest with you. I never want to have one of those rocks stuck in my esophagus again. And one other thing, what was the name of the doctor who removed the stone?"

"Dr. Kugelman, Dr. Norman Kugelman, he's one of the best gastroenterologists at the hospital," replied Sally.

CHAPTER SIX

Zeus settled himself into the celestial tub just after his assistant, a nubile nymph from the island of Samos, finished scenting the waters with jasmine and myrrh. He was about to invite the winsome maiden into the royal receptacle when his lavation was abruptly interrupted by Hermes, who had arrived to deliver the ominous news. The messenger had long ago eschewed the ablutionary privacy of his leader, and Zeus didn't seem to mind. In fact, he actually welcomed an audience when bathing, particularly on the now rare instances when he could entice a young female into his perfumed water. But on this occasion, Hermes had a rather grim countenance, and his porkpie hat was not at its usual jaunty angle. Zeus waved the young maiden out of the room, put on his ermine robe, and after toweling down, accompanied

Hermes into his boudoir to hear the report from the messenger.

"We've had a bit of a setback in New Jersey, sire," announced Hermes in his most tactful tone of voice.

"How's that?" responded the Omniscient One.

"One of the stones that Midas was turning to gold caught in his gullet and had to be removed by a gastroenterologist. The procedure was quite ingenious. He put a flexible scope in his esophagus, snared it with a wire trap, and pulled it out. Kevin, that's his American name, was eating flapjacks two hours after the procedure."

"A what?" responded Zeus with a baffled look on his visage. "We have some satyrs around the place, creatures that are half goat and half man, and there's a Minotaur with a head like a bull and a body of a human. Is that like a gastroenterologist? This being must have some magnificent wizardry at his disposal. Does he have a name?"

"His name is Norman Kugelman and he's a physician just like Hippocrates or Asclepius, only they call him a gastroenterologist. Amazingly, he owns a business called the Uranus Land Company even though he's a Jewish fella. No, this isn't magic. It's called technology, but it's too complicated to explain. Still, there's a bit more to the story. It seems that the same conundrum that befell Hercules has engulfed Kevin and that problem is an arrow from Eros into his heart."

"You mean love?"

"Yes, Your Excellency, just as Hercules became enamored with Alice. By the way, your four hundredth grandchild was born in New Jersey. He's already walking at six months. Anyway, your golden King has also been smitten. He's found a gal by the name of Sally Simpson. They are engaged to be married."

"By Jove, I can't blame the man. The first woman he meets in almost an eternity, and as us gods always say, he's only human." Zeus chortled while Hermes didn't crack a smile.

"Kevin's promised her that he won't produce any more gold and he's been attending the Christian church on a regular basis. His proselytizing for our faith seems to be over, at least for now."

Hermes braced himself for the Supreme Being's temper. He dug his wings into the well-worn regal carpet anticipating a tantrum, similar to the one Zeus had thrown when his son Hercules had disobeyed his commands, but to his discombobulation, Zeus just sat in his chair with his eyes closed and started to whistle a tune that his son Apollo often played on his lyre. The melody was "The Impossible Dream" from the "Man of La Mancha." After a few bars he opened his eyes and stared at Hermes. And then he spoke.

"I'm not shocked. That ass-faced clown never had his heart in the pagan program. I figured that I had nothing to lose by sending him to earth even though it's against my scruples to reincarnate the mortals. Then the guy meets a woman and screws her and screws up. This thing called Christianity has got us beat, but for the life of me I can't understand the special attraction. Jesus Christ is a Greek name, Joshua the Anointed, while those tenets of Christian theology, the epistles of Paul, were written in the Greek language. And remember when my mother hid me from my evil father Cronus who wanted to swallow me? Similarly, Jesus was concealed from Herod after the monarch was apprised that the infant would become King of the Jews. Then there's the flood that I created after that stupid king, Lyacaon, sacrificed his son to me. I became incensed over his display of barbarism. My deluge was as powerful as Noah's inundation, O.K., it only lasted nine days, but it was a hell of a flood, wiped out everyone except two humans. And don't ever forget that the box opened by Pandora brought the same tribulations to mankind as the apple that Eve ingested."

"But tell me more about the doctor. Is he as wise as Hippocrates, the sagest physician that ever lived? Does he know of the four humors: blood, black bile, yellow bile and phlegm that the great physician expounded upon? Yes, those four bodily fluids elucidate the workings of the human body, and they of course correlate with hot, dry, cold, and wet, and the four elements air, fire, earth, and water, marrying with *winter, spring, summer, and fall*, so said Hippocrates long before these words were used in the song *You've Got a Friend* recorded by James Taylor and written by Carole King, only he wasn't a tailor and she wasn't a king. I hope this Kugelberg's taken the Hippocratic Oath where he vows not to do harm to any patient, and treat all of them as if they were his parents. No euthanasia allowed, be chaste and religious--you said this guy is Jewish--and respect patient confidentiality. Does he follow these doctrines? You bet he does! He must know the ancient Greek civilization or he wouldn't have venerated Uranus by naming an important company after grandpa."

"He has a medical license in the state of New Jersey, sire, but I couldn't tell you if the four humors are still taught in today's medical schools," responded the noncommittal messenger.

Zeus ignored him and continued on. "When Hippocrates died, he was ensconced in the Elysian Fields, and Hades kept him for his own medical needs. I probably shouldn't be telling you this, but my brother has always been troubled by a formidable case of hemorrhoids, most likely from all that sitting on his throne. Come to think of it, all of my siblings suffer gastrointestinal ailments, it's kind of like our Achilles heel, and of course there's my problem with excessive flatus that you've experienced firsthand. Hippocrates knew how to treat my farting. He recommended that I avoid beans even though I loved a juicy lima or a scrumptious lentil and forget cabbage. When I stopped gorging on those suckers all that gas just melted away. But guess what? I became constipated from lack of fiber. I know it sounds strange, a god, let alone the numero uno, who can't move his bowels. I consulted with Hippo--all his friends called him that--and he gave me some therapeutic herbs, thapsian, and hellebore, and when that didn't work some daucke and cuckoo-pint. Soon I could poop like a goose. I should have made him a god but I didn't. Did I already say that? The problem now is all the pain, borborygmus, and belching, with the occasional loud fart--no, it's not thunder--is extremely embarrassing and I can't forget the stinker that I expelled during the recent war counsel for Titan unrest. I blamed it on my son Ares, god of war, but I doubt anyone believed me. And where is Hippocrates? He's in fricking Greek heaven. But as you know, we already have a bunch of gods around here to help the sick. Panacea prescribes a tonic for the infirm and the disabled, but it's no good for a god with a belly ache. Her sister, Hygea, pats me on the head and tells me that I get myself all worked up when the frustration with the meager fortunes of my religion start to eat at me, but maybe someone with a fresh approach like Kugelmeister might be just what my sorrowful gut needs."

"Kugelman."

"And then there's Asclepius, my grandson from Apollo and a woman named Coronis. When Apollo discovered that Coronis had been unfaithful, he killed her during childbirth. Asclepius was raised by my cousin Chiron, son of my father Cronus, half man, half stallion. Some families have a black sheep in the family. We have a horse's ass. But this equine oddity was very gentle, and he was adept with medicinal herbs and the like. He taught little Cleppy about how to heal wounds, quell fevers and treat plagues. One afternoon Asclepius killed a serpent which had wrapped itself around his staff. Another snake appeared with a special herb in his mouth and restored the first snake to life. After that, he used this substance to resurrect the deceased, particularly a man named Hippolytus who had suffered an unlucky misfortune. This fellow was all man. I mean he was a stud. Anyway, this Hippolytus was so good looking that Aphrodite wanted him for herself, but when Hippolytus gave her the cold shoulder she had a sea monster kill him. Asclepius experienced remorse for the chap, and used the snake potion to bring him back to the living. But this act made me god damned mad, for if nobody ever dies what good is any religion? It's the fear of the unknown after departing from the earth that requires man to pray for his soul in the hereafter, and that's where gods come in to do their job. So maybe I was a bit hasty, but I blasted him with a thunderbolt. In those days, I was silky smooth with that weapon, very accurate with pinpoint precision. I catapulted him into the heavens and made him a god. Now he sulks all day reading his medical journals and feeding those snakes. When I show up for my annual checkup--Hera insists I make a yearly appointment even though I'm immortal--he just stares at me and tells me all my symptoms are in my head. Oh, he's prescribed all sorts of different herbs that he grows in his garden but none of them have ever worked. I even had one of those snakes wrap around my belly for a few days looking up at me and sticking out his forked tongue, but that reptile didn't have a clue as to how to treat my symptoms. One day, after I erupted with a large belch, he became so annoyed that he slithered away and never returned. That's the problem with doctors. They tell you it's all in your head, O.K., so fix my head! The guy doesn't like me after I shot those thunderbolts, and I can't blame him but don't spread rumors to the other gods that I'm washed up. The other day, Apollo told me that Asclepius suggested that we have elections to pick a new leader and get some new blood at the top. Hey buddy! This isn't a democracy. And I picked this morose moron over Hippocrates? Do you think I could get an appointment with Kugelberg and tell him about my bloating, pain, constipation, and humiliating flatus?"

"His name is Kugelman, Your Lordship," responded Hermes. "As your messenger, the logistics would be daunting. He's already had a consultation with Morris, the Hebrew underangel, when he was injured in a car accident, and I'm not sure if he treats pagan patients."

"Moe? How's he doing? Good spirit that one. I

wanted to hire him years ago. I would have promoted him up the ladder but he went with Yahweh and he's still stuck there in a rut. Maybe he'll put in a good word for me."

"Well let's not rush into anything right now, but what do I tell Midas about his fling with the Christian lady?"

"Tell him, I don't care what he does with her. Let him try Christianity and sample those stories of kindness, charity, and faith. If becoming a Christian can cure that ignoble noble of his selfishness and deceit, I'll pay homage to Jesus myself and check my mythology manual at the Pearly Gates!" And with that, Zeus disrobed and headed back into his bathtub, but the water had cooled and the damsel was nowhere to be found.

CHAPTER SEVEN

Four years had passed since Kugelman's accident and his subsequent infatuation with Polly Polk. In that time, he had endeavored with some success to keep his mind engaged with other tasks, and he made an effort to avoid all but strictest professional contact with the bewitching nurse for fear of stirring up his latent desire. His only son, Adam, had recently been Bar Mitzvahed, and Selma had been preoccupied with the planning of that event, which in their social circle, and in Selma's view of her status in that circle, required an evening affair at the country club after the morning service in the synagogue. The entertainment included a jazz trio during the cocktail hour followed by a twelve piece band for the pubescent and prepubescent guests and their parents, complemented by marvelous food that only Jews know how to prepare and eat. Their son's Bar Mitzvah mandated a sit down dinner with an appetizer of chopped liver followed by an eggplant and couscous salad. The main course offered a choice of either wild Sockeye salmon caught the previous day in Alaska, or a Cornish hen that had been exercised on a regular schedule. Sitting nearby, on each plate, were knishes supplied by Goldberg's Catering while a medley of organic baby carrots and white beets bathed themselves in an Amaretto sauce. For dessert, a delicious chocolate soufflé had been baked with an assortment of Jewish pastries. The overall theme was basketball--Adam was an aspiring although rather short point guard--and each table was adorned with a different major league team with the New Jersey Nets motif reserved for the Bar Mitzvah boy and his family. Kugelman believed that this glorious extravaganza was more than a tad over the top, and he remembered his own modest affair, a kosher buffet lunch in the bad smelling Orthodox synagogue. But the party seemed to make Selma happy. He was making enough money that fifteen grand for his only son's entry into manhood was no big deal. Naturally he was extremely proud of the kid.

At the morning service, Kugelman had stood up in front of the congregation, reciting the short prayer before one of the seven Torah segments sung by the rabbi. Then he and Selma dressed the holy scroll in its velvet cover, and gently placed it back into the ark where it would sleep for another week until the next Sabbath. Adam had diligently studied his Bar Mitzvah portion under the tutelage of Rabbi Joseph Cohen, the assistant rabbi. Norman had observed the boy tussling with the unnatural Hebrew alphabet with the script travelling from right to left instead of left to right, but Adam had performed well on this special day except for his slightly off-key chanting, which was no surprise, as singing voices in the Kugelman clan were distinctly below average; but this boy was destined to be a physician, not a cantor.

Over the previous months, as he observed his son preparing for this important day, Kugelman recounted his boyhood: spending two hours at heder (Hebrew school) five days a week after eight hours of public school, trying to master the labyrinthine language and the myriad of laws and customs, enough to satisfy the most obsessive compulsive personality. As a schoolboy, he had resented the time spent in the musty synagogue when he could have expended that time polishing his skills in baseball or hockey. Later in life, he remarked to his mother that attending college seemed like a vacation

After his son's performance, the congregation hushed as Rabbi Horowitz delivered the sermon. The Rabbi droned on, examining the portion of the Torah that had been read that day. It was the familiar story where God directs Abraham to sacrifice his son, but at the last moment the Almighty spares Isaac from being killed by his father. Kugelman had heard that story many times before, and on previous occasions, as he slumped in his seat in the synagogue, his mind had been far away: as a young boy, thinking about the prospects of the New York Rangers, or in later years, pondering over a difficult patient, or most often, combating hunger, and wondering why the rabbi couldn't just sit down so they could get something to eat. But on this day, he tried to make sense of the words of Horowitz. Testing Abraham's faith in God? Really? Now what father would kill his only son just to prove he was a devout Jew? And what kind of a god would present a choice like that to a father? Kugelman looked with love at his own son sitting next to him. Are we to thank Him and believe Him merciful by letting Abraham off the hook at the last second? Alright, these are just allegorical stories. We don't take the Bible literally, some scribe writing down a story in 100 B.C. But was there any meaningful message that Kugelman could take from that tale? That God's a mean guy and takes pleasure in having poor Abraham sweat bullets for three days while trudging up a mountain with his unsuspecting son. How about the trauma to the psyche of Isaac? Don't worry kid. It was just a joke. Forget about it. Finally, the Rabbi finished up and blessed Adam and his family. Kugelman reentered the present, his mind focused on the welcoming speech he would make to the guests at the party that evening.

Unhappily, after the lavish event, Selma suffered a letdown. Kugelman presumed that a weight would be lifted from her shoulders now that the pressure of planning such an elaborate festivity was over. Judging from the rave reviews of the attendees, it had been a remarkable success, but for some reason, she didn't take much satisfaction from a job well done. If anything, she was tetchier toward Norman than normal, if you can ever call that normal. She followed the previous pattern of their marriage, directing her infelicity to her preoccupied husband. She bitched about his long hours, constantly comparing him to other doctors that she knew, whom she imagined arrived home much earlier in the evening to be with their family, which in truth they probably did. And try as he might, Kugelman arose earlier and earlier and arrived home later and later, but when he did manage to come home at an acceptable hour, he would fall asleep right after dinner. This made Selma even angrier than on the evenings when he came home late.

To cheer his wife up, Norman decided to take her to Atlantic City for a long weekend. The first few days were idyllic. It appeared that they had recaptured some of the magic in the marriage. But on the last day, Selma wanted to attend one of the very late shows and afterwards hit the Black Jack tables, but the staid Kugelman had begged off, claiming his never ending quest for a good night's sleep before returning to work the next day. Selma, hearing another plea for sack time, took this as a personal insult, as if in his slumber he was blocking her out of his life. Her smoldering fury rekindled. She stayed up all night in their hotel room blaring the TV as loud as possible. Kugelman had to wrap a pillow around his head and slink under the blankets in order to catch a few *zzzz*'s, so that the trip which had initially showed such promise turned out to be a fiasco.

On a late afternoon, Kugelman was called to see Mr. Johnny Franklin in the Intensive Care Unit. As he had predicted, Franklin had suffered another attack of pancreatitis, except this time his condition was much more serious. The pancreas is a cryptic organ that sits behind the stomach and in front of the vertebrae and major blood vessels. It is divided by convention into the head, body and tail, like some species of salamander. In reality, it's a sack of chemicals which are needed to digest the foods that we eat. There are specific enzymes present to digest fat, carbohydrates and sugars, the basic building blocks of the mammalian diet. A pancreas can be found in almost all vertebrate species, and thus it was a gland that developed early in the evolutionary chain. The islets of Langerhans, small collections of cells that secrete insulin and control blood sugar, are also present in this enigmatic structure almost as an afterthought. Kugleman often wondered why those little islands couldn't have been inserted somewhere else in the gut, but these were the silly thoughts that sometimes protruded into his consciousness. In a small percentage of alcoholics, after chronic heavy drinking of ten years or longer, the pancreas spills out its enzymes into the surrounding cytoplasm. For unknown reasons, an explosion occurs in the gland, and the pancreas actually starts to digest itself causing acute inflammation.

According to his wife, Franklin's drinking had caused him to be fired from his job as a used car salesman and as a result, he had "tied one on" for two weeks, downing a fifth of gin daily. The night before, he had experienced relentless abdominal pain, and by the time he showed up in the Emergency Room, he was gravely ill requiring admission to the ICU. His kidneys and lungs had failed from the toxins released into his blood stream, necessitating emergency dialysis and placement on a respirator. Kugelman looked at his patient's CT scan. It appeared that a volcano had erupted in the head and body of the pancreas. Where there had once been normal tissue, there was now an amorphous mass of inflammation. Some areas were frankly necrotic, a medical term for dead or dying. There is no specific treatment for acute pancreatitis. The medical plan is to support the patient's other vital organs until the inflammation subsides, which in severe cases can take four to six weeks if the patient doesn't succumb before that time. Kugelman examined Mr. Franklin, and the wretched man's bulging abdomen felt as if a bag of cement had replaced the normal flesh. The gastroenterologist had seen this problem several times in his career, although not usually this life-threatening, but unlike the bleeding ulcer, there was no scope procedure that needed to be performed. He dictated his consultation note, talked to Mrs. Franklin who was anxiously camped in the waiting room, and hurriedly wrote some orders to start intravenous nutrition. He was already late for his own nutrition at the Kugelman household; nothing new there. On his way out the door, he spotted Polly tending to a patient a few beds down the hall.

Maybe it was the recent blowout at the casino or his desire to be polite, or his desire period, but he found himself in a conversation with her.

"How's it going?" he asked nonchalantly.

"Oh, the usual routine, nothing as exciting as when you were one of our patients." She smiled that beautiful smile in concert with her long eyelashes that batted her lower lids in an innocent, but, for the forlorn Kugelman, captivating way. Despite his hidden passion for her, Kugelman was careful in his phlegmatic monotone not to betray himself.

"You know, Selma and I never thanked you for the dedicated care that you gave me after my accident," Kugelman offered, hoping that by bringing up the topic of his wife he could mollify his overdeveloped guilty conscience. "As a matter of fact, I'm feeling better than ever. No residuals from the fractured hip. I try to work out a few times a week, but my schedule is even more demanding than before the crack-up."

"Yes, that's all I hear, 'paging Dr. Kugelman, paging Dr. Kugelman.' All the patients that we see rave about what a wonderful doctor you are." The tone of her voice was almost reverent. At that moment it became apparent to Kugelman that she truly liked him. All at once, the possibility that they might be a couple one day didn't seem so farfetched, and of course this caused an element of exhilaration and anxiety to course through his body, as his pulse began to race.

"Well, maybe we'll go out and have a cup of coffee someday and talk about old times when you were my scope assistant." Kugelman was shocked by his boldness.

"That would be great, I'm sure Selma wouldn't mind. I got to know her when you were a patient here. She seemed a very devoted wife."

He wanted to say, "I was just kidding. Out for coffee with a gorgeous babe like you? Let me know any wife who would approve of such a meeting even it was just innocent conversation over some stale java," but instead he replied, "I'm running a bit late, my son has a Social Studies test tomorrow and I need to quiz him."

"Oh, if he's half as smart as you, he'll ace the test," replied Polly, and the look of admiration left no doubt in Kugelman's mind where she stood on the subject of Norman Kugelman. He gave her a final short wave as he shot out the double doors of the ICU.

After dinner, Kugelman went through the motions of helping his son prepare for the test which was Selma's idea of keeping Norman busy during the evenings for the kid was more than "half as smart" as Kugelman, probably considerably smarter. Clearly, he didn't need any assistance at all. The tired father managed not to doze off, so the evening went surprisingly well. Selma was planning an elaborate trip for them to Italy. She seemed to have snapped out of her post-Bar Mitzvah depression. As she bubbled on and on about Florence, Rome and Venice, Kugelman nodded his head with feigned enthusiasm, his mind wandering to the annual hospital golf tournament which was taking place the next day. He had planned to take the afternoon off.

Norman had been a fairly proficient athlete as a kid although he was small for his age. But as previously mentioned, he spent so much time at his Hebrew and secular studies that he never acquired the skills to play high school sports. Golf was a little different. His father was an avid albeit terrible golfer and Norman began to accompany him to the golf course when he was just twelve years old. Being introduced to this frustrating sport at a very young age allowed him to become a mundane but not a great or even good golfer. He could break 100 with regularity, executing four or five powerful strokes and sinking a few putts out of the ninety-five that he played. This was just enough to "bring him back" as the saying goes. The tournament took place on a hot and humid New Jersey afternoon, but just getting away from the office and concentrating on his golf cleansed Kugelman's cluttered cerebrum. Even the many bad shots with the accompanying curse words were more enjoyable than the buttoned up demeanor that he displayed on the job, for he always thought of the profession as a stressful occupation, not a calling, or an exalted position in society as some of his colleagues imagined; only a tough slog to get through each day doing his best, and hoping not to commit a major mistake. But maybe it was just this humility that had contributed to his success. His golf group that day consisted of some of his friends on the medical staff, but not the greatest of players, consequently, his team placed fifth which was out of the money. Nonetheless, he was able to add another golfing photograph to his collection in the office. At the banquet afterwards, Kugelman's entourage amused themselves with stories of previous golf outings, the usual hospital chitchat, as well as sexist comments concerning the pulchritudinous young ladies who had supplied refreshments on the golf course that day.

It was almost ten o'clock before the party broke up. As Kugelman settled into his car, he realized that he had forgotten to call Selma and notify her that he would be arriving home late. In his mildly inebriated state he said to himself, "no big deal, Selma will understand." He couldn't have been more wrong if he had played the string bass in the symphony that day instead of playing golf. The house was eerily quiet as he entered the kitchen. Norman knew from previous experience that this often portended a looming catastrophe. He opened the refrigerator door and avulsed the cap on a can of Diet Coke to quench his thirst from the hot day and the diuretic effect of one too many beers. He tiptoed toward the bedroom, turning the knob on the door ever so slowly so as not to awake Selma if she had fallen asleep, but Selma hadn't fallen asleep. No, she had been stewing for several hours. Her obtuse husband had been gone for the whole day and not once had he contemplated giving her one stinking phone call, not one. Never mind "I love you" before hanging up. The man who slept through Hamlet, the opera, the symphony, and could only think about sleep in Atlantic

City, was suddenly able to find the energy to play golf all day and then drink with his buddies all evening. And who knew who else was with them?

So as Norman opened the door and Selma observed his sweaty face with his sweaty golf shirt and his sweaty pair of shorts, the light bulb that is programmed to go off in a person's brain shattered into tiny pieces in the frontal lobes of Selma Kugelman. She went berserk. All her frustrations about her inattentive, preoccupied, robot through-the-motions spouse exploded, erupting in a torrent of profanity, "You bastard, you god-damned bastard. Not one fucking phone call. Who were your with? The blond at the bar? Or Zimmerman's wife who you fawned over at the holiday party? Were you screwing her?" She yelled these epithets at the top of her voice. Then she charged at him, kicking and punching. Kugelman scrunched into a peek-a- boo defense a la Muhammad Ali to deflect the blows. As he stepped back into the hallway Selma slammed the door as hard as she could and the entire house shuddered at the force of the impact. Adam awoke to see his dad out in the hallway with a pained look on his face. Kugelman told him to go back to bed. His mother was just in a bad mood.

The chastened husband slunk to his study and sat there in his smelly clothes. He had blown it. If he had just called her before the dinner, this wouldn't have happened. If he could just be more fun-loving, no, more fun and loving; if he could just get home on time; if he wasn't so exhausted; if she had pursued her acting career and not married him, if, if if, and he felt guilty for all his failings as a spouse. He put his head in his hands and he wept. For despite all the success he had accomplished in his life with only his brain and his hands, he had made a complete mess of his marriage. He tiptoed back into the bedroom. It was dark and he couldn't tell if Selma was asleep or not. He began to profusely apologize and apologize and apologize. *He was entirely at fault. He should have called. He'll start coming home on time. He'll turn over a new leaf.*

Finally Selma spoke. "Get out your clothes for tomorrow and sleep on the couch." That was it.

The next several weeks were uneventful. Kugleman rose at the crack of dawn, forgot about his workouts and focused on following Selma's rules to the letter. He called her two or three times per day, never failing to say "I love you." He arrived home exactly at six in the evening even if he had to leave work over to the next day. Eventually, Selma allowed the hapless Kugelman to rejoin the marital bed. Her mood improved, and the Selma that he remembered from college re-emerged for a time. On her birthday, he bought her a diamond necklace. She seemed pleased when she opened the gift, but during the subsequent dinner at a posh restaurant, Selma fumed when she noticed Kugelman's eyes wandering to the next table to fix on a sensuous young woman with a revealing décolleté. These few seconds of out of bounds viewing were enough to place a pall on the occasion, such that Kugelman gave up any hope of getting lucky that evening.

Mr. Franklin had been in the ICU for almost six weeks, but slowly he turned the corner. His kidney function reverted to normal and he was weaned from the ventilator. The hard mass in his abdomen slowly diminished in size, while his CT scan improved except that a large pseudocyst had formed where the pancreas had once resided. The medical profession loves the mystery of the word "pseudo," meaning "false" in Greek. *Just call it a god damn cesspool in the belly* mused Kugelman on more than one occasion. Norman was grabbing a quick bite at the hospital cafeteria before his office hours when he noticed Polly walking toward him. "Can I join you for lunch?" she inquired, then sat down next to Kugelman before he could reply.

"I hope there's no pork in that sandwich?"

"No, it's all beef but probably not kosher," Kugelman laughed.

"How's Mr. Franklin coming along?"

"He's doing fine. We're transferring him to the university hospital tomorrow. They're going to drain the pseudocyst on his pancreas."

"Yes, he was one sick cookie when he arrived, but you did a phenomenal job in pulling him through."

"I didn't do much, just kept him alive during the acute phase of his illness, and nature took care of the rest if you know what I mean.

Why do you always sell yourself so short? Do you act that way with Selma? I bet she admires your skill and intelligence just like the hospital staff."

"As a matter of fact she doesn't." Kugelman was as stunned as Polly when he heard himself say that.

"I don't follow," she said as her limpid blue eyes blinked unconsciously.

"We're going through a rough patch. My long hours and preoccupation with my job have gotten to her, I guess. We're trying our best to fix the problem and the problem is mostly me."

"That just amazes me," answered Polly. "Of all the doctors at the hospital you are the kindest and most thoughtful. All the nurses I know would kill to be married to you."

"I might look good on the surface, but underneath it's pretty empty. I'm really not much of a husband. I'm so wrapped up in my work that I don't seem to have anything left for the marriage."

"There you go again, always running yourself down. I never knew that about you. Maybe you need counselling or a talk with your minister. I'm sure you can work this out. I recalled that Selma was such a caring person."

"She is for everyone else, but you're right about the counselling. And by the way, we're Jewish and he's called a rabbi." Kugelman instinctively placed his hand on hers and she didn't pull away. He endured the same rush in his groin that had emerged when he hugged her after the accident. "As a matter of fact, talking to you has made me feel better. Maybe we can get together for that cup of coffee."

"That would be great," replied Polly, making eye contact for the first time. She couldn't hide the eagerness in her face as she wrote down her cell phone number on a napkin and handed it to him. "Give me a call anytime." Kugelman hastily rose from the table. He was late for office hours plus he had to be home promptly at six.

It was Selma that brought up the possibility of marital therapy after another argument where she had thrown a full bottle of milk at him, rupturing the container on the floor. Kugelman couldn't remember the

THE MYTH OF DR KUGELMAN

cause of the spat, just cleaning up all the milk with the help of the dog, who was happy to play her role in lapping up most of it. Norman willingly agreed. They decided to make an appointment with Rabbi Cohen, the associate rabbi. Kugelman had treated the principal spiritual leader, Myron Horowitz, as a patient, and he thought it might be inappropriate to use him as their therapist. Rabbi Cohen was about forty years old. His family had been congregants of the synagogue, and he had been Bar Mitzvahed there. After rabbinical training and a stint as an assistant rabbi in Cleveland, he had returned to New Jersey to become the associate rabbi and heir apparent to Horowitz. He was a pious individual, strictly orthodox. His wife wore a wig as is the custom with the very observant, and they didn't practice birth control. It seemed that every year another Cohen was added to the family until they had six kids. Then it was rumored that his wife Esther had a hysterectomy and the number of children stopping multiplying. Cohen's lips were thick and sensitive. He talked with a mild lisp. Although his nose had a Semitic bend, it didn't dominate his face and certainly couldn't compete with Kugelman's for size. His jaw was weak and his eyeballs were prominent, bulging under his hooded lids. His large black satin yarmulke perched on his head like a shell. The image of a Jewish turtle manifested itself in Kugelman's mind.

Selma made the first appointment for noon on Kugelman's afternoon off. The gastroenterologist scrambled to make his hospital rounds and complete his paper work so that he would be on time. Cohen introduced himself even though they had met several times before. He immediately got down to business, delving into the details of their marital discord. Selma did most of the talking while Kugelman sat there stoically listening to the painful recounting of all his failings. He mostly nodded in agreement with her assessment of his miserable performance as a husband: never on time, not calling her, no excitement in the marriage, lack of affection, just hold my hand, a little gift here and there to surprise me, put me up on a pedestal, and make me feel like a woman. He had heard this laundry list of dissatisfactions and remedies a thousand times, or so it seemed. When it came time for Kugelman's side of the story, he was apologetic for his lapses, agreeing wholeheartedly that Selma had pinpointed all his faults. He expressed his desire to learn how to become a better husband, at the same time emphasizing the importance of saving the marriage.

At the end of the session, Cohen spoke. He tried to find a balance, pointing out to Selma that her husband couldn't always supply her with the love that she craved, commenting that she was overly obsessed with his tardiness; after all, he did have an unpredictable profession. Kugelman was advised to show more affection and work harder on the little things, like a kiss on the lips, and a pat on the cheek. He encouraged both of them to reserve time in the week where the two of them could just be together and talk. He went on to emphasize the importance of God in the relationship and that prayer could help heal their differences. The rabbi suggested attending the synagogue on a regular basis and observing the religious holidays together. He made an appointment for the following week.

As the conferences continued, Norman expended

great effort (or at least great to him) to follow Cohen's advice. He put his energy towards buying tasteful if not mind blowing gifts, and sending her flowers when he remembered. The couple became regulars at the Friday evening services. Kugelman closed his eyes as he recited his prayers, trying to bolster his faint faith while tightly holding Selma's hand as if he was fearful of letting her go. Occasionally, he heard a little voice in his head. "Don't give up on the marriage. Don't leave your wife and child. Stop obsessing over Polly Polk." Was this God talking to him or just the insistent voice from nowhere? He became rather fond of the amphibious-faced Cohen, as he sometimes stuck up for Norman in their meetings, trying to find the root of Selma's anger toward her husband. More than once he remarked, "surely it can't be just Norman coming home late for dinner, it must be something more than that. Could it be that you resent his career and the fact that you never had one of your own?" Try as he might, Selma wouldn't allow the rabbi to probe deeper into her psyche. She insisted that she wasn't jealous of his profession and his status as a doctor, nor did she wish that she'd done something different with her life. Her desire to become an actress was now long past, or so she said, and she didn't blame her mother for advising her to give up her budding career on the stage and marry Norman. And no, she didn't have another marital interest. If the truth be told, she had difficulty admitting any blame for the precarious state of their union except that she was in desperate need of a loving husband. Their leaky matrimonial boat continued to meander along, until one day Selma announced that she didn't particularly care for Cohen and the counselling sessions ended. Kugelman was disappointed, but he agreed that the meetings with the rabbi didn't seem to be going anywhere. As usual, he resolved to try harder to satisfy his unsatisfied wife, for divorce to him was an admission of failure and went against all of the ethics that had been instilled by his parents and his religion.

CHAPTER EIGHT

After the fiasco with Midas, Zeus pursued his quest to re-establish his timeworn religion with renewed zeal. He tried to curb the wild parties and his gourmandizing, and for a time his intestinal disorder improved although his pains never completely subsided. The Don Quixote of divinity decided he needed a consultant. No, not his son Apollo, who had mismanaged the Hercules adventure so badly, nor his brother Hades, who was content with his deathly life in the underworld, with no interest in additional business that might accrue from new converts. Confiding in his wife Hera would only lead to further arguments, plus his dalliance with the Samian nymph had resulted in the conception of his one hundred and third child, and despite his excessive pullulation, he wasn't about to turn his new sweetheart into another cow. No, he had no doubts about his choice for a public relations specialist. He had selected his daughter, the beautiful Athena, the goddess of wisdom and the patron of the great city of Athens, the most intelligent of all the gods and goddesses in the Pantheon. Besides, she was the only child of all his offspring that Zeus had birthed himself. Yes, himself.

Eons ago, Zeus had spotted her mother, the goddess Metis, and was enamored by her beauty. In those days, he was more lustful and more persistent. She turned into a bird to flee from him, but Zeus became a fowl and flew after her, then she became a fish so Zeus transfigured to a sturgeon and swam to her. She morphed into a snake and Zeus converted into Monty, the python, and slithered after the tight ass Titaness. The following day, Metis did not flee and they serenely copulated. In spite of that magic moment, Zeus then opened his mouth and swallowed the young maiden, for he was fearful that if she bore a male, this child would depose him and become the supreme god (like father, like son). Shortly afterward, he developed a terrific headache. His head hurt so badly that he summoned another son, Hephaestus, the god of blacksmiths and neurosurgeons, who split his father's skull with a very sharp ax, and out popped Athena, his comely and brilliant daughter. The fate of Metis is unclear, but Zeus blamed her for some of the gastrointestinal problems that now afflicted him, for there's nothing like a kick in the gut from the inside. Athena became the instructor of man. She taught the earthlings how to sow, harvest, sail, and solve mathematical problems. If anyone could spread some polytheistic propaganda, it was Athena.

When Zeus expounded his dilemma to his daughter, she frowned and then proceeded to tell Zeus the unpleasant truth.

"Dad" she announced in a matter of fact voice, "you're a fuck up."

"A what?" thundered Zeus, looking around for some thunderbolts to hurl at his insolent daughter.

"Calm down Pop, and hear me out. How many children do you know that were delivered by cranial section? And when the other gods ask me about my mother, I have to tell them that she lives in your intestines, and someday I hope to meet her, except only if you puke her up. I suffered my entire adolescence without maternal guidance and most likely wouldn't have turned that lovely maiden Arachne into a spider if I'd had more ego strength. And I've never told anyone before, but after ten thousand years, I'm still a virgin, but maybe it's this body armor and helmet that doesn't attract the guys, gals or gods."

"I'm sorry about that," responded Zeus, blushing slightly, and he continued in a more contrite tone. "Anytime I belch or cramp or suffer from heartburn, I'm reminded of my misdeeds. I loved your mother very much particularly when she was a sparrow, and I, a lovesick robin."

"And how have you lived your life since I was born? You've been travelling around the universe with your concupiscence as a guide instead of your conscience. While you were off somewhere behaving like an ungodly fool, the rest of us had to fill in for you. As for your barbarity and ruthlessness, how do you explain all that? You appear mighty tawdry compared to the likes of Jacob, Job, Jesus and even Joel Olsteen. How many times does Sisyphus have to push that large boulder up the promontory? His sole crime was revealing the whereabouts of a concubine that you were screwing. Then there's the luckless Ixion. I'm aware that he hit on my stepmother Hera, but chaining him to a burning wheel for eternity isn't going to get you any converts in this day and age. And what about Tantalus, residing deep in the underworld with that cup of water ever so close, and not able to imbibe of it. I'm aware that he boiled his son and fed him to the gods, but this is the kind of tale that just doesn't resonate in the modern world. I haven't even mentioned Prometheus."

"I know, I know, I have my peccadillos and these stories are dated, but I'm determined to change my ways. Who should know better than you about the great contribution to civilization by my flock, the ancient Greeks? Remember *feeling good is good enough for all* just like that fellow Bobby Watchamacall." As Zeus struggled to remember the Janis Jooplin hit, Athena became pensive and then she formulated a plan; not to exalt the gods themselves, but to highlight all the famous scientists, mathematicians, and philosophers that had contributed to the advancement of mankind while they worshiped the Olympians as their deities. She came back in a few days with a treatise extolling the brilliant minds of the golden age of Greece and she started reading her text to Zeus.

"Let's start with Pythagoras, a mathematician who lived around 500 BC. He is famous for his study of the triangle, in which he stated that the sum of the squares of the two sides of a right angle equal the sum of the square of the hypotenuse. This axiom is taught to every high school student in every geometry class in the modern world. Despite that, it's not generally known that Pythagoras believed in the immortality of the soul. His followers would not eat meat or fish, similar to the vegans of today, and no eggs, so they were very strict. Still, they had an abhorrence of beans, possibly from the gas produced," and Zeus eagerly nodded his head in agreement.

"He was followed by Euclid who coined such terms as "parabola" and "ellipse." He studied optics and vision and thought that discrete rays emanated from the eyes. Well, nobody's perfect. And Archimedes, who is best known for his famous epiphany, while in the bath tub; that a submerged body would displace water according to its volume. At that discovery, the excitable mathematician yelled 'Eureka--I have found it' as he nakedly bolted from his dwelling to announce his discovery. One of the early astronomers was Aristarchus, the first stargazer to postulate that the earth revolved around the sun. There is evidence that Copernicus of Poland read his work two thousand years later when he proposed the same concept. Remember Eratosthenes. Most people don't. He calculated the circumference of the earth by looking at the sun's reflection in a well during the summer solstice, proving that the earth was a sphere. All these discoveries occurred at the same time that the Old Testament was describing this planet as flat. And who can forget the venerable Empedocles? He had a fantastic theory of evolution. In the beginning there were tribes of grotesque creatures: some with heads but no necks, arms without shoulders, and limbs in odd places with multiple hands. There were bodies of oxen with faces of men, and bodies of men with the head of a cow. With passage of time, these freaks were eliminated and modern animals developed. He was the first proponent of the air, fire, earth, and water theory, in conjunction with Love or Strife which ascended or diminished according to an eternal cycle. Lamentably, with time, Empedocles fancied himself a god. He leaped into an active volcano to prove he was immortal, but was never seen again prompting the famous couplet, 'Great Empedocles, that ardent soul, leapt into Etna, and was roasted whole.'

"That was a mistake," tittered Zeus, "but I wouldn't give up on the four elements theory, it may yet prove correct," but as he voiced this opinion, he emitted a prodigious yawn.

"I haven't finished yet father Zeus. I've documented fifteen more scientists followed by philosophers, architects, and playwrights."

"Let's give it a rest for a while. I'm craving a little libation. Then it will be time for my afternoon nap followed by my soak in the tub. Just leave the rest of the manuscript with me and I'll read it when I get a chance."

Athena threw her document at Zeus, and stormed out the door.

One year after the start of their courtship, Kevin Midas and Sally Simpson were married in the evangelical church located in an industrial part of Bergenfield between an auto repair shop and a vacant lot growing thistles as tall as an elephant's eye. The house of worship looked out on a picturesque little stream which was in fact a sluice for runoff water. After a heavy rain, a distinct odor of sewage could be detected, but fortunately not on this day. It was a cloudless spring afternoon with the sun benignly showering its rays through the open church windows onto the loving couple, while the cawing of a crow perched on a nearby telephone wire could be heard when the slightly out of tune organ wasn't playing. Kevin, despite his mandibular malocclusion, was a handsome groom in his newly tailored suit, one of three that he had a purchased at Joseph Bank Clothiers for the price of one, while Sally was resplendent in her elegant but frugal wedding dress from JC Penney. George was the best man. He was clean shaven and his hair was stylishly tied in a chignon bun. He prepared himself for the task at hand by nervously fingering the rings in his right pants pocket, constantly checking to be sure that he hadn't forgotten them. Sally's younger sister was the matron of honor. She and her husband had arrived the previous evening from Idaho where they made a living guiding float trips down the Salmon River and growing marijuana in their back yard. But today she wore a conservative shift dress that barely hid her fourth pregnancy.

In attendance was Polly Polk, radiant in a delicate sheer blouse and a tight fitting long skirt which did nothing to hide her generous god given attributes. She was accompanied by a friend, Doug Armstrong, a coworker from the hospital. Polly denied any romantic attachment to the handsome nurse, and to be honest, there were rumors that the man was gay. Herky and Alice sat in the first pew. In two short years, the brawny fellow had become a pillar of Christianity. He had recently become a deacon in the St. Patrick Catholic church in Hoboken. With a loving wife and adorable children, the Frum family was an exemplary model for traditional Americana before the advent of single parents and same-sex marriage. The reception was held at a Mexican restaurant near the church. Kevin wasn't interested in advertising his Greek roots or religion anymore. After the wedding, the couple spent a week at the Waldorf Astoria, ate at expensive restaurants, visited all the Manhattan museums and attended three Broadway plays. Sally worried that all this spending was beyond their budget, but Kevin argued that this honeymoon was the last one for both of them, so they might as well blow what little money they had saved.

Disturbingly, their business enterprise had begun to flounder now that the former gold bug was no longer fabricating any more of the yellow metal. The jewelry business had always been very competitive, but the Great Recession had seen many individuals cut back on nonessential items now that they were no longer able to pay for these possessions with home equity loans. Although the would-be customers admired Sally's skill, they often didn't buy. She contemplated returning to the nursing profession to make ends meet and applied for a job at her former hospital working the night shift so she could still mind the store during the daytime hours. Sally urged Kevin to talk to Herky about hiring him back at the turkey plant, but her freshly minted husband refused to follow her advice. To her astonishment, the Christian teachings captivated and inspired the one-time Greek monarch. In a short period of time, he became a regular at the weekly services in contrast to her sporadic Christmas and Easter attendance. One Sunday morning, he was baptized into the Christian faith.

Kevin read the bible stories, comparing them to the ancient Greek polytheism, noting that many of the words such as Genesis and Exodus were words of Greek origin. He learned that one all-powerful God created the world in just six days. This seemed a lot simpler than the quarrelsome divinities and monsters: Uranus, Cronus, Rhea, the Titans, the Giants and the Cyclops, with the ingestion of children, incestuous marriage, and nurturing goats, with no definite blueprint of how and why the world came to be. He read about the intrepid Moses parting the waters of the Red Sea, and his successor, Joshua, blowing down the walls of Jericho. The onetime king studied the book of Job, impressed by the misfortunes that the pious man endured to test his faith by an all-powerful god. At bible class, Kevin was an avid student, as the pastor explained the exegeses of the New Testament, and he reveled in the devotion of Jesus to the poor and the hungry. The ex-king studied the Messiah's miracles: exorcising demons, feeding the hungry, walking on water, re-ascending to heaven, and realized that the Christian savior was infinitely superior to the clown crew on Mt. Olympus. When he discovered that Christ died for man's sins, he was relieved, for he had done a whole lot of sinning. Kevin listened intently on Sunday morning when the preacher exhorted the flock to put their faith in Jesus Christ, for if they adhered to His teachings, the congregants would spend eternity in the blissfulness of the hereafter, but if they rejected the Savior, Hell would be their destination on the Day of Judgment. Midas recalled his struggle in Hades and his failed quest for admission to the Elysian Fields. Even Homer's inspiring prose could never lift his spirit as did the gospels of Matthew, Mark, Luke and John. And how could Zeus ever compare to the real God?

Kevin spent most days studying scripture, and to Sally's annoyance, completely lost interest in the struggling bauble business, leaving the entire operation to his new wife. He began to teach his own religious class. One Sunday morning, when the preacher was called out of town to attend to his ill father, Kevin gave a sermon to the congregation. His topic was the Good Samaritan. To his amazement, and maybe it was the regal bearing that he had inculcated centuries ago, the worshipers were moved by his exhortations. At the end of the service, the men patted him on the back while the women hugged him tearfully, implying to Kevin that his preaching was more effective than the resident reverend. One of the attendees was visiting that morning from Dover, NJ in the next county. He suggested that Kevin might come to preach to a few of his friends in that community. Once again, he was enthusiastically received. Kevin impetuously decided to open a new church there and rented a rundown building in the old part of that town. The practical Sally was wary of this venture, but she agreed to sell her mortgage free house and withdrew her application at the hospital. They moved to a dingy apartment near the church where Kevin could be closer to his parishioners, and Sally commuted the thirty miles to their jewelry shop in her old Dodge Neon. It wasn't long before their modest little building was overflowing with parishioners searching for answers to life and death, while seeking reassurance that their soul would be saved in the hereafter. Kevin's comforting homilies and optimistic message soothed their anxious inner selves. They could sleep at night knowing that faith in their preacher and faith in Jesus would keep them from perdition.

And then a strange thing happened. The previous vice that had gripped the former sovereign in ancient times reasserted itself in spite of his discovery of Christ: this shepherd to the lost sheep of humanity, this man walking in the footsteps of God, this beacon of illumination for darkened souls, succumbed to the very depravity that had risen up and consumed him in antiquity. Not surprisingly, this recurrent evil was greed. For it soon dawned on the Midas mentality that establishing himself as a super star salvation maven could make him buckets of money, maybe even more money than turning stuff to gold, for didn't the bible state, "if you have not been trustworthy in handling worldly wealth who will trust you with true riches" (Luke 16)? And that's what he set out to do.

He and the reluctant Sally broke their leases in the apartment and jewelry store, packed up, and departed New Jersey. They settled in Texas, a hot bed for evangelism and unbridled capitalism. He borrowed some of the cash that his Dover parishioners had tithed to their church--some might construe this as "stole," despite his promises to pay it back--and used the money as a down payment on a large abandoned Circuit City building in the suburbs of Dallas. He renovated the edifice and extravagantly decorated his office with oil paintings and statues of Jesus and his disciples. A large antique oak desk was purchased to sit on an opulent Persian rug. Lush velveteen covered seats with drink holders were installed in the auditorium. The lectern where he addressed the congregation was constructed from the finest marble while the lighting overhead could be adjusted to set the proper mood depending on his themes. Preacher Midas established a website, took out full page advertisements in the local newspapers, and without any formal training or accreditation, he began to preach to the multitudes.

His message was clear. If they would place their faith in Jesus, their entrance through the gates of heaven was a slam dunk, but not only would they obtain the immortality of their soul, they would attain success in the here and now, accumulate wealth, and have all the worldly possessions imaginable. To accomplish all this, they needed to confirm their faith in Pastor Midas. The congregants were therefore obligated to generously support his teaching, preaching, and beseeching, by donating as much money as possible so their minister could continue to deliver his divine message. And if this required some plastic, there was even a special form on the tithing sheets where they could write in the numbers of their debit or credit cards. The thoughtful shepherd accepted MasterCard, Visa, and American Express, and he reminded them not to forget the little number on the back of the card and the expiration date. If they didn't possess any plastic or a bank account to write a check, they could obtain a payday loan with a thirty percent interest rate, but of course Pastor Midas left out that salient bit of information.

As the money began to roll in, Kevin purchased a six thousand square foot home in a tony suburb with a lap pool, putting green, and a tennis court. Sally was skeptical, yet she had to admit that Kevin had a real talent for his new profession. Maybe it was love for her new husband or their luxurious life style, but she overlooked his dishonesty, his disingenuousness, and his hunger for the almighty dollar. Kevin bought an expensive Maserati for himself and a Porsche SUV for Sally. Soon he was receiving invitations from all over the country to deliver his message, so he leased a private plane to avoid the inconvenience of commercial air travel. Sally disliked flying and didn't accompany him on these preaching trips. Kevin felt a need to change his image. He bought a closet full of Armani and Ermenegildo Zegna suits with impeccably matched handmade ties, and the Men's Warehouse and Joseph Bank wardrobe was shipped to Good Will (about the only donation that the disadvantaged received from the Midas' that year). At his urging, Sally bought Oscar de la Renta dresses, Yves St. Laurent perfume, and Judith Leiber handbags. Kevin visited an oral surgeon and had his jaw and teeth worked on so that all the donkey remnants on his face disappeared, and his mien acquired the look of a man communicating with God.

Their lavish spending eventually began to catch up with them. The money that they were raking in from their constituents could not keep up with their exorbitant expenses, particularly the second home in Aspen, and the small yacht anchored in Key Biscayne. Thus, Kevin came up with a new wrinkle to augment their income. He hit upon faith healing as a way to produce more revenue. Disabled individuals were brought on stage during his preaching, usually folks who were crippled or blind, some ailment that could be easily discerned by the congregation. Kevin would pray and wail and implore the Savior, often speaking in tongues. Remarkably, their afflictions would melt away and they would be healed, but of course unbeknownst to the rapt audience, these infirm characters were paid actors and the script was rehearsed well in advance of their "cures." Kevin raked in the cash from the hordes of sick men and women who were easily duped by these unethical if not criminal schemes. The fraudulent preacher knew that he was falling into a trap that he had been in before, but the acquisition of wealth was a potent aphrodisiac to his soul. He couldn't stop himself, even though he prayed diligently to God to help him find a way to desist from travelling down this evil path, but he received no answers from the Almighty, just like he had received no answers from Zeus, Apollo or Hades.

On one of his trips to Los Angeles, Kevin met a young woman by the name of Jessica. She was tall, of mixed race, part Latino and part black, a former beauty pageant winner and a runner-up for Miss California. This alluring vixen regrettably became addicted to prescription drugs and cocaine, followed by a failed marriage. She was confused and searching for meaning in her life. On a whim, she decided to attend a mega prayer meeting where Pastor Midas was the main attraction. So enthralled was this needy woman with the power of his words that she returned the next evening to hear his uplifting message. Jessica, like many beautiful women, wore clothing which accentuated her voluptuousness, consciously or unconsciously requiring the gawking, head-swiveling stares of men, whether studs or scumbags, to validate her attractiveness to the opposite sex and maybe to her inner self. On her second visit, she went backstage to meet the mesmerizing preacher. Kevin couldn't take his eyes off

her as she breathlessly announced that she had decided
to find salvation and become a born again Christian after
hearing his message from the pulpit. Kevin suggested that
they continue their dialogue at a quiet bar not far from
where he was staying. There, he repeated his Christian
themes to the impressionable young lady who listened
raptly. One thing led to another and Jessica spent the
night in Kevin's hotel room, but it didn't end there. After
the evangelist returned to Dallas, he received an endless
stream of communication from the besotted girl, hungry
for his attention. He tried to put her off but his flesh was
weak. Will power was not his strong suit. The next time
he was in Los Angeles they met for a torrid weekend
of debauchery and Jessica introduced the supposed
holy man to the drug scene. They smoked marijuana
and popped Vicodins while talk of Jesus was put on the
back burner. This was the first, but certainly not the last
adultery that Midas committed in the cities where he
preached.

It took some time, but Sally ultimately found out
about her husband's sexual misdeeds. One afternoon
while Kevin was taking a swim in their pool, his cell
phone on their kitchen table erupted with the incessant
buzzing that ensued from multiple text messages. Sally
picked up the phone and, in a state of shock, read the
sexually explicit missives from Jessica, repeating the
same theme: her loneliness and desire for him, while
begging Kevin to be with her that weekend. Sally didn't
say anything right then, but it didn't take long for Kevin
to tell her that he had just received an emergency call
to fill in for a colleague in Los Angeles. Over time, she
surreptitiously searched through his carry-on bags and

found negligees along with other bawdy items from Victoria's Secret accompanied by scented cards addressed to Jessica, but occasionally Paula or Christy were the recipients of his largesse. Sally had been so caught up in the life of the rich and famous that she had become blind to Kevin's philandering. Now she became furious and confronted her husband. Kevin tried to placate her by buying his disillusioned wife a five carat diamond ring while swearing on the bible to mend his profligate ways, but the desperate Jessica resorted to calling their home phone at all hours of the day and night when Kevin threatened to break things off. After another year of his excuses and itinerant infidelity, Sally finally decided to leave him. She headed back to New Jersey with her dog, and temporarily moved in with her friend, Polly Polk. She went back to work in the Intensive Care Unit, but obviously she was no longer the head nurse, and accepted a significant cut in pay. The ring and all the extravagant clothing that Kevin had given her was sold to pay her debts. The distraught woman filed for divorce, ashamed and humiliated that she had ever fallen for such an avaricious scoundrel as Kevin Midas.

CHAPTER NINE

At one time, Asclepius had been a famous physician. Lamentably, he made a grievous error in judgment when he decided to bring dead people to life. As stated previously, this power angered Zeus, for he had planned for man to live and then die, and he resented Asclepius' interference in the order of human existence. After Zeus booted Asclepius upstairs to the heavens, temples were erected to celebrate the physician's healing powers. The populace frequented these hallowed sanctuaries to affect cures for their ailments and pay homage to the snakes that were often kept in these holy places. However, that had been ages ago. In modern times, the image of Asclepius' staff with the entwined serpent was still employed by physician societies and medical schools to adorn their letter-heads and yearbooks, but in today's medical community, most contemporary practitioners had scant knowledge of this eminent healer's accomplishments.

Asclepius had never liked Zeus; never liked his boorishness, his promiscuity, or his petulance, plus he was tired of his incessant carping about the loss of the great Hippocrates to the Elysian Fields. The snake charmer was jealous that the top-god had always favored the other physicians in the pantheon, who were in fact Asclepius' female children: Panacea, for remedies, Hygea, for cleanliness, Iaso, for recuperation and Aegle, for good health. He had taught these gals all he knew about doctoring, but never received any credit for his mentoring. One stinking mistake in judgment in an otherwise unsullied career of ministering to the sick; was that enough reason to completely ignore the most talented doctor in the celestial medical group? He had seen Greek mythology crumble in its relevance to the mortal world under the stewardship of Zeus and he felt there was a need for a change at the top. He had some candidates in mind, including himself. He grumbled to the other gods about the incompetence of their leader and found some sympathetic ears amongst the lesser deities, including Atlas, who had become fed up with holding up the earth, complaining that his joints were stiff from standing in one spot for so long. Asclepius had even taken a secret trip to mythological hell, Tartarus, and had exploratory talks with some Titans for another war and the overthrow of Zeus and his minions. However, to his disappointment, these fellows had aged and their zeal for battle had waned. Even Prometheus had lost his fire.

In his heavenly residence, Asclepius watched the superstar clinicians perform their art: Hippocrates,

Aristotle, Galen, as well as Benjamin Rush and William Osler in the United States. He observed Harvey's studies of blood circulation, Jenner's development of the smallpox vaccine, Fleming's discovery of penicillin, Banting's formulation of insulin and even Doogie Howser's success as a teenage intern, but Asclepius still believed that the ancient ways of medicine were superior to modern methods and he dreamed that someday he would get a chance to once again prove his mettle.

He made a point of avoiding Zeus and his hypochondria, leaving his daughters to manage the day to day gripes of the Supreme God, but today was the date of the annual physical so he put on his cleanest white toga, coiled his most energetic snake around his staff, and trudged to the palace along the cobblestone road which was badly in need of resurfacing. Zeus was annoyed when Hera reminded him of his check-up, for he had planned to share an afternoon snack of goat's milk and honey--yes, there was milk and honey on Mt. Olympus too--with a young naiad that he had recently met in a nearby pond. He had no use for the arrogant reincarnator and his foolishness. Instead of sticking to his knitting and helping to heal the human race, this busybody had interfered with the love life of Aphrodite, and involving himself in the business of gods was none of his god damned business. Asclepius entered the royal chamber and promptly got down to the task at hand with barely a hello.

"Any new complaints?"

"Nope, same old problems. I still have the cramps and bloating, maybe a little better than last year, but not much. Got any new remedies?"

"Nothing specifically that I can report today, but as I've outlined to you in the past, in exquisite detail I might add, most of your problems stem from an imbalance of the four humors gyrating around your heart and into your gut. The black bile has mixed with the liver blood in a frightful proportion, and the phlegm, oh the sticky phlegm, has coated your spleen and replaced the yellow bile in your choledochal duct. As a result, your moods are up and down with the phases of the moon. After careful annotations and observations of the planets Mars and Venus, particularly when Orion is high in the winter sky, I've come to the brilliant conclusion that you suffer from a bipolar disorder. Unfortunately, there's not much you can do about that. Yes, the psychiatrists nowadays claim that lithium or Prozac can help, but I'm skeptical of these twenty-first century shrinks--a bunch of charlatans with no scientific basis for their treatments."

"Could they be any worse than those herbs that you prescribed from your garden? Talk about bitter, you know my tongue burned for days after that last concoction...."

"Excuse me, Great God, but I resent your attitude toward my buckthorn berries. If you had taken them as I had prescribed instead of feeding them to the Olympian goats, I'm positive that in time your gut would have improved. When I gave them to Poseidon, his hemorrhoids shrank in three days. And of course, the theriac gave you headaches, and Trigonella, the rash. I'm sorry. None of that was my fault."

"Look, great healer," and Zeus let out an irreverent grunt. "Maybe I should get a second opinion. Hermes was telling me about a doctor called a gastroenterologist that could examine my gut."

"Let me tell you about these men that look into intestines. You might think I don't keep track of the new advances in my profession, but I certainly do. I'm proud to announce that I've been reading about the colonoscope in my medical journals. I feel I am uniquely qualified to use this instrument because of my vast experience with the healing power of snakes." This imperious pronouncement grated on Zeus's nerves, and the Preeminent One laughed the derisive laugh that he reserved for people and deities that aggravated him.

"That's technology, you numbskull; it's got nothing to do with your snake or snake oil crap. Hermes tells me that you need special training called a fellowship to put that thing in a human. What are you going to tell some medical board? That you obtained a degree by apprenticing to a centaur?"

"What's wrong with Chiron? He knows more about pharmacology than anyone in the universe except for me. And as you remember, I have the power to raise the dead." Asclepius instantly regretted this outburst, but his pent up animosity was hard to stifle.

"Don't bring that subject up again!" thundered Zeus. "I employed a few lightning bolts on Hercules not long ago--I'm sorry to say they were ineffective--but I'll use them again if necessary."

"It's just that I've hung around on this moldy mountain forever. You have no need for me, preferring my daughters to my best efforts."

"Your offspring were way ahead of their time. Do you know that more women are enrolling in medical school these days than men? At least they listen to my complaints and seem genuinely concerned about my excess gas and borborygmus even though they aren't able to cure me. Your youngest, Aegle, she's a cute and perky little thing. She cheers me up, always trying to get me into the gymnasium for a workout. But if you can't do me any good, you best be on your way."

"I bet I could go down there and operate those scopes and show those gastromythologists or whatever they're called a thing or two about how to heal the sick."

"You can't be serious."

"No, those doctors will be shocked when they see the great Asclepius back at work, performing his diagnosing and his healing."

"Let me tell you something, old sawbones. Hermes has been educating me on the practice of medicine in the twenty-first century. Believe me, it's much different than when you hammered up the shingle more than a few millennia ago. It's very complicated and stressful. You can't see one or two patients a day. You've got to churn out the production. Then there's paper-work, bill collection, law suits, continuing education seminars, and you need permission from higher authorities to prescribe a medicine or order a test. You wouldn't believe the bureaucracy in managing a patient these days. I'm told that even treating a cough is Kafkaesque, and there won't be any time to grow all that damn spinach in your garden."

"They're called herbs," retorted Asclepius.

"Whatever they are, they won't do you much good in today's health care environment."

"But what about Hermes and Mars, they've developed product lines like clothing and candy bars that have sold very well in the modern world."

Zeus was becoming terribly irritated, wishing that he'd never have to deal with this pain in the ass again. "O.K., you've got a bet. You go down there and show those doctors the ancient ways of medicine, and if you're successful then I'll retire and you can take over. You don't fool me. That's what you've been planning for a while. But if you fail, then I'll banish you from the sacred mountain, take away your snakes and ship you to Tartarus to be with your Titan buddies. I know you were recently down there stirring up trouble. And remember, no bringing the dead back to life. Is that clear?   I'm going to send you to the United States. I know just the fellow you need to work with. His name is Dr. Norman Kugelman. This guy is a magician with the scopes. There's a rumor abounding that he's looking for an associate. I'll contact Demetrius Georgopoulos, the distant relative of King Eurystheus, who will prepare some documents indicating that you have a license in New Jersey and are board certified in gastroenterology. Stay down there as long as you want."

"You've got a deal. I'll show these Johnny-come-latelies a thing or two." Asclepius shook Zeus's hand, sealing the bet, then waved goodbye to the naked Naiad who was about to serve her lord some fresh baked cookies from the Olympian oven.

CHAPTER TEN

Zeus had been correct. Norman Kugelman was urgently searching for an associate. The practice was busier than ever, and he was arriving home later than ever, and thus Selma was more disgusted with him than ever. One of his partners was on leave after suffering an almost fatal heart attack, and with subsequent open heart surgery, the likelihood of him rejoining the practice full-time was in doubt. Just this past week, the junior associate announced on short notice that he was moving to Florida to join a lucrative practice in Boca Raton where he could earn more money while seeing less patients. Kugelman was desperate to find help. He placed ads in all the medical journals and attended Digestive Disease Week, the national convention of gastroenterologists, seeking a subordinate to join him. A few applicants showed interest, but when they observed the seedy location of the building and the indigent clientele, they were so unimpressed that Kugelman never heard from them again. He mulled over the possibility of selling the entire operation to a hospital or large clinic, and moving his practice to a more affluent town nearer their home. Selma had encouraged him in this endeavor, but in spite of that, he was reticent to make such a change. His idealistic streak was against abandoning his patients just to earn more money and his lifestyle was more than comfortable. Miraculously, a few weeks later, he received a call from a physician recruiter, a Mr. Georgopoulos, who told him that a gentleman from Greece was interested in the position and would be coming for an interview.

When the fellow arrived for his appointment, Kugelman was taken aback by his appearance. He had the swarthy complexion of a man from the Mediterranean. He spoke with a Greek accent, and emanated a faint smell of body odor. His hair was preponderantly grey, slicked straight back. His nose was refined, aquiline in shape, while his dark eyes stared out intensely like a mythological eagle. He wore open-toed sandals and a faded sport jacket with leather patches on his elbows, a style that was popular in the 1980's, and Kugelman could have sworn that he was wearing a toga. He leaned on a cane adorned with an image of an animal, possibly a serpent of some sort. An odd shaped satchel was slung over his shoulder that Kugelman found out later was a goat's bladder. When the gastroenterologist asked him his name, he responded, "In this country I go by Dr. A.S. Clepius, but you can just call Cleppy if you so desire.

Kugelman inquired about his training. "I worked

with the famous Chiron in Greece and acquired most of my gastroenterology knowledge in Macedonia near Mt Olympus." The American had no familiarity with Greek teaching programs, but in the U.S., Chiron had been a biotechnology company before being bought out, and Olympus Inc. was the largest manufacturer of colonoscopes. Asclepius added, "I have been in the United States for three months to learn English. I've obtained a temporary medical license until my references arrive, which might take some time as they have been archived for many years."

Kugelman took the Greek on a tour of the facility. Asclepius seemed intrigued with the equipment, particularly the scopes, and although his dress and mannerisms were a bit odd, he was polite and respectful, carefully hiding his streak of arrogance. Kugelman was willing to overlook his obscure training and bizarre persona, plus he was desperate. The next day, after discussing the candidate with Selma who was naturally skeptical, he offered the man a job, with the opportunity of a partnership in the near future. To the doctor's astonishment, Dr. Clepius immediately accepted.

Three weeks later, Asclepius showed up for his new employment. He was still wearing the same peculiar outfit. Kugelman advised him to take off the sports jacket, and handed him an oversized lab coat to cover most of his gown along with a stick of deodorant. There were three patients in the holding area awaiting colonoscopy. Kugelman was on his way to a hospital for an emergency so he turned them over to the Greek. Dr. Clepius worked slowly on the first case. The nurse assisting him noticed that he was unfamiliar with the technique for as he started up the colon, he kept banging against the walls, making little progress. She was about to place a call to Kugelman, when out of the blue, he began to hum a strange tune, almost like a chant. Immediately the scope started to advance, albeit slowly, ultimately reaching the cecum (the end of the colon). The following two examinations proceeded in the same manner, but it had taken him the whole morning to complete just three procedures where Kugelman normally did ten or twelve.

That afternoon, Cleppy saw a few patients in the clinic. As luck would have it, the first patient was Bertha Tootle, the patient with the fifteen-year history of irritable bowel syndrome. The yogurt had improved her bloating for several months, prompting her to pronounce Kugelman a genius, but grievously the baby elephant stomping in her belly had returned from his vacation while the ten pound Buddha had been employed again to sit on her abdomen, this time without much success, so she was eager to see the new associate. After listening to the recitation of her ailments, Cleppy pulled out some greenery from his sack. "This is thapsian, a plant that I used in Greece for just such a problem. Make some tea from these leaves instead of the kudzu. Hippocrates used this remedy and he was quite successful." Mrs. Tootle left the office pleased that her new physician had confidently come up with a novel remedy for her long standing complaints. The next patients included: Mr. Orville Lush with cirrhosis of the liver, Ms. Lexy Forsythe complaining of a stomach ache, and an eighteen year old, Pedro Sanchez, with acid reflux. Asclepius went through the same routine, reaching into his bag for an herb or an ointment. He even sang a song for the young man with heartburn.

A few problems did crop up. Asclepius told the patients that they could pay whatever they determined was appropriate. If they had a few pieces of gold, a chicken, or some vegetables, it was fine with him. Obviously, none of these folks had any of these objects in their possession, so they ended up paying nothing. He didn't take any notes on the computer during these visits, but wrote down a few words in Greek on a scrap of paper. At the end of the day, Kugelman was informed of his new associate's clumsy colonoscopic technique as well as his unorthodox performance with the clinic patients. He brought Dr. Clepius into his office emphasizing the need to fill out the billing forms so that insurance would reimburse the practice, while stressing that barter was not an acceptable method of payment. Kugelman reviewed the computer program with him again, and underscored the need for precise entries, emphasizing the consequences of their absence if there was ever a malpractice suit. The Hellene was baffled by these criticisms, and didn't comprehend the words "insurance" and "malpractice suit." He kept repeating that he was gratified to work with a snake again, even if it was a mechanical one. Kugelman ruminated that hiring Dr. Clepius might have been a mistake.

A month went by, but Cleppy's production was still below par and his new employer was disheartened by his sluggish progress. Kugelman signed the new physician's first paycheck and handed it over to him. After looking it over, Dr. Clepius was surprised with the paltry sum. Although the gross pay was the amount that he had agreed to, after deductions, there was only sixty-five percent remaining. The senior partner patiently explained the withholding of Social Security, Medicare, and income taxes, and mentioned that after paying the secretary and nurse's salary, along with the hefty malpractice bill, he was actually losing money on his new assistant. Cleppy did not grasp most of this elucidation, and furthermore, he yearned for the days when he could collect some virgin olive oil or goat cheese for his services, while partaking of ripe basil and oregano leaves from his garden to enhance a delicious lunch. It didn't take long for him to recognize that a manufactured scope could never replace his faithful serpents.

Kugelman's personal life remained in turmoil and eventually his time at work became more of a respite than the continual conflict at home. He had discontinued his regular attendance at the synagogue, but like most Jews, even the least observant, he showed up at the High Holiday services, Rosh Hashanah and Yom Kippur, just to validate that he was of the Jewish faith. After almost six thousand years of misery he wasn't about to abandon the old religion, even though his mind often wandered in the service except to assiduously keep track of the number of pages left in the prayer book so he could head for home. As they were leaving the morning prayers on Rosh Hashanah, Rabbi Cohen, resplendent in his white gown and yarmulke, looking like an albino turtle, came up to Selma and Norman with a New Year's greeting.

"Shona Tova Kugelmans. I haven't seen the two of you for months. How are things going between you?"

Kugelman blocked an urge to blurt "like crap" but he waited for Selma's reply, not wanting to make an unnecessary mistake.

"Oh, we're doing just fine!" responded Selma in the breezy and carefree manner that she reserved for everyone other than her husband. Kugelman smiled in concurrence as the rush of other congregants pushed them aside, but he made a resolution to make an appointment with Cohen on his own.

A few weeks later, he sat in the Rabbi's office bemoaning the continuing dysfunction of his marriage. He had more tales of petty arguments surrounding his errant punctiliousness along with the more pointed accusations regarding his paucity of puppy love. As Selma's dissatisfaction amplified, his sleep-time on the couch had risen. Cohen pursed his prominent lips and tugged at the back of his oversized skull cap. He seemed generally concerned, and Kugelman was fond of him for his sympathetic attentiveness.

"I don't know what to tell you at this point; I don't seem to have the answers. You know, Selma strikes me as a decent person. Yet she has never accepted any responsibility for your marital difficulties, and you seem to blame yourself entirely. I firmly believe that neither one of you are being honest with each other. Doesn't her constant carping and dissatisfaction make you angry? Surely you can't believe you're that bad of a husband? Look at all your strengths--your integrity, your faithfulness, and your ability to make a living for your family. Maybe only so-so or worse in the romantic department, but overall a mensch. You remind me of Sisyphus pushing that boulder up the hill but never reaching the top, if I could use a mythical analogy." Even rabbis need a Greek myth to sometimes illustrate a point.

"I suppose I'm angry at times, but when I do get

upset with her, things just get worse between us. I keep thinking that I can fix this thing but frankly I fear that the marriage will break apart. You know, I made those wedding vows forever."

"Maybe you require more professional help, a psychologist who has training in marital therapy or maybe it's never going to work for the two of you, and you should consider a separation at least for a period of time. In the Jewish faith we accept divorce and there's even a ceremony called a "get" to make it all kosher."

Kugelman was taken aback by the rabbi's candid confession. For the first time, he had heard the ugly "D" word from somebody other than his innerself. Instead he answered, "That's what we need to do. I'll run it by Selma. Maybe she'll agree to further counselling." He was not about to accept the end of his marriage.

One morning, Kugelman was making his rounds when he ran into Sally Simpson. He had not forgotten about the curious object that he had removed from her boyfriend and now husband, Kevin Midas. He was often called to the Emergency Room to remove hot dogs, sirloin, turkey or the odd chicken bone from esophagi, but he had never encountered a stone, never mind a gold one. He had worked with Sally for many years at the hospital. She was always good for a joke or two and often had Kugelman in stitches, but she was also a very knowledgeable professional. He placed great trust in her assessments of their mutual patients, which made him wonder how a level headed person like Sally had ever fallen for this Midas chap who appeared to be a real oddball. He remembered that as the fellow was being anesthetized, he kept muttering about swallowing shards of gold and why hadn't Dionysus warned him not to drink from that cup. Sally had told the nurse in the ER that Kevin had ingurgitated a piece of meat while eating a late night snack, but instead he had found the golden sphere. She seemed bewildered when he showed the object to her. Now why would anybody swallow something like that, let alone put one in his mouth at one a.m.? Then Kugelman reminded himself that he had retrieved equally strange objects in the past. Some goofy folks jammed things up their rectum for a sexual thrill, while a few psychotic individuals ingested screw drivers, forks, spoons, and even scissors, but Mr. Midas didn't seem to fit those categories. He had heard that they had married and moved to Dallas where he preached the gospel. Kugelman had once seen him on television on a Sunday morning as he was surfing through the channels trying to find Meet the Press, so he was surprised that she was back in town and working at the hospital.

Sally filled him in on her unfortunate time with Kevin. She related his success as a preacher, then his branching out into faith healing while becoming unfaithful to her. Now they were going through a painful divorce. But to make matters worse, her soon to be ex-husband had been indicted for tax evasion, for unbeknownst to her, he had never paid anything to the IRS on all the money that he had made and subsequently spent. She became a bit weepy as she related this sad tale. Now she was starting over with a pile of debt, while Kevin could be looking at multiple years in prison. Kugleman told himself, "now there's an unscrupulous character, how would Selma like to be hitched to that crook?" After staying with her old friend Polly Polk for two months, she and her poodle were about to relocate to a rented house in her old neighborhood. Kugelman's heart performed a flip-flop with the mention of Polly, but he was genuinely distressed by Sally's misfortune.

"Did you ever find out why he swallowed that stone?"

"Oh, if I told you, you would never believe me," and Kugelman changed the subject. He couldn't resist the urge to inquire about Polly whom he had not seen at the hospital for several months.

"She's very happy. A man has come into her life, Dr. Percival Dredge. You know him, the cardiologist that used to be on staff here until he moved to a better location in Paramus. She quit here about a month ago. She's working as a nurse in his office. No weekends or holidays, and she arrives home every day at five p.m. The woman loves the job and I think she loves Percy. They've become engaged. The wedding is set for the end of the summer."

"Dredge, that schmuck!" burst out Kugelman in a voice that caused a few heads to turn at the nursing station. "When I was on the executive committee here at the hospital, we had to discipline him for reaming out a nurse in front of her colleagues. He used the "C" word, a word you can never use when yelling at a female, if you know what I mean. It was rumored that when he was married, he had sex in the doctor's on-call room with a few of the techs. And talk about unnecessary procedures, this guy was putting stents in the hearts of demented patients from nursing homes just to collect the fee. We were all relieved when he left the staff before we had to take away his privileges. She's marrying *him*?"

"The man has reformed, now that he's met Polly, at

least that's what Polly tells me. He's been divorced for a few years and has joint custody of his children. Polly's become quite attached to Jason and Kristen. They all just returned from a hiking trip in Colorado, and Dr. Dredge bought her an enormous diamond engagement ring. The stone is even larger than the one Kevin bought for me. Now that I'm moving out, Dr. Dredge--I keep calling him Dr. Dredge but he wants to be called Percy--will be moving in."

Mrs. Tootle revisited the office a few weeks later, with a huge smile on her face. Her pain had markedly diminished with the medicine given to her by Dr. Clepius. The juvenile pachyderm was nowhere in the vicinity of her abdomen, and the religious statue was back on the shelf. Similarly, Lush's jaundice had receded, Ms. Forsythe's pain had abated, and Pedro no longer had indigestion. The office staff was impressed with Cleppy's treatments, and word got back to Kugelman, who was pleased that the eccentric practitioner had actually achieved some success. He felt encouraged enough with the progress of his new partner to take the long anticipated holiday in Italy, which they had put off until he could find some help with the practice. The Levys would be going with them, which Norman hoped would limit their arguments to a minimum, although he wasn't enthralled to hear about the lucrative buyout of Levy's company by Schnitzer Steel.

But Kugelman's confidence in his new partner may have been wishful thinking, for although his bedside

manner was effective, Clepius' haphazard management
style persisted. His slow pace had left many irate patients
fuming in the waiting room as they fasted for their
colonoscopies which were three hours behind schedule.
He had difficulty finding time to call patients back with
answers to their questions or complaints which frustrated
the nurses and medical assistants trying to cover for the
disorganized doctor. Lab work and pathology results
piled up on his desk. Stacks of patient files--the office
was not yet paperless--began to grow up from the floor
like tall weeds, making it difficult to navigate to his desk.
Cleppy enjoyed performing the colonoscopies, albeit
rather awkwardly, and his interaction with his patients
was gratifying, but as Zeus had predicted, practicing
medicine in modern times was more demanding than he
had anticipated. Eventually the arrogant god began to
ponder a return to the ancient mountain, but the notion
of facing Zeus and admitting that he had lost the wager
was enough to keep him at his job.

One morning while Kugelman was still on vacation,
Asclepius was performing a colonoscopy on Mr. Milton
Snodgrass when he encountered the largest polyp that he
had ever seen in his short career. It came upon him like
a giant mushroom on a stalk, but when he approached it
with the scope it frustratingly slithered from his grasp. It
reminded the Greek of Tantalus down in Hades trying
to drink that cup of water. After about fifty minutes
without success, the veteran nurse who had worked with
Kugelman for several years suggested that he perform a
biopsy on the lesion and leave its removal to the senior
gastroenterologist. The Hellene, embarrassed by his lack
of skill, readily agreed. Snodgrass was very understanding

when told that he would need to come back for Dr. Kugelman to complete the procedure. He would be called with the biopsy result in the next week.

Kugelman returned from his trip to Europe, rested and refreshed. He was eager to get back to work. Ominously, the first few hours of the morning were taken up by his office staff complaining about Dr. Clepius. When Kugelman took a peek into the Greek's office, he was astounded by the mountains of papers and documents overwhelming the small room. On top of that, computer entries of Clepius' office visits were mostly blank, while the billing forms were not filled out for many of the procedures that he had performed. Cleppy had told the office manager that he would complete the records when he could find the time, but Kugelman wondered how this could be possible two and three weeks after the encounters. It began to dawn on him that he might need to let the junior man go. Dr. Clepius was an honorable and empathetic fellow, but often he was obstinate, and just a little too cocky. Some of the patients had been helped; still, it was apparent to Kugelman that Dr. Clepius had large gaps in his scoping technique, almost as if he had never had any formal training, never mind his organizational befuddlement. However, the harried gastroenterologist didn't have any other candidates for the job, and he couldn't make it home at the appointed hour without an associate, so he opted to put off any decision on the Greek's future employment.

CHAPTER ELEVEN

Selma was amenable to resuming their counselling as long as it was someone other than Cohen. She did some research and came up with Dr. Penelope Jost, a marital therapist with a PhD. in psychology. Kugelman was hopeful that Dr. Jost could untie the Gordian knot of their tangled marriage, and being a woman, she might have better communication with Selma than the Orthodox rabbi. Within a few weeks, they had their first meeting with the new psychologist. Dr. Jost was not exactly the person that Kugelman had in mind when he contemplated a marital specialist. She was tall, her hair dyed an ash blonde, and she wore a heavy foundation which Kugelman suspected was to cover adolescent acne scars but he couldn't be sure. Her grey-green eyes were surrounded by mascara, complemented by an unstinting application of crimson lipstick with matching fingernail polish. Kugelman estimated that she was about forty years old. She had on a silk blouse, with maybe one too many buttons undone at the top, revealing more of her chest than professionally necessary, and she wore a well-tailored shortish skirt which outlined her athletic figure. Norman couldn't help staring at her long legs crossed directly in front of him, and he feared that their shapely contours might be a distraction from the work at hand.

After the perfunctory introductions, Dr. Jost rambled on about her qualifications, emphasizing her experience and success as a therapist. She spoke with a slight southern drawl, informing them that she had grown up in Nashville and was a fan of the Grand Old Opry and President Andrew Jackson. She had married her husband Albert ten years ago. Albert was appreciably older, a retired investment banker, who had bought a dairy farm and moved to rural Warren County, but they also rented a garden apartment in Hackensack where Penelope--she asked to be called that--lived during the week. Near the end of the session, she finally got down to the marital conflicts that were facing the couple, and she began to ask a few questions. But as Selma was winding up and about to gush forth with her usual litany of complaints, Penelope stopped her. Time was up. As they trooped out, Kugelman realized that the entire hour had been taken up with the therapist talking about herself and Albert. He suspected that they were in for a long siege of appointments if this was the progress that was to be made in each session.

They met weekly. As usual, Kugelman's faults as a husband took the center stage as Selma disgorged all of his marital short-comings, not mincing words to express her dissatisfaction with his imperfections. Norman chimed in with a few mea culpas, and knowing nods of his head, but mostly he stared at the beguiling Dr. Jost. After each complaint, Penelope prattled on about her own marriage and how she and Albert had had similar disagreements, but now that Albert was not stressed by the pressures of Wall Street, he spent more time thinking of her, making delicious salads from the dainty cucumbers, crispy arugula and multi-colored heirloom tomatoes that he grew organically on the farm. She recounted in endless detail about the time he bought a suckling pig from the neighbor and amazed her with a pork roast on her birthday. Last October they had driven to Vermont and stayed at a bed and breakfast where they could look out on a cemetery that contained the dead from the Revolutionary War and Robert Frost's grave. They read "Stopping by Woods on a Snowy Evening" curled up together in front of a roaring fire. Norman mused to himself. *How has this idyllic union got anything to do with my rotten marriage? While this babe and Selma are yukking it up, I'm paying the meter for this bullshit at a hundred bucks a pop. And how does a guy like Albert, milking cows on a farm compare to the day to day stress of a doctor?* But he kept silent, fixing his gaze on Penelope's femurs and tibias while occasionally glancing at her bosom under the revealing tops that she wore, trying not to think bad thoughts, but in truth, he was jealous of Albert and the fun that he must be having every weekend.

In due course, all of Kugelman's malignant miscues as a husband came to light, but his inability to improve his lackluster performance continued. He persisted with the same lame excuses that even he had become bored with hearing. Yes, he admitted, the life of a physician had taught him to be guarded in his emotions, and he had not seen much affection from his parents although by his reckoning they had always seemed happy together and were married for almost sixty years. His problems with fatigue and lack of sleep, a product of long hours at work, were certainly factors that had led to the current situation, for on vacations and some weekends they got along fairly well, but it was the day to day living that seemed to be the main source of friction. Lamentably, those days outnumbered the other ones by a wide margin.

After a few meetings, Dr. Jost turned her attention to Selma and like Cohen asked the same questions about her childhood and adolescence. Selma became somewhat testy when the queries were directed at her, and the bubbly rapport that she had with the therapist when Kugelman was getting grilled wasn't so bubbly when the spotlight was turned on her. Penelope took the same approach in the therapy that Cohen had pursued. She pointed out that Selma would have to be more accepting of Kugelman as a husband even if he had some obvious faults. Maybe cultivating other interests, such as resuming her acting career, would enable her to obtain fulfillment, and that her regret in not pursuing her passion was being directed at Norman. She pointed out that Albert had done just that. He had retired and bought the farm, learned to fly an airplane, hunted moose in Maine in the autumn, and their marriage was so much stronger … and Kugelman wanted to scream. *Forget about Albert, I don't care if he's fucking a goat or reading poetry all day. Your god damned marriage is perfect and ours is shitty. Does that sum it up?*

How many more sessions do we need of St. Albert?

Selma was unwilling to accept Dr. Jost's analysis of her anger, and eventually Norman appreciated that they were heading down the same dead end street that they had travelled with the rabbi. One day the therapist announced that their sessions would come to an end. Kugelman speculated. *Even Dr. Jost, collecting her generous fee, has decided to throw in the towel. It's a hopeless mess, the Kugelman marriage.* But no, that wasn't the reason at all. Dr. Jost was moving to Paris! She had met a banker years ago when she lived in Manhattan. The relationship rekindled after they serendipitously attended the same hot yoga class. One thing led to another, and now he had been transferred to France, so this would be their last session. Kugelman ejaculated, "What about Albert?"

"Oh, Albert will be alright. You know over the past few years we had grown apart, and Albert living on the farm just didn't work out."

Kugelman instantaneously realized that the malarkey about Albert was a cover up for her own unsuccessful marriage. How could Selma and Norman ever get any help from this confused bitch? He contemplated asking for his money back. No, she should having been paying them for all these sessions, but he and Selma had a good laugh when they walked out the door. Selma told him that if he would just pleasantly surprise her from time to time with a little present of some sort, this would go a long way to increase her affection for him, but Kugelman knew that when he did bring flowers or gifts, there wasn't much thrill for Selma, for how could she be surprised when she had requested to be surprised.

Several weeks later, a call came in from Milton Snodgrass for Dr. Kugelman. He told the senior physician that he had undergone a colonoscopy six weeks ago by Dr. Clepius, but he hadn't been called to schedule the repeat procedure, nor had he received the results of the biopsy. Kugelman was distressed by this lack of communication from his junior associate. He told Snodgrass that he would personally search for the report and get back to him. He asked for the patient file and was told that it was somewhere in Clepius' office. His associate was at the hospital making rounds and the secretary was hesitant to search through those charts without his permission. In spite of that, Kugelman and the office manager entered the Greek's office and rummaged through the helter-skelter piles of documents heaped up on his desk, book shelves and the floor. Finally, the communication from the pathologist was located under a small mesa of papers. Then, like a springtime plunge in a cold Canadian lake, Kugelman received the shock of his medical career. The reading on the biopsy stated "a focus of adenocarcinoma in an adenomatous polyp." There was a note by Clepius in the margin dated five weeks previously, "will talk to Kugelman next week when he returns." The polyp contained adenocarcinoma--the medical term for cancer--but the report had been submerged in his office, and the Greek had forgotten to bring it to Kugelman's attention. He sat down in Clepius' chair, and stared up at the veteran employee who had helped him start the practice years ago.

"What will I tell Snodgrass?" he wailed. "I'm sorry you have colon cancer but your report was lost. We're liable for a horrible lawsuit if this malignancy has grown into the wall of the colon and he'll need major surgery. It's been a month and a half. Suppose the cancer has spread to other parts of his body and he dies!" Kugelman was now in a panic, fearful of a horrible malpractice judgment. And what defense would they have? "It got lost under a mound of other paper-work, your honor, and it took six weeks and a patient's phone call to find it." No, there would be no trial, only a settlement for one million dollars, the maximum amount that the practice carried. But in extreme cases, the plaintiff could be entitled to the doctor's personal fortune, and as Clepius had zero net worth, they could go after Kugelman's savings. The insurance company might drop him from coverage, and if he couldn't find a malpractice carrier, he would be out of business. A cold sweat erupted in his palms and blood pounded against his skull as he pondered these awful possibilities. He decided that the only recourse was to call Snodgrass back, apologize profusely for the lost document while not exactly telling him the reason for its misplacement, implying that it could have been the pathologist's fault, the dumb U.S mail, or a dog roaming through the office that might have eaten the report. Anything, but that it sat under a stack of papers on Dr. Clepius' desk!

And that's what he did. Fortunately Snodgrass was a trusting fellow. Kugelman reassured him that if he could remove the entire polyp with a repeat colonoscopy, the problem would be solved without major surgery. But then his wife came on the line. She had numerous questions about whether the cancer could have spread during this delay, and how could a thing like this have happened? She repeated more than once that she didn't want anything to do with Dr. Clepius ever again. Kugelman tried to assuage her anxiety, informing her that the odds of the cancer spreading were very unlikely, but this was exactly the scenario that he most dreaded. He would perform the colonoscopy himself, as soon as possible. Mrs. Snodgrass replied that her husband had a lot of faith in him, implying that her faith in him was not so great after this debacle, but they agreed that he would submit to a repeat examination. The doctor's hands were shaking as he hung up the receiver.

Kugelman confronted Clepius that afternoon. He shoved the fateful document under the Greek's nose accompanied by an expletive. Clepius turned white. He profusely apologized as Kugelman pointed out the potential of a law-suit, and the more Kugelman talked, the more he raised his voice and soon he was screaming at the poor man-god. Finally, Kugelman told him to pack up his things and get out. He was done in the practice. With that, Kugelman stormed out of the office. That evening, when he told Selma about the horrible fiasco, she scolded her husband for hiring that idiot, and not listening to her when she advised him to sell his practice and move to a prosperous exurb which didn't give Kugelman much consolation but he couldn't deny her logic.

Kugelman repeated the colonoscopy a few days later. As he manipulated the colonoscope on its route through the colon of Snodgrass, he made sure to have his best technician assist him just in case this sucker was difficult to remove. When he approached the S-shaped turn known as the sigmoid, the polyp came into view. It had grown minimally since the Greek had been there as judged by the photographs from that exam. The polyp had a long stalk, attaching the head where the cancer was present to the wall of the colon. It flopped around in response to contact with the scope as Clepius had noted in his report. With Kugelman's many years of experience, he seized upon the best method to excise it. He started by removing small bits at a time to make the remaining portion smaller. When he had removed about a third of the lesion that way, he pushed a large snare through the channel of the scope, similar to the basket that he had used to remove the sphere from Midas, and expertly placed it around the stalk like a lasso. He plugged the other end of the snare into the cautery unit, then put his foot on the pedal to activate the current. He closed the snare, slowly burning through the stalk and cutting it in two. Pressing hard on the suction button located on the handle of the instrument, he sucked the excised polyp into the end of the scope. Then he removed the colonoscope with the accompanying polyp and plopped the tissue into a formalin jar.

Snodgrass went home with Kugelman's assurance that the cancer was most likely removed. He and his wife seemed satisfied with the result, but Kugelman spent extra time schmoozing with the couple, hoping to win back their confidence. The final pathology report confirmed that the cancerous part of the polyp had been completely extirpated, and no further treatment was required except for a follow-up colonoscopy in six months. Kugelman breathed a sigh of relief. His fears had been overblown. There would be no law suit and Mr. Snodgrass was cured of his cancer.

Asclepius went back to his apartment utterly dejected. He had put a patient's life in danger, opened up the practice to a law-suit, and revealed his gross incompetence. All these eons he had been kidding himself. He was an idiot to think he could arrive in the twenty-first century and be a success at practicing medicine. What a colossally stupid bet he had made with Zeus and why hadn't he listened to Kugelman, an ethical man with a successful career who had tried to instruct him in the complexities of the job? He wished for guidance from a higher power, but when you're a god, a former god, or a quasi-god, who do you pray to? He had a small statue of Athena in his goat bladder. The Greek deity pulled it out and intoned an old chant that Chiron had taught him when he was still a boy. He heated a gyro in the microwave for himself and thawed a frozen mouse for the pet python that he kept in the apartment. He tried to sleep, but kept waking up, chastising himself for his abject stupidity and arrogance. After a few days of moping around the place, he resolved to meet with Kugelman the following day and beg for one more chance to redeem himself, at least until he could make plans to return to Mt. Olympus and prepare for his trip into hell, which he justly deserved.

After the Snodgrass colonoscopy, the staff straightened up the Greek's office. Although a number of missing reports were found as well as some charts that had been lost for months, no other potentially litigious documents were located. Kugelman began to feel some remorse at the harsh treatment that he had meted out to Clepius. Now that it had all worked out for the best, he recognized that he had overreacted to the Snodgrass incident, but the fear of a malpractice judgment was always in the back of his mind, as it was in the minds of most physicians who practice in the U.S.A., for the courts and the lawyers do not always distinguish between gross negligence, human error, poor judgment, or just plain bad luck. The physician was at the mercy of a jury trial preceded by several months or years of depositions and motions where the plaintiff's attorney endeavored to scare the hell out of the doctor. He had settled a case a number of years ago and to this day was still having nightmares of that experience.

When Asclepius showed up at the office the following day, Kugelman was remorseful for his harsh behavior toward the Greek, and was willing to take him back. Dr. Clepius was contrite, the proud god humbled, as Kugelman went over the mistakes that he had made. This time, he was more receptive to the valid criticisms and vowed not to repeat them again. Kugelman suggested that they hire a nurse practitioner to help both of them with their phone calls and paperwork and they talked well past six in the evening. Kugelman felt a weight had been lifted. He would not be sued, at least not this time, while his associate had hopefully learned a valuable lesson.

On the way home, Kugelman relaxed to the dulcet notes of Mozart's clarinet quintet that piped through the Bose speakers in his luxury car. It had been a difficult day. But as he turned into his driveway, he suddenly recalled that this afternoon was his son's graduation from Junior High School. With all the tumult at the office, he had completely put it out of his mind. The house was empty, and he surmised that Selma and Adam were still at the graduation. He resigned himself to a tongue-lashing or worse from Selma, so he made sure that a blanket and a pillow were on the sofa in the study for use that night. Uncharacteristically, he poured himself a tumbler of Wild Turkey 101 and gulped it down hurriedly. Then he rummaged through the refrigerator looking for something to eat, discovering some roasted chicken and a spinach salad that they had carried in the previous evening. As he was noshing on his dinner, the twosome returned from the school. Kugelman immediately began his apology, acting more penitent than a Trappist monk, relating the events of the day to his spouse, and hoping for some sympathy. However, the only comment from Selma was to reiterate that she had told him not to employ such a worthless piece of shit--Selma could swear like a sailor when she was angry--and she didn't care about Kugelman's feeble justifications. He hadn't bothered to show up to share an important day with his son, and as a father, *he was less than a worthless piece of shit*, but Kugelman was hurt more by the disappointed look on his son's face than by Selma's tirade.

The following morning, Kugelman was taking a shower still thinking about the near disaster with Snodgrass when Selma burst into the bathroom. Kugelman had slept peacefully on the couch, having inured his body to the minor discomfort over the years. He had not appreciated that Selma had been in the bedroom all night pacing the floor. Her sister had undergone elective gall bladder surgery the day before, and not only had Kugelman forgotten about his son's graduation, but he had failed to look in on his sister-in-law at the hospital. Moreover, there had been complications during the night. She opened the shower door and shrieked,

"You rotten son of a bitch! You rotten son of a bitch!" She grasped his right arm with her long, recently manicured finger nails and dragged them down his shoulder, leaving four superficial scratches on Kugelman's biceps. Then she stormed out leaving him to mop up the blood as best he could.

He got dressed and drove into work, his mind numb from the abuse that he had just received. For even if his performance as a husband was substandard, he couldn't believe that he deserved this kind of punishment. Norman cogitated on the hours wasted seeing the unhelpful therapists, searching the high-end stores for expensive gifts, and calling florists to buy those feckless flowers. He was at a loss to explain why Selma hated him, hated him enough to become physically violent. But then he pondered, *if I had picked up the phone and called her, inquired about her sister, and attended the graduation, this might not have happened.* Guilt once again found its way into Kugelman's brain, creating abject confusion. When he entered his office, he slumped in his swivel leather chair, removed the gold encompassed bifocals, and covered his face with his palms shouting *fuck, fuck, fuck!* For his greatest fear was now upon him, the dissolution of his marriage.

A few weeks later, Kugelman announced that he was leaving, at least for a while. Selma, for her part, was exceedingly calm, telling herself that Kugelman would tire of the single life, and soon beg to come home. When he asked to watch a televised Yankees game with his son, she was quick to tell him that he could never enter the house again unless he moved back permanently. Norman was tempted to give it one more try but he was hurt that

Selma never once apologized for her angry outburst and so he didn't. One evening, as he sat in his Courtyard Suite by Marriott, he dialed the number of Polly Polk that he had kept in his wallet all these months. The sweet familiar voice answered.

"Hello this is Dr. Kugelman" he stated in a matter of fact voice. He was conditioned to calling himself "doctor" to any nurse, no matter the circumstance.

"Yes, Dr. Kugelman, it's good to hear from you. Why are you calling?"

"Well, it's a long story and I need to talk to someone. I remember you told me to call you if I ever needed someone to talk to and that someone is now you," he fumbled. "Can we get together maybe tonight?" the tone of his voice rising with anticipation.

"This is rather sudden. Percy and I were going furniture shopping for our new home. You did hear about Percy and me? We'll be getting married next month."

"Yes, I did. Sally told me." His heart sank. He had been hoping that she had seen the true Percy Dredge and had broken off their relationship.

"How about tomorrow after work, at the Starbucks in Hackensack."

"Fine, see you then," answered Kugelman, and he quickly hung up the phone.

Now that there was no need to rush home in the evenings, he found more enjoyment in his work. His terrible battles with the clock that he fought when he lived with Selma began to dissipate. But the next day, as he methodically worked through his patients, some of the old anxiety recurred. He became apprehensive that he might be late for his date with Polly as he had been late for Selma on so many occasions. Fortunately, his schedule went smoothly with no emergencies, and he found himself sitting at the Starbucks five minutes early with a Venti skinny vanilla latte in his hands. He saw her come through the entrance, gorgeous as ever, still wearing her nursing uniform, which in the twenty-first century had changed from white to a shade of pink. He caught her attention with a welcoming wave. She ordered a mocha, before sitting down with the love-starved gastroenterologist.

"So tell me Dr. Kugelman. What is it that you need to talk about so urgently?" inquired the doe eyed nurse, "Is it about Selma?"

"As a matter of fact, it is," replied Kugelman, "and please call me Norman." He started into the entire story about his failed relationship, as newly separated and divorced people tend to do, recalling every slight and insult that had transpired between them. Polly stared at him intently, and as the sorrowful recounting poured forth, she became more sympathetic. The admiration that she had for him going back to when she was a young graduate resurfaced. Kugelman could see in her eyes, or imagined that he could see in her eyes, some affection for him, more than just respect for his abilities.

"But tell me about yourself. You can't be serious with that Dredge fellow?" and the still hopeful Kugelman couldn't hide the disdain in his voice.

"Well, I'm delighted to tell you that for the first time in my life, I'm genuinely in love. You know I was married once before, just out of high school, but we were way too young. Percy has been so kind. He's lavished me with expensive gifts, escorted me to the finest restaurants, and taken me on fabulous trips to Colorado and the Bahamas. Last week we saw a performance of Aida at the Metropolitan Opera. Can you believe it, a simple girl from New Jersey at the Met? We're to be married next month."

"Congratulations, but don't be flattered by all of his wealth. His morals are suspect. I could tell you some stories about him. Plus, I'm not sure he comes by all that money all that honestly. I'd be careful if I were you," and Norman kicked himself for so obviously showing his contempt for her soon-to-be husband.

A flush filled her perfect face as she stared at him, the long eyelashes remaining stationary. "No one has ever treated me the way he has. And what would you know about scraping and saving every penny just to make the mortgage on your house and the payment on your car, while giving your widowed mother some cash every month to supplement her Social Security income. My father had three kids to feed, and he couldn't save a dime for retirement. He died on the job of a heart attack at age sixty-one. Now I have a chance never to worry about finances again. Percy has generously invited Mom to move in with us after the renovations are complete. So don't you tell me about money, Dr. Big Shot Kugelman!" As she stood up to leave, the crestfallen physician, desperate for her love, understood that he had probably blown whatever remote possibility that he might have had with Polly by bad mouthing the devious Dredge. He impulsively grabbed her, and kissed her full on those beautifully full lips. She didn't pull away at first, and Kugelman knew that he had struck a chord in the limbic recesses of Polly Polk. Then she broke from his embrace and left the Starbucks without finishing her mocha or saying goodbye. Kugelman sat there in silence, slowly drank his latte, then rose up from his chair and left. His marriage was floundering on the rocks with a gaping hole in its hull, and the ravishing Polly had not even thrown him a life preserver.

CHAPTER TWELVE

Zeus was relaxed after his back rub performed by a woodland sylph. As he rolled off the massage table, he noticed the treatise that Athena had prepared still sitting on the celestial coffee table. He picked it up and turned to the section on the philosophers, (philo--lover, Sophos--wisdom). Socrates was the first topic, the most famous of the group. Although Socrates never committed any of his concepts to paper, or in those days papyrus, his ideas were preserved through the writings of his student Plato in a series of conversations known as *dialogues* where a character named Socrates carried on a conversation either with himself or interrogated other people. Socrates didn't teach in a classroom, but wandered about the marketplace in the city-state of Athens, conversing with the rich as well as the poor. The former stonecutter was not a handsome man; some described him as ugly. He did not deign to dress in the fashions of the day. He had a tolerance for the cold and harsh conditions so he often went barefoot. As a young Athenian soldier he had been commended for valor in the Peloponnesian wars.

Socrates was driven by an inner voice that told him what he shouldn't do, but never what he should do. His idea of knowledge was primarily concerned with ethics such as friendship and courage and how to live a life of piety. He instructed his students by repeatedly asking them questions, then challenging their logic with more questions, the so-called Socratic Method, a process of teaching still in use today.

The former marble shaper was tried in an Athenian court for the charges of corrupting the youth of the city and being a gadfly--a busybody--but in reality this was a political trial based on his association with several aristocratic citizens who had fallen into disfavor. He was convicted, and offered a choice of death or exile. Socrates chose to drink a cocktail containing hemlock, a poisonous plant related to parsley. He had no fear of death, and believed that the soul was immortal, but if wrong, he would fall into a dreamless sleep.

As Zeus read on, he thought of the spirit of Socrates, now in the Elysian Fields, still asking a myriad of questions. He remembered the deliberations of the gods after his death. Several of his colleagues condemned Socrates as irreverent toward the deities, possibly an atheist, but Zeus promoted him to heaven because of his virtuous life: modesty, honesty and sexual purity, attributes that Zeus and his minions were severely lacking but appreciated in the earthly human. As he continued his study of the text, he ruminated about the inner voice that enabled man to lead an honorable life; one might call it a conscience. Some men had one inside them and some didn't. Yet in many individuals, a belief in god, any god, a scripture, or a myth, might enable the sinner or the sufferer to hear that small utterance and gain some solace. After this profound notion, Zeus fell asleep while the papers that Athena had given him fell to the floor and lay there in a higgledy-piggledy pile.

When Zeus awoke, it was early morning. He had slept in his favorite chair all night, and guessed that Hera hadn't missed him in the empyreal bed because she never did. He called in his slave, the eunuch Castro, to retrieve his daughter's manuscript from the floor, and the Preeminent One began to read again. After skipping through Plato, the stoics, the cynics, and the sophists, he came to Epicurus, a later philosopher, who cautioned against excessive amounts of food, alcohol or sexual encounters. Yet in the modern world, epicurean is synonymous with *a lover of indulgence and sensual pleasures*; in fact, the man lived a life of temperance. He didn't subscribe to the belief that gods bothered with the day-to-day tribulations of man, thus, humans couldn't provoke their wrath. His comments on worship were unorthodox. "If the gods listened to the prayers of men, all men would quickly have perished: for they are forever praying for evil against one another." This phrase aptly summed up most of the wars and vendettas in the history of the world. He was famous for his four part cure for human beings. "Don't fear god, don't fear death, what's good is easy to get, and what's terrible is easy to endure." Wretchedly, the man died from a kidney stone obstruction which is as painful a death as one can envision.

Finally, Zeus reached the last few pages concerned with Aristotle-- the great philosopher and scientist. Aristotle, unlike Socrates or Plato, engaged in scientific inquiry. He regarded the accumulation of empirical facts as an end in itself rather than the Socratic idea to acquire knowledge just to "know oneself," and where Plato was mathematical, Aristotle was biological. He divided the animal kingdom into invertebrates and vertebrates, describing their anatomy, physiology and social habits. His hypothesis that bits of matter called gemmules were passed from generation to generation was confirmed by the discovery of DNA in the twentieth century, but many of his pronouncements were completely wrong such as his theory that the human mind was seated in the heart. Aristotle believed in a god, but his perceptions of god or gods were not of the Olympian sort. This philosopher proposed the *unmoved mover* where everything is in motion except the Supreme Being. God is pure thought, the rational soul, the celestial, and the immortal. Zeus groaned when he came across this passage.

The god put down the manuscript, appreciative of his daughter's scholarship; he would have expected no less from the goddess of wisdom, but he was not particularly encouraged by the paragraphs that he had read. For although these men were brilliant and developed concepts which are still applicable today, and none of them denied the presence of god or gods, there was nothing in their writings that would point to Zeus and his querulous pantheon as the driving force behind their postulates, and he was unsettled by the recurring thought that the Greek gods with all their vices and imperfections imitated man as whom he was, not who he wanted to be.

After he left Selma, Kugelman groped into the far corners of his psyche, trying to make some sense of his muddled life. He had subconsciously pinned his hopes on Polly to find happiness, and after the kiss in the Starbucks, his yearning for her increased even more. To add to his befuddlement, he never completely abandoned his thoughts that the marriage could somehow be salvaged. He couldn't motivate himself to find an apartment and continued to live at the Marriott. Selma, for her part, did not want to live as a divorcee with the stigma that would redound in her social circle, and the downgrade in her life style that would result. She was confident that her wayward husband would eventually return home, forgetting about the flaws in his character that provoked her fury when they lived as a couple, and not having any ideas about how she could improve their relationship once he was back in the nest. Neither of them considered whether there was any affection for one another still remaining in their relationship. Kugelman stopped by on a regular basis to pick up his son for dinner or take him to sporting events. At that time, the couple would have civil conversations about their offspring, but after the kerfuffle in the shower, they both seemed hesitant to engage in any discussions about reconciliation, so their ship of misery drifted aimlessly as more water passed slowly under the bridge.

Word of their separation reverberated through the

community: the synagogue, the country club, and at their son's school. To Kugelman's amazement, but probably not to anyone else's, their friends all sided with Selma, for how could fault be apportioned to this respectable woman, so attentive to all, who never forgot a birthday, an anniversary, or a condolence call, if god forbid, someone should die? Why would Kugelman, who was sitting on top of the world, with a revered profession, a lucrative practice and a loving family, just up and leave? Rumors spread that the doctor had an affair with a nurse at the hospital, and if there was one woman, there must have been several, going back years probably to the beginning of their marriage. He had finally decided to leave before his devoted wife kicked him out. A few weeks later, he was purchasing some microwavable dinners at the grocery store when he ran into the heavily perfumed and perfectly coiffed Cynthia Levy who gave him an obligatory hug in the frozen pizza aisle. They exchanged some pleasantries about their kids who had played junior high basketball together, but Kugelman could see that her voice strained to be civil and he knew she was thinking. *You selfish putz. How could you leave your wife and son to satisfy your mid-life crisis?*

Kugelman performed a follow up colonoscopy on Mr. Snodgrass at his six-month follow up and he was cancer free. Recently, he had seen Johnny Franklin in the office; the pseudocyst on his pancreas had been successfully drained, and there was no smell of alcohol on his breath. Mrs. Tootle continued to improve with the herbs administered by Dr. Clepius, with only an occasional reappearance of the elephant. The office clerk had switched the designation on her chart so that she was now the Greek's patient, not his. Sadly, Daniel Stewart had not been as fortunate. On his last visit, Kugelman had given him free samples of the expensive medication for his colitis, and his disease had remitted. Yet, like many young adults with a chronic illness, he had no compulsion to visit the doctor when he was feeling well, and he hadn't seen the gastroenterologist for almost two years. Kugelman received a call from the young man one evening. He complained of fever, belly pain and worsening diarrhea with the passage of blood; all typical symptoms of a flare of his colitis. When Kugelman saw him the next day, he immediately sent him to the Emergency Room to be admitted. In the United States, if a patient shows up in an ER, by law he cannot be turned away for lack of ability to pay, and therefore can obtain admission for free care from the hospital and all of the doctors. Oh sure, they can bill these individuals, but most people without health insurance also have very little net worth or more likely no net worth, so these bills are never paid and are ultimately written off. Kugelman didn't expect remuneration for his services. Although he could have punted him to a free clinic or a university hospital with a long waiting list, his conscience would never allow him to desert a patient in need.

The exacerbation of Daniel's disease had been more severe than previous episodes. He was feverish and pale from loss of blood. Kugelman noted that his abdomen was slightly distended. He feared that his young patient might be developing toxic megacolon where the bowel becomes so inflamed that it overinflates and may actually burst causing peritonitis and even death. He decided to transfer him to the ICU so he could be watched more carefully by a physician who was present twenty-four hours a day, which was not the case on the non-acute hospital wards of his community hospital. Kugelman infused high doses of hydrocortisone which have been used to treat this complication for over fifty years. He obtained a stat X-ray which showed that the bowel was not swollen and the gastroenterologist was relieved as he reviewed the images with the radiologist.

Within forty-eight hours, Daniel had markedly improved. All of his symptoms had diminished and he complained of hunger, always a good sign in a gastrointestinal patient. Kugelman felt a little sheepish, having placed a non-paying patient in the ICU costing the hospital thousands of dollars per day, but he had learned through long experience that it was better to be cautious than overconfident of one's abilities to treat patients. He had gone through that phase shortly after starting in practice, when like many young doctors, he presumed that he had all the answers to every individual that he attended, but over time, the practice of medicine had become a very humbling profession, and Kugelman now had great respect for all the pitfalls that can occur in an illness. He had seen a few colons perforate from ulcerative colitis and he didn't want to repeat that scenario with Daniel Stewart.

As he was writing the orders for transfer to the medical floor, there was a tap on his shoulder. When he looked up, there was Sally Simpson-Midas, whom he hadn't seen for months. "Hi Dr. Kugelman, how are you? It's been awhile." Kugelman noticed that she seemed happier, and maybe it was some application of makeup and a new hair style, but she appeared more attractive than on their last meeting.

"I'm doing OK," he replied in a laconic voice. "I don't get down here too much and it's a good thing. ICU patients are not my cup of tea and I try to avoid this place if at all possible. I imagine the same thing can't be said for you, if you know what I mean." He had tried to make a weak joke, but Sally laughed as if he was Johnny Carson and it dawned on him that she knew he was separated from his wife.

"You know we should probably get together and renew old times," she offered. Kugelman was surprised by her forwardness, but he heard himself replying, "That's a great idea. How about later in the week? I have Wednesday afternoon off. Let's catch an early dinner at Delmonico's."

"I'd love that!" enthused Sally, and Kugelman silently reflected, *Wow this woman's pulling out all the stops,* no *doubt what's on her mind,* as she rummaged in her pocket for a piece of paper and wrote down her address with instructions to her house along with her cellphone number.

Wednesday came quickly, and soon they were seated at the trattoria, perusing the menu, and engaging in the usual hospital gossip. Kugelman found himself enjoying her company and laughing at her imitations of the doctors that they knew. He couldn't help notice the tight sweater and the glossy lipstick that she wore for the occasion. Eventually the conversation turned to his failing marriage. Kugelman was at first guarded, but he soon warmed to the topic, describing each and every battle in exquisite detail, enough to bore even the most interested party. Despite his ramblings, Sally was an understanding listener. Kugelman revealed his innermost feelings which were not what he had intended. Finally, Sally couldn't resist asking, "So have you filed for divorce?"

"Divorce?" Kugelman responded, slightly indignant. "We are not yet officially separated. Selma and I haven't ruled out the likelihood of a rapprochement." Sally pursed her lips as if that wasn't exactly what she wanted to hear and Kugelman scolded himself. *You idiot. This woman is practically throwing herself at you and you come up with a dumb statement like that.*

"The way you talk, it sounds as if your marriage is kaput."

"Well you're probably right but I'm just a bit confused right now." Then Kugelman hastily changed the subject. "So tell me about yourself."

"There's nothing much to tell. I'm renting a house in Bergenfield, naturally not as nice as the home that I owned before I met Kevin, but my poodle Elmo keeps me company, and I've started making jewelry again. I've enrolled in night school to obtain my master's degree in nursing. You know, I'll be on my own from now on, and I have to maximize my income. My daughter Amy will graduate from college this year but she's not sure if she can find a job. Unfortunately, her major is philosophy, and I might need to support her for a while. Thank god she had that soccer scholarship. My divorce with Kevin is finalized. He pled guilty to tax evasion and has started his three year sentence in federal prison."

"Speaking of Kevin, has he swallowed any more gold stones? I just can't fathom why he ever did that. You've never told me the real truth behind it."

Sally laughed. "I told you once before that you'd never

believe me."

"Why don't you try me," answered Kugelman.

"Did you ever hear of King Midas?"

"Sure, the fellow from Greek mythology, everything he touched turned to gold."

"Yep, that's him. Kevin is a reincarnation of King Midas, only now he needs to put the stones in his mouth in order to turn them partially into gold. The process can take hours and that's what he was doing when he swallowed the rock that stuck in his goose (a term professionals in the gastroenterology business often use for the esophagus). The one you had to fish out."

"That's the weirdest thing I've ever heard" Kugelman remarked. *This woman isn't only starved for a man, but she's a little nuts too, but then again, how exactly did the golden nugget land in Midas' esophagus?* He couldn't think of a plausible explanation for it.

Sally saw that her comment had disturbed him so she didn't elaborate further, and she decided to drop the topic of her ex-husband.

"I had lunch with Polly last week. The wedding was beautiful, and they've moved into a million dollar home in Old Tappan. We hadn't talked since they returned from their honeymoon in Spain," offered Sally, not aware of Norman's secret infatuation or of their meeting at the Starbucks a few months previously. With the mention of Polly, blood rushed to his cheeks, but he kept his face hidden in the menu staring at the list of pastas: the spaghetti, the linguine, the fettuccine, and the ravioli. "How's she doing with my old buddy Dredge," he remarked in as off-hand manner as possible.

"Since the wedding things have not gone according to

plan. It seems that after Polly started working at his office, she noticed that when patients paid in cash, the receptionist put the money in a pouch. Then one day she saw Dredge putting those bills in his wallet and marking the patient's account as unpaid, and in due time, it was written off as a loss. Then Percy instructed the clerk to bill all the office visits as "extensive" instead of "moderate" or "limited" which of course entitled the practice to a higher fee, even if the people came in only for a blood pressure check. She noticed that Dredge performed "copying and pasting" in the computer from previous visits so that it appeared that he had spent considerable time examining each patient even though there were times when he hadn't seen them at all. When Polly confronted him with these facts, Percy moaned that his expenses were out of control and the practice needed more revenue. He told her that all the doctors did the same thing. Polly says he has promised to stop these practices and find other ways to generate income. Sadly, it gets even worse. Just yesterday, I saw him sitting in his Mercedes in the hospital parking lot when one of the techs with whom he had a previous affair, got into the car, gave him a kiss, and they drove away. It didn't take a genius to figure out where they were going. They've been married less than two months and I haven't decided whether to tell Polly."

"She'll eventually find all this out for herself. Dredge's a despicable louse." Kugelman was concerned that Polly had made such a terrible mistake in marrying the corrupt cardiologist, but he couldn't stifle an irrepressible flicker of hope that he might yet have a chance to win that winsome heart. Surely his infidelity couldn't go on forever without her finding out.

He drove Sally back to her place, and was invited in,

ostensibly to show him some new jewelry designs. But no sooner had they walked through the door when Sally embraced him and kissed him full on the mouth, and he could feel her tongue exploring the upper third molar on the left. Kugelman for his part began groping her, feeling her breasts that pressed against him, and he became aroused. She led Kugelman to the bedroom, and he followed her there, but as she lay in the bed, waiting for his advance, he suddenly blurted out, "I'm a married man, I can't do this."

"Can't do what? You're a mature adult separated from your wife. You're lonely, and you need female companionship and god knows I need a man right now. Why can't we just have some fun?"

"I don't know. I'm just a prude I guess. I had a great time tonight. Let's just be friends for now until I sort things out." All at once, Kugelman experienced the same twinge of the guilt that had engulfed him years ago when he had eaten the ham out of the office refrigerator, only this time he didn't partake of the forbidden flesh.

Sally rose from the bed and straightened her sweater and skirt. She showed him her basement studio where the bracelets and rings were crafted. They joked and laughed some more before Kugelman said good night and gave her an obligatory peck on the cheek that even Plato would have been proud of. As he walked toward his car in the cool night air, he wore a silly smile on his face, and he commenced to whistle a tune, "Ode to Joy," from Beethoven's ninth symphony, something he hadn't done in years.

CHAPTER THIRTEEN

Zeus was famished after finishing Athena's thesis. He ordered his slave to bring him some of his favorite delicacies: spanakopita, moussaka, a large plate of spicy shrimp, a few pints of olives, and several baklavas for dessert all washed down by a bottle of excellent Euboean wine. To cap the delicious meal he downed a large helping of ambrosia, ingested by all of the gods and said to confer immortality. A few hours later, he perceived a rumbling and tumbling in his gut. Within minutes, he had the sensation that a large mammal was charging around in there, similar to the pachyderm in Mrs. Tootle's belly, but this was more like a wooly mammoth, make it ten wooly mammoths and a mastodon. If only he could just pass some gas, the pressure would be relieved, yet try as he might, even straining on the divine commode, he was unable to produce even the tiniest of farts. He summoned Panacea and begged for relief. As a last resort, the goddess had him drink a combination of cumin, goose-fat, toad skin, and wasp wing, but with no results. He sent her away with a few choice curses which he later regretted, for despite remaining silent during his diatribe, Zeus could see tears well up in her plaintive eyes. He had a bath drawn by a lovely sylph and the warm water afforded him temporary relief, but upon emerging from the tub, his distress recurred. Finally he summoned Chiron, the old centaur and master pharmacologist, who administered an enema that he had invented, the 3H: high, hot, and hell of a lot. This occasioned a Jovian passage of flatus, which finally rid him of his agony, and he took to the deific bed and slept.

When he awoke, he was determined to achieve respite from these dreadful episodes. He decided to obtain a second opinion. Yes, even gods need a second opinion. The name of Norman Kugelman cropped up in his immortal brain once again, and he convinced himself that a consultation and a colonoscopy might find the cause of his visceral vicissitudes. At first, his plan was to shoot a thunderbolt at the gastroenterologist and propel him into the heavens, employing a similar maneuver that had been successful with Asclepius, yet it was obvious that these missiles lacked the effectiveness of 1200 B.C.; furthermore, there was no colonoscope on Mt. Olympus. In addition, Kugelman was a Jew, and Zeus wasn't at all sure that a non-believer could be brought to his court, for no Jewish soul had ever inhabited Hades after death.

Zeus was on a first name basis with the angel Morris, whom Kugelman had conferred with after his car accident. They had been on opposite sides of a religious conflict over two thousand years ago. In 198

B.C. the Seleucids, a Greek monarchy, conquered Judea. At first, the king, Antiochus III, was favorable to the Jews, allowing them to practice their customs. However, his successor Antiochus IV saw the Jews as a cash cow to fund his many campaigns. He heavily taxed them while attempting to convert them to the pagan ways. This new Antiochus transformed the Holy Temple in Jerusalem to a shrine for Zeus, and banned several Jewish customs: observing the Sabbath, circumcision, the interdiction of pork, and he put Torahs to the torch. The Jews rebelled, led by a man named Judah the Maccabee (Judah the hammer). This fearless warrior defeated Antiochus IV, exterminated the pigs in the Temple, and lit the menorah to dedicate the victory. There was only enough oil for one day but a fantastic miracle took place, and the fuel lasted for eight days. Since then, those of the Jewish faith have celebrated Hanukkah, lighting candles in a menorah for a week and a day commemorating the victory of the Maccabees. This holiday has now become the Hebrew surrogate for Christmas. Jewish kids receive presents on each night that the candles are lit, and thus don't miss out on the crass commercialization of the Yuletide.

Of course, at the time, Zeus was dismayed at the power of the Jewish god, for not only had he defeated the Greeks, but to rub salt in the wound, he had created a supernatural hoo-hah after the battle. Zeus never met Yahweh during the conflict. Instead, the Jewish god had sent Morris as his envoy to do the negotiating. This offended the Olympian who expected a more prominent being in the Hebrew hierarchy than the lowly cherub. Zeus stated his territorial demands before a conditional truce could take place, however, the under angel reported back that Yahweh had said *no dice*. Well, he didn't really say that, but Zeus soon understood that in Antiochus he was backing the wrong horse, and the anti-Antiochus forces were the victors. Shortly thereafter, the Romans arrived with their gods identical to the Greeks, albeit with different names, and then came Christianity. At that point the pagans could have turned off the lights, Hanukkah or no Hanukkah, for it was downhill from there.

Zeus decided to ask Morris about contacting Kugelman. He arranged for a meeting with the heavenly being on neutral ground, just outside the Pearly Gates, in a little café known as God's Half Acre. St. Peter was host. The usual pleasantries were exchanged, some fish and loaves of bread were served, and the holy beings discussed the empyreal news: a plan to construct a new ark in response to rising seas from global warming; the botched revisit of Hercules to earth which had even reached the one-god crowd in heaven; and the resurgence of creationism, which St. Peter bragged was now taught in the Texas public schools and thirteen other states as an alternative to evolution. Then Zeus got down to the business at hand. He wanted to know more about this fellow Kugelman. Morris answered somewhat apologetically, "Well, he's not a religious fellow. I wish he would spend more time in the synagogue, but he's an upright man with the essence of God inside him. In Hebrew, it's referred to as the Shekinah. The guy can't be corrupted."

"We Christians like to call it the Holy Spirit," interjected St. Peter.

"I know all about that inner voice," rejoined Zeus.

"It could be the reason that our mythology went belly-up. All those philosophers with their quest for knowledge and the righteous life, hey, just a few prayers and sacrifices at any Greek temple would have been adequate, and they could have done all the whoring they desired. The Olympic deities, including myself, misread mankind. Nowadays, humans want gods to help them find their conscience and the meaning of their existence. They don't want to hear about all those battles and concubines and the gods' petty squabbles. But let me ask you fellows a few questions while I have you here. Have your religions improved the human experience for the better? Were the Crusades, the Inquisition, or the Thirty Years War any better for man that the Peloponnesian War? Did the destruction of Troy by the ancient Greeks compare to the genocide of the Jews, the Rwandans or the Native Indians?" The other deities stared at their feet, nervously rustled their wings, and kept silent.

"But getting back to Kugelman, will the man take me on as a patient, if I bring him to Mt. Olympus?"

"Oh, he'll treat you," responded Morris. "He never turns down a patient, but a trip to your place is out of the question. In any case, Yahweh would never allow it. Why don't you travel to New Jersey? Make an appointment and describe all your ailments. Then he will probably schedule a colonoscopy. You're ten thousand years past fifty so you shouldn't have any problem meeting the guidelines. Afterwards, he'll sit down with you and hopefully have the answer to your intestinal woes."

"Moe, that's a great idea!" exclaimed the Greek top-dog god. "I'll travel down there, stay with George for a few days, obtain some fake ID and a Medicare card including parts A, B, and D. Perhaps buy some new clothes, maybe meet a fraulein or two, and finally find out why the old gut is in a rut. Why didn't I think of that?

"That's what separates the gods from the God" answered Morris with a sardonic smile.

"You know Moe, you're a pretty sharp apparition. Let me know when your contract with Yahweh is up. I could use someone like you around the mountain." And with that, Zeus travelled back to his palace and made plans for his trip to earth.

Daniel Stewart's condition improved and he was released from the hospital five days later. He was started on prednisone, the oral form of hydrocortisone, but Kugelman knew that he couldn't take this medication indefinitely for there were severe long term side effects including acne, diabetes, and thinning of the bones. He counselled Daniel to keep his office appointments, and the boy was thankful that Kugelman would continue to see him as a charity patient. This time he evinced a determination to follow up on a regular basis after Kugelman's previous prediction of a severe recurrence had been on the mark. The gastroenterologist felt genuinely sad for this likeable kid who had been cursed with such a debilitating illness.

Kugelman continued to see Sally. She was soothingly empathetic after going through two divorces herself, although she often found him annoying, spouting on and on about Selma and their relationship. Kugelman invited himself into her home to enjoy her Irish stew or chicken with dumplings, almost as tasty as his mother's matzo balls. One Sunday evening he arrived just in time to partake of a guiltless baked ham with sweet potatoes, and he offered to set the table. While rummaging in the breakfront to pull out the china, he noticed four golden spheres, and brought one over to Sally.

"Is this the stone that I extracted from your ex's esophagus?"

"Yes, the very same. I'm keeping them for him until he gets out of jail."

"But how did he come into possession of them?"

"I told you, Norman. He was King Midas in ancient times. He was hanging around in limbo, just outside the Elysian Fields, you know, Greek heaven, waiting to gain entrance, but after three thousand years he was starting to despair. When Zeus contacted him to produce more gold for the gods, he jumped at the opportunity. I'm sorry to say, he stepped on the toes of Apollo. That deity wanted him off the mountain, but rather than another trip to Hades, Midas elected to be reincarnated. He promised to bring Greek mythology back to the modern world. Except he turned to Christianity and became a dishonest preacher, where before he had only been a grasping king. Of course you've heard of Hercules? He also came down to perform some modern day assignments. Do you remember when that guy who was trapped under a steel girder? An unidentified man lifted the beam and freed him."

"Yes, I recall that. As a matter of fact, my former nurse assistant, Alice Kapusta, married the fellow. We were invited to the wedding but we didn't attend. You're telling me that guy was Hercules?"

"Yes, that's him. After he met Alice, he quit the god profession. Zeus became ticked off and hurled some thunderbolts at him. They caused that awful storm that we had a few summers ago, but luckily they did no damage. Herky is now in the food business and doing very well selling Herky's Jerky Turkey. He doesn't want anyone to know his former identity, but of course Kevin told me the entire story. I heard that the wedding was lovely with ice sculptures of the Greek gods and delicious ethnic food. You would have enjoyed it."

"I doubt it. These people wouldn't be the types that Selma found interesting. The long trip home would have been miserable listening to her complaints, if you know what I mean."

"And another thing, don't be astonished if that fellow in your practice is one of them as well, that Dr. Clepius."

"You've got to be kidding. I'm flabbergasted that you fall for all that malarkey."

"Have you ever seen his medical degree or the certificates from his fellowship?"

"Well, not exactly, You know I'm a pretty busy guy. He told me that he would forward the transcripts when they arrived and for all I know, they're at the office," but Kugelman mentally kicked himself for not demanding more documentation of the Greek's education. "But he does have a medical license otherwise he couldn't practice in the state." As he was saying all this, it dawned on him that he occasionally wondered whether Clepius had ever received any formal scope instruction, never mind the toga, the goat bladder, the odd looking cane, the snake references, and those weird herbal remedies, but he put all of this out of his mind. It was just too preposterous.

After dinner, Kugelman started back on his favorite subject, "I've been seeing Selma. She's found a psychoanalyst who has helped her gain some insight into our problems, and she wants me to start couples therapy with her. The shrink has recommended a short vacation together, but I've suggested that if we are to have a vacation, let's do it right. We're flying to Maui next month and taking Adam as well. I bought Selma an emerald broach for her birthday which really surprised her for once. She really wants me back. I plan to move in if the trip to Hawaii goes as planned."

Sally frowned perceptibly at the mention of the expensive gift. "Has she told you what might be different this time around? Is she working on the anger issues-- your unpredictable hours, and your self-absorption?"

"No, she doesn't tell me about the topics they discuss. Just that she thinks we could make it this time, and I'm a man who takes his wedding vows seriously.

"Does she love you and you her?"

"Yes I loved her very much, and I guess she loves me or she wouldn't want me back."

"Loved? Guess?"

"No, I meant love. I love her very much," but the lack of conviction in his voice was quite embarrassing. Sally could always find his weaknesses, just like a therapist, no, better than any therapist.

"Sure, take the trip. It's obvious you still want the marriage to work. You would kick yourself if you didn't give it another chance, but remember, your problems always resurface when you are back at work, enmeshed in your practice. At some point, you might need to accept the fact that your relationship just isn't a go anymore."

"I don't think you understand, this time will be different. The separation has done us some good. Selma understands that without me, her life is pretty miserable. I'm going to find more associates to join the practice. I'll take more time off, buy her flowers every week, and give her a kiss on the lips, none of that pecking the cheek, when I leave the house every morning. I can do it. I just need to work at it a little harder." And Kugelman blathered on, in a hopeful childlike tone.

"Well I don't think it would be a good idea for us to see each other again. Selma will blow her stack if she finds out, even if we're just friends."

"You know, I wouldn't be so sure of that, Selma can be charming, particularly if she knows how much you've helped me. I can't thank you enough for listening to my endless nonsense about me, me, me, and she, she, she, if you know what I mean." He grasped her hand and looked into her understanding eyes with the little crow's feet just starting their ambulation along the edges of each lid, "and if it wasn't for my commitment to my marriage, I would have had sex with you that night and probably more than once," he foolishly announced.

"Save that for your wife," she joked, "but I'd like you to have the gold stone that you removed. Kevin will never miss it." Kugelman protested, but to please Sally, he took the sphere with him. The next morning, he placed it on the bookshelf behind his office desk.

Before he left for Hawaii, the senior physician met with Clepius, and reviewed all the additional duties required while he was absent, attempting to prevent the pratfalls that the Greek had committed during the last vacation. The reincarnated man had progressed as a gastroenterologist. His colonoscopy skills improved steadily, while his office management was adequate although lapses occasionally ensued. Stacks of charts still accumulated, and the nursing staff was constantly on his case. Nonetheless, he was considerably more amenable to criticism than before the Snodgrass debacle. Then, just for his own curiosity, Kugelman asked the Hellene about his training in Greece: the names of the professors in the gastroenterology department, the number of colonoscopies he had performed in training, and the location where he had taken the certifying exams. Asclepius seemed flustered and then blurted out;

"The Academy, The Colonoscopy Academy, I learned much of my gastroenterology from professor Chiron, and some of the other physicians, Dr. Pontia Panacea and Dr. Hypsipyle Hygeia. These are some of the greatest gastroenterologists that Greece has ever produced. Believe me, I received better training than any doctor in this country!" and as Clepius raised his voice, Kugelman backed off.

"O.K., just asking. You seemed very inexperienced when you started, if you know what I mean."

"Yes, I had a difficult time adjusting to American medicine, the profession here is not what I expected, and I thank you for your patience. I miss my practice in Greece where the pace is much slower. I can see two or three patients a day, and work in my herb garden."

"You know, I can't say I blame you," replied Kugelman, "but how will we replace you if you decide to leave? I was hoping to find an additional associate so I could slow down a bit and spend more time with my family." *And put my marriage back to together*, Kugelman mused silently.

"I haven't made a final decision, in fact I'm not sure if my old position is still available," as Asclepius reminded himself of his wager with Zeus.

"Just think about it, in another year I'll make you a full partner," as Norman made a mental note to google The Colonoscopy Academy of Greece when he returned from Hawaii.

The following week, Hortense Polk, Polly's mother, arrived for an office visit. She had been referred by Dr. Zuckerman, who had initially suggested Dr. Katz, Kugelman's gastroenterology rival, but Polly had intervened insisting that she make an appointment with Kugelman. Hortense had expected to find the senior physician, but instead Dr. Clepius entered the exam room, informing her that Kugelman was on vacation and apologizing that she hadn't been notified by the office. Hortense was in her late seventies but acted much younger. She was a short woman and walked with the characteristic stoop of a septuagenarian, but even so, her eyes still had a sparkle and at one time she must have been a knockout, for she had a distinct resemblance to her daughter. Hortense frequently emitted an infectious laugh, and her voice had a sweet tone, not the raspy quality that sometimes affects the elderly. When she found out that Cleppy was from Greece, they had a lively discussion about Greek mythology, a subject that had interested Hortense since she had been in high school. She always regretted that she and her late husband had never saved enough money for a trip to Greece. Cleppy immediately sensed a connection with this woman, while her unruly grey hair reminded him of the goddess Medusa who had once helped him with his medical studies.

Recently, Hortense had developed fatigue and shortness of breath when she was in the yard attending to her tea roses. Last month she had passed some blood from her bowels. Dr. Zuckerman had drawn lab work which revealed a low percentage of red cells in her blood and a low iron count. A common cause of this type of anemia is blood loss from the colon. After examining her, the Greek recommended a colonoscopy after Kugelman returned, but there would be a six-week delay before the procedure could be scheduled. Mrs. Polk didn't want to wait that long, besides, she had bonded with the Greek physician. She requested that Dr. Clepius perform the examination.

The colonoscopy was done a few days later. Asclepius was becoming more adept with the workings of the instrument and managed to reach the cecum in twenty minutes, which was a marked improvement in his performance. He was congratulating himself on his success when he saw a reddish protuberance in that area which resembled a large piece of beefsteak with a central depression. When the scope contacted the tumor, the lesion bled easily, and there was no doubt that this was the source of her anemia. Ominously, its appearance was suggestive of colon cancer. The growth could not be removed with the colonoscope, so Clepius obtained biopsies for pathologic confirmation. Polly was at the bedside when he reported his findings, and he showed them pictures of the lesion. It was obvious to the former colonoscopy nurse that the tumor was malignant. She blamed herself for not insisting that her mother have a screening colonoscopy many years ago which probably would have prevented the cancer from developing.

A few days later, the results from the pathologist confirmed the diagnosis. Clepius contacted Mrs. Polk immediately--he had learned his lesson from the Snodgrass episode--and referred her to a surgeon after conferring with Polly and Dr. Zuckerman. Hortense underwent the operation soon afterwards. The news was dire. The cancer had spread into the liver and throughout the abdominal cavity, and the surgeon was unable to remove the primary tumor from the colon. He closed her back up and relayed the bad news to her daughter in the surgical waiting room. Polly didn't say anything as she listened to the surgeon recite the devastating prognosis, acquiring the vacant stare that people evidence when their worst fears are confirmed. Then she quietly started to sob.

Dr. Clepius visited Hortense frequently while she recuperated in the hospital. The elderly woman had been told that the cancer was inoperable. In spite of that, she remained cheerful and continued to have lively chats with Cleppy about his country of origin, displaying a thorough knowledge of the Greek gods including the physician deity Asclepius. She made a satisfactory recovery from the operation, and was referred for chemotherapy, but as the oncologist, Dr. Montgomery, explained, the chance of obtaining a durable remission with this type of advanced malignancy was slim. Although Hortense had decided against further treatment, Polly encouraged her to choose the cancer therapy. Like many loved ones, even nurses, she held out the hope of a long shot cure, rather than accept the fact that her mother's condition was terminal, and so the elderly woman acquiesced with her daughter's wishes.

The Kugelmans' holiday had been uneventful if not spectacular. Norman enjoyed spending time with his son as the couple once again tried to renew the romance that had eluded them for so many years. He pronounced the trip a success, convincing himself that the old spark had been lit and the fire re-ignited, although conceding that the wood was pretty damp. Upon arriving at the office, he was immediately notified of Mrs. Polk's surgery. The gastroenterologist rushed over to the hospital after completing his morning colonoscopies. Polly was there, a worn look on her beautiful face, gained by many hours sitting at the bedside. He came over to her and gave her a little hug with a pat on the back, forgetting the last time he had embraced her. This was the professional Kugelman at work, not the star-crossed lover. Polly informed him that her mother had made an appointment to see the oncologist after discharge. Despite the fact that her prognosis was hopeless, he didn't want to interfere with a decision that had already been made, so he reassured her that if there was a chance of a remission, she should give it a try. You could always stop the treatment if the cancer drugs couldn't be tolerated, and he employed the word you as if Polly herself would undergo the chemo, employing his best physician-speak.

The following morning, Polly called him on his cell phone. He had assumed that it was regarding her mother, but to his bafflement, she requested an urgent meeting in private. They agreed to meet at 5:30 that evening at the Starbucks in Ridgewood now that Polly was living in the well-heeled northern suburbs. When he arrived, she was already there with the mocha in hand. Kugelman ordered some black coffee and a bran muffin--his fiber intake had dropped off appreciably while living at the hotel. The restaurant was crowded and they located a small table near the entrance. Polly was still wearing her nurse's uniform, but even after a long day at work followed by a visit to her mother, she looked as fetching as ever to Norman.

"You look great, as usual," offered Kugelman and he immediately bit his tongue. *The woman's mother is terminally ill, you dolt.*

"Well, I don't feel great," admitted Polly, seemingly not upset at his faux pas. "The news about my mom was a total shock. The woman has never been sick a day in her life and now the time left to her is to be measured in days. But that's not why I'm here. It's about Percy. After we got married, I discovered things about him that I never knew. Did you realize that his license was suspended in Nevada before he moved to New Jersey? And then I learned that he was inflating his office charges and keeping patient cash in his pocket. I told him he could go to jail for fraud. At first he vowed to stop this practice, but he never reformed and when I brought the subject up again, he became very angry. You know he has quite a violent temper. Lately, he stays out all night playing poker with his buddies, or so he tells me. Last week he took a trip to Las Vegas with a few of those friends and left me at home. I need your advice," as her voice started to crack with emotion.

"As a matter of fact, Sally mentioned you were

having some problems," he said. *Now that I'm going back to Selma, this gorgeous woman wants a relationship with me.* His heart started beating rapidly while some extra beats intervened, as they usually did when he was excited. "Do you think he has been cheating on you?"

"Well, he has admitted to one fling with a call girl in Las Vegas. You know, one of those expensive dating services, but he denies any other women. He's promised me that nothing like that will ever happen again, and I trust him." Kugelman knew from Sally that this was another one of the lizard's lies, but instead he responded.

"So you want my advice. How can I help you?"

"I was hoping you might give me the name of your marital therapist. Sally tells me that you're getting back together and I think that's great. If I could just get poor Percy to a counselor, I think we could work things out. You know he had a troubled childhood. His father was a drunk, and his mother died when he was ten years old. He was raised by an aunt who already had five children. It was a miracle that he made it through medical school, but he's brilliant, graduated top of his class. Deep down he's a terrific guy. He's been so generous to me and my family. You know I just adore his children. I didn't want to talk to you about this in front of my mother. Goodness knows she has enough on her mind already."

Kugelman remained stoic, but his hopes were dashed. *That's it. We're here together so I can give her the name of a shrink for Percy the prick. She could have just asked me over the phone. That skunk won't reform in a hundred years and this babe thinks she can fix him. I should straighten her out; tell her she's barking up the wrong tree, not only the wrong tree but she's in the wrong forest on the wrong continent.*

Nope, she doesn't want me, just the name of some therapist for her fraudulent and philandering husband.

"You're right. Selma and I are getting back together. I firmly believe that the therapy eventually achieved results. She's visiting her mother in California who's in a nursing home. She's staying with an old college roommate of mine, Howard Fishman and his wife.

"Not *the* Howard Fishman, the fellow who produced modern versions of Hamlet and Othello and won Oscars for 'Sleepless in Cleveland' and 'Fatal Repulsion'?"

"Yeah, hard to believe that little Howard made it so big, no one could have guessed. When Selma returns, I plan to move back in. Penelope Jost was our first professional therapist, but she's left the country. Now Selma is seeing Dr. Samantha Gregory, whom I have never met, but Selma seems happy with her. We'll be starting couples therapy soon. Before that, we went to Rabbi Joseph Cohen but I doubt a Jewish clergyman is for you, if you know what I mean," and he laughed a little too heartily.

"I guess not, but I'll definitely get in touch with Dr.Gregory, thanks. You know, I always admired you, Norman. Sometimes I even wish that we had become an item. After you kissed me, I thought long and hard about what you said, and I almost called you back. For now, I think Percy and I need to try to work things out, but you never know. Let's keep in touch." *You flirtatious Cleopatra*, agonized Kugelman, *bringing me here with that wide-eyed innocence, oozing sensual pheromones, to talk about your unfaithful husband even while your mother is terminally ill, and then you throw that coquettish curve ball at my phallus that never committed adultery. What am I? An insurance policy if things don't work out with Dredge? Am I to hibernate at the Marriott like a love-sick bear waiting for you to bring me a honey pot after the spring thaw?*

"Yes, things might have turned out differently, but now you have your marriage and I have mine. Please don't hesitate to call me if I can be of help." He sounded like the doctor he was--ending a patient interview. As they got up to leave, he gave her a hug and longingly looked into those beautiful baby blue eyes, but what he didn't see were the eyes of Cynthia Levy, sipping a latte in a rear corner of the restaurant, and witnessing the embrace.

CHAPTER FOURTEEN

Two months later, at three a.m., Zeus arrived on earth. The conversion into a human form had taken longer than anticipated. He had transformed himself into all types of animals: birds, snakes, oxen, dolphins, and of course man, but this transfiguration was relatively tricky, because Zeus needed to keep his godly intestines intact for the colonoscopy. The chariot from Helios had already left for the day so he hitched a ride with Selene, the goddess of the moon, who also drove a celestial cab. Selene had once been one of his lovers, and Zeus, as always, anticipated that she still had some feelings for him. However, she rebuffed the Top-god, refusing to be enticed into the back seat, claiming that the carriage would fly off course, and so the disappointed Zeus sat politely in the passenger seat gazing at the constellations until the vehicle touched down on Flatbush Avenue, near the apartment of Mr. Georgopoulos.

When the sleepy hot dog entrepreneur turned mythological ambassador opened the door, he was befuddled to see a short balding man with a long beard, wearing a hooded cloak and sandals, and smelling of goats. Only his penetrating stare indicated that he might be something more than a peasant.

"Excuse my appearance, my good man," offered Zeus in a rather quiet voice speaking English with a pronounced Greek accent, "but I needed to reincarnate into a man somewhat urgently. A shepherd near Mt. Olympus died a short time ago, and I took on his physical traits. I'm still working on my English. I presumed that the Rosetta stone was an ancient granite with Hieroglyphics translated into Greek, but I discovered that it's also a language company.

"Hey, Zeus. Good to have you aboard. Welcome to the good old USA!"

"Do you have my papers ready?"

"You didn't give me much time, but yes I went to my engraver in the Bronx, and he has your terrestrial name, Aristotle Yanakakis. He stole the Social Security number from a deceased homeless man in that borough. I've obtained a Visa card with your new name on it. I'll take your photo on my phone in the morning and we'll have a picture I.D by the afternoon. Your Medicare card should soon be ready along with your AARP supplement so you'll be covered if Kugelman wants to have a look in your colon. By the way, I recently underwent a colonoscopy myself. The procedure was a breeze. The doctor found two polyps, and I need to come back in five years. The prep is somewhat of a challenge, but for a god like you, it shouldn't be a problem."

"What do you mean by the prep?"

"That's the laxatives you must take to be clean inside. You know, get all the poop out so the doctor can see inside your colon."

"Can't he make an exception for a god?"

"I doubt that. Remember, he mustn't know that you're from heaven or wherever you come from. You have an office appointment scheduled for Friday at four o'clock. Sally Simpson-Midas, Kevin's former wife, remember her? She's a friend of Kugelman's receptionist. She was able to get you squeezed in on short notice. You know I asked her out a few times after she separated from that Midas rascal, but she put me off. Told me she wasn't ready for a new relationship, but maybe she's tired of Greek men. I can't say that I blame her."

"Don't bring up that venal king turned preacher. Pretending to heal the sick with his magical powers, that's something I wish I could do. In which case everyone would have a Greek temple or shrine in his backyard instead of a barbecue pit, and paganism would really be cooking with gas. Do you think this Sally girl might be interested in a date with me tomorrow night? I heard she's a real sweetheart."

"You've got to be kidding. I don't think one night stands are her thing."

"Oh you never know about that," replied Zeus with a puckish smirk on his shepherd's face.

"Never know about what?"

"About the one night stands. I hear she loves dogs, and I could transform myself into a sexy Rottweiler, just for the evening...."

"Forget it, pal. You're not here for that," George replied with some irritation. These mythology types were getting on his nerves and he vowed that this would be his last rodeo with the deities.

"You're right, my good man. I'm on this planet to get a second opinion for my troubled innards. The bloating the constipation, the gas, and the odor you wouldn't believe! Those quacks on Mt. Olympus aren't helping me. I need an expert, an august healer such as Kugelman."

George was blown away at the admission of vulnerability from the god, and he quit picking at the hairs in his nose to respond. "I didn't realize that even gods have medical issues. I was taught in bible school that the Christian god was all knowing and all powerful. There's nothing about him getting sick."

"Well, us Greek gods are a bit different. We're more like men and women, almost brothers to humans. Sometimes we behave well, sometimes not so well, and sometimes we have health issues. If a mortal screws up, he can always find one of the gods who's made the same mistake, and maybe he doesn't feel so much like a sinner. Kind of takes those guilt feelings away; god knows I've made my share of boners. Just ask my wife Hera."

George softened a bit at the honesty of his new charge. "Maybe I can arrange a visit with Sally, but I need to be there to supervise."

"By Jove! That'd be great. I can always stay a few more days if she and I hit it off. Show me to my quarters. We have a busy day ahead, and I've got some shopping to do. I can't look like a goat herder when I have my appointment with the great doctor."

The following morning, a Saturday, the god and his handler headed to the same second hand store where Hercules had purchased his clothing. Zeus looked through the pile of used T-shirts somewhat disdainfully and tried on a pair of sneakers.

"This won't do, George. I need to look like an executive, not a schlepper shepherd. Is there a Brooks Brothers around here?

"We'll have to go into Manhattan. There's a store on Madison Avenue in midtown," responded George. After dealing with Hercules, Midas and Asclepius, nothing mystified him. On the subway, no one glanced at the odd looking man in a goat herder's attire. He was sitting beside a young girl with at least ten rings attached to various orifices on her face while an even larger collection of body jewelry clustered in and around her navel exposed by a meager halter top. Her hair was dyed a bright pink with emerald streaks. Black polish burnished her finger and toe nails while her arms were adorned with the tattoos of two large angel wings and a large serpent arose from her midriff toward her breasts.

"I'll have to tell Aphrodite about these fashions when I get back home," Zeus stated in a rather loud voice, as he stared over at her cleavage, where the serpent's head was ostensibly buried. Nobody looked up from their smart phones. The passengers were too busy texting their friends, viewing You Tube, or playing Candy Crush.

At the clothing store, Zeus picked out two of the most expensive suits, a grey herring-bone, and a navy blue. He purchased two dress shirts of the finest pima cotton, along with a pair of classic Brooks Brothers ties, green and silver, and red and blue, both with wide diagonal stripes. He went next door to the Johnston and Murphy shoe store to buy an expensive pair of cordovan tasseled loafers, then visited an exclusive men's salon, where his beard was shaved, and a bit of Grecian Formula was added to his hair. Eureka! He was Aristotle Yanakakis, billionaire shipping magnate, recently arrived from Greece to see Dr. Kugelman for an answer to his gastrointestinal afflictions.

On Sunday, George drove him to Hoboken to visit with Hercules, who immediately recognized the sartorially dressed man as his father. The former strong-god ushered them around to the tiny back yard behind the duplex and beckoned Zeus and George to sit at the small patio table with an overhead umbrella.

"Hello Father, what brings you all the way to New Jersey? It won't be long before we have the entire pantheon of gods down here on earth. Are you still looking for some more converts to paganism? I haven't seen anybody embracing the old mythology." Hercules couldn't resist a dig at his father now that he no longer feared the jolt of a bolt.

"I'll tell you why I'm here," explained Zeus, ignoring his son's insolence. "I've been getting some pretty severe pain in the gut, except now that you're gone I no longer have a pain in the ass," and he guffawed with gusto at his own joke as was his custom. Zeus could still throw the verbal barb if not the thunderous one. "I've come for a consultation from a gastroenterologist. I'll be seeing Dr. Norman Kugelman tomorrow, and you're right, the ancient religion isn't gaining much traction. You weren't any help, and that avaricious bastard Midas is in prison, but as you know, hope springs eternal even in the breast of a god. I understand you're doing very well in your new career as a chicken producer."

"It is the venerable turkey, Father, Herky's Jerky Turkey." He introduced him to Alice and his stepson Jimmy and the toddler Uri (nobody called him Uranus). Zeus was happy to meet this latest addition to his family; he now had over four hundred grandchildren.

"By Jove, the kid looks big for his age. He already has a strong chest and legs and that head is the size of a six year old. He could be another Giant in the making. We could use some new blood on my team," remarked the Supreme One as he hoisted him into his arms. "Reminds me of you at that age, although I wasn't around much to see you grow up. If you recall, your stepfather, whom I impersonated to seduce your mother, thought you were his offspring for many years. Wow, was that guy hot when he found out that I was the real dad. It's a good thing I'm immortal or he would have killed me!" And Zeus let out one of those hearty roars that scared the tot, and he began to bawl.

"Herky honey, I'm taking Uri inside. Let me know when you father has left." Her icy tone did not belie her dislike of the obnoxious top-god.

"You want to play some catch, Papa Zeus "asked Jimmy. "Herky can really throw the ball. He's like stronger than any man on the block, maybe the universe."

"No, my boy. I sort of threw my arm out tossing those electric missiles from heaven. Maybe later."

"I remember the one you threw at us. That was like really, really scary, but my step-dad was super smart and we never got hurt." Hercules groaned when he heard this bravado from young Jimmy, and feared that the awful

Jovian temper would surface, but Zeus just chuckled.

"You've got a spunky kid there Hercules, or should I call you by your new name, Herky Frum. It's a good thing we're not up on Mt. Olympus or the lad would get a good whupping from me," as he hugged Jimmy good-naturedly. "But tell me, if you're no longer a pagan, are you practicing any religion?"

"Yes, I've become a Christian, a Roman Catholic. I believe in my salvation through Jesus Christ and I hope to go to the Christian heaven one day. I've given up my sinful ways, no more drinking, smoking or whoring. I'm leading a good Christian life, working hard and trying to be a loving husband and a role model for these children."

"Did you ever hear of the Septuagint?" asked Zeus.

"I'm afraid that word is not in my vocabulary."

"The Septuagint was the translation of the Hebrew bible into Greek. In the time of the great city of Alexandria, the pagan king, Ptolemy, had seventy-two Jewish scholars translate the entire Hebrew scripture. That was the Old Testament that the Christians used for years, and of course all the epistles and gospels were initially written in Greek. It was Plato who first described the "oneness of god," but much to my dismay he eschewed the rest of the pantheon, yet I flatter myself that I was the *one God* similar to Aristotle's *unmoved mover*. For two thousand years the Christians used Aristotle's theories, rightly or wrongly, to explain the physical world, and the Popes burned men at the stake for questioning his writings. And the democracy that's so popular in your new country? You think Americans invented it? Think again, my boy. It was the Greeks. And with all these women's rights that are now in vogue, you haven't forgotten Aphrodite and Athena and the other goddesses, including your stepmother Hera, have you?

"How could I forget Hera? That bitch, if you'll excuse my vulgar language, made my existence miserable for ages, but can you blame her? I was the product of your infidelity," grumbled Hercules, anticipating more lecturing from his father, and he was not disappointed.

"And if I'm right, you Catholics don't allow a woman to be a priest, let alone a god," Zeus retorted, ignoring his son's pointed criticism. "We accepted homosexuality 2500 years ago. Alexander the Great was one great gay guy, and I've had a few male lovers myself. So if you throw away your pagan heritage, remember, many of our customs and beliefs were copied by the modern age. I wish you good luck in your new life, but don't ever forget your polytheistic polygenesis. Now I'm hungry and thirsty so let's crack open a good bottle of Greek wine with some tasty sardines followed by a large leg of lamb. Where are your slaves?"

"There aren't any, and that's one cruelty of ancient Greece that we Americans no longer tolerate. We fought a civil war over it. You know, Father, sardines and mutton aren't popular in this country, but I can heat a pepperoni pizza in the microwave with a frosty bottle of Budweiser."

Zeus didn't complain. He was hungry and devoured the pizza and pronounced it to be excellent. The beer reminded him of the batch that Dionysus had once brewed for one of his famous orgies, but he didn't relate this fact so as not to offend the Christian Hercules with his wife and children within earshot. Then they played ball in the parking lot behind the house, with Zeus watching, and Uri came out too. It was amazing how far the little one could throw a baseball, and it wasn't until after dark that he and George left the Frum home.

As they clambered back into the car, George remarked. " Hey, I called Sally this afternoon and told her that you were in town for a few days and wanted to meet her. She invited us to stop by this evening. It's a thirty minute drive to Bergenfield."

"That's great. Did you tell her I was Zeus or Aristotle?"

"I just stated that you were a friend from Greece. I didn't mention who you were, only that you were an associate of Herky Frum and Kevin Midas, so maybe she figured out that you are some kind of king or god."

"Or king of the gods," interjected Zeus. "I should have splashed on some extra cologne, as he checked each armpit with his nose. "These modern gals don't like any body odor."

"You've got to be kidding me. What makes you think you'll get that close?"

"I'm Zeus, with over one hundred concubines. You bet I know how to seduce a wench."

George pulled his 1995 Mercury Marquis up in front of Sally's house and parked the car. They trudged up the sidewalk while Zeus adjusted his tie and slicked back his hair with his hands. Sally was waiting for them at the door, having been alerted by the vociferous barking of Elmo. As they walked into the foyer, she gave George a hug. Zeus was about to embrace her as well, but she stuck out her hand instead, and the Immortal One shook it with a slightly crestfallen look. The two Greeks plunked themselves down on her sofa, then received a thorough sniffing from Elmo. Sally went to the kitchen for some cheese appetizers and wine.

"I'm sorry, but George didn't tell me your name," posited Sally, as she reentered with the refreshments and sat down in a chair across from them.

"Aristotle, Aristotle Yanakakis from Athens. I'm a shipping magnate in Greece. Some people call me a shaker and a mover in that country," bragged the god with a silly grin.

"No, I mean who *really* are you?" asked Sally, ignoring his empty boastfulness. "I'm well aware of the Mt. Olympus cabal that's recently been coming to see us. You must already know that I was married to Kevin, who was one of you. Let's see. You could be Apollo or Dionysus, but I would have expected them to be more handsome. Herky has told me about the ankle wings of Hermes, and I don't see any. If you were Pan, I'd suppose some goat-like features, and I doubt that Poseidon would leave the ocean to visit me in New Jersey. I'm going to presume that you are the chief himself, Zeus, who's come to seek a second opinion for his GI complaints from Dr. Norman Kugelman. I called his office last week and scheduled your appointment."

"You betcha, that's me, Zeus. The top guy in charge of the whole shebang, the one and only, and the big man on campus. In haste, I stole this visage from a dead shepherd or otherwise you'd be knocked off your feet by my regal presence."

"Well welcome to America, Zeus. Is this a short visit just to see Kugelman or will you be passing out some of those Greek mythology pamphlets like Kevin did before he became a preacher and then an inmate. Maybe he still has some copies that he's distributing to the other jailbirds," and Sally laughed that infectious laugh, maybe to hide the hurt.

Zeus joined in the joviality. "Nope, I'm just here to see Dr. Kugelman, and find out about what's causing all that grinding in my gut. You know, you have a great sense of humor, reminds me of Leda, Queen of Sparta. That woman was a hoot. In fact, I transformed myself into a swan, and we had sex. Talk about kinky. She hatched two eggs, my children, Pollux and Helen. Did you know that the dazzling Helen of Troy came from an egg? We could have some fun together, you and I, maybe I can stay over for a week or two, borrow George's car. We could drive up to Nova Scotia, and I could become anything you want and…" George grabbed the god's knee and frowned at him. Then he looked at Sally and shrugged his shoulders as if to say, *I'm sorry that I brought this ignoramus to your place.* But Sally seemed to enjoy the uncouth god's garrulousness, and she cracked up at his outrageous anecdote.

"I don't think I'm the egg laying type Zeus. I've had one child, by natural childbirth, and that's enough. I don't think you and I would be compatible, but someday I might be interested in a jackass again, and I'll give you a call." George practically split a gut laughing while Zeus sort of snorted not knowing if she was making fun of him. Then Zeus became serious.

"I just want you to know that I'm terribly sorry about King Midas. If I'd known that his vices would cause you such grief, I would never have sent him back to earth. Apollo had it right, send the sleazy monarch to Hades and be done with him."

"Well, thanks for your concern, Zeus. I'm getting

over the shock of it all, and back to my old routine, but I guess a rotten apple is a rotten apple. It doesn't matter on which religious tree that apple has grown. But tell me, this fellow Dr. Clepius that works with Kugelman, is he one of…"

"Yes, that's the physician-god Asclepius back on earth working with the mechanical snakes. He thinks he's a better doctor than anyone living today. Did you ever hear anything more ridiculous?"

"I *thought* he was one of you. I've cared for some of his patients in the Intensive Care Unit at the hospital. He's a decent fellow, and with Kugelman's tutelage, he's turning out to be a pretty fine physician. He's got a real feeling for his patients, not like some doctors."

"You don't say. Perhaps I've been too critical of the ancient medicine but god knows Asclepius didn't help me. I made a bet that he wouldn't be able to practice medicine down here. It could be that I was a little hasty in my judgment of him."

At that point George let out a loud yawn, "We'd better be on our way. It's getting late and we have a long drive back. Nice bottle of wine, thanks."

"Yes, nice meeting you Sally, you're a real pussycat. If you ever change your mind about that trip to Canada, and you decide to be my kitty or my turtle dove, I could become a lion or a lynx or a swan again. George will know how to get hold of me." And as he was about to put his arms around her, the hot dog vendor hustled the deity out the door, and into the humid summer air.

Zeus arrived at Dr. Kugelman's office the next day. As he approached the building entrance he noted with pride that below the names of Drs. Kugelman and Clepius there was a small inscription in fine print, "This building is the property of the Uranus Land Company." He threaded his way through the crowded waiting room populated by a young black woman with three noisy kids playing on the floor, an elderly male in a wheel chair accompanied by his attendant, and an auto mechanic just off work still smelling of oil and grease. Zeus was perplexed that a physician of Kugelman's stature would attend to these lower class patients. He had assumed that only the rich would be his new doctor's clients. He strode to the front desk and announced in his customary booming voice. "My name is Yanakakis and I have an appointment with the eminent physician, the great Dr. Kugelman. Is there a quiet area where I can wait for the doctor, and maybe partake of some pastries and a bottle of sparkling water? You don't expect me to sully my clothes and my reputation in the presence of these people, do you?"

The receptionist gave him a cold stare and in her best New Jersey accent replied, "Etha yuh sit in that cheah over theaah," and she pointed to an empty seat next to the mechanic "or yuh leave. It's yoh choice, bustah." Zeus was taken aback by her authoritarian voice. In a way she reminded him of his wife, as he meekly took a seat and thumbed through a worn copy of last year's Sports Illustrated swimsuit edition, making a mental note to subscribe to this publication when he returned to Mt. Olympus.

Ultimately, the receptionist called out his name,

"Mistuh Yana Kock Ass, right this way," and he was ushered into a small room with a scale and a blood pressure cuff. "Take evathing off cept yuh undaweah and put on this paypeh gown." She tossed him a paper bundle that had the texture of ancient papyrus. It unfolded into a cape, and he put it on, open in the back. After about fifteen minutes of sitting and sweating, the gown became damp and soggy under his arms, such that Zeus regretted wasting time buying those fancy suits. Finally, Kugelman knocked on the door and briskly entered. "Good to meet you, Mr. Yanakakis. Who sent you over to us?"

"I got your name from your associate Dr. Clepius. We grew up together in Greece. He told me that you were the best. While I was in the States on a business trip--I'm in shipping--I decided to contact you for a second opinion."

"Tell me about your symptoms," began Kugelman.

"Well, all this started many, many years, probably centuries ago," started the Greek. "Terrible, terrible pains in my gut," as he pointed to his lower abdomen. "I become horribly bloated and I can't pass any gas. If I soak in a hot tub and take an enema, in about six hours I begin to feel better. Recently these episodes have worsened and so has my regularity. Eons ago, Hippocrates told me to avoid beans and started me on the root of the cuckoo-pint plant. I did well for some time, but then he died, sad to say, and I haven't been able to find anybody else. Old Chiron is past his prime and just between you and me, Dr. Clepius was too preoccupied with the dead to give me his full attention."

Kugelman was puzzled by this bizarre story. He attributed some of the nonsense such as eons and centuries to his poor grasp of the English language, but he couldn't resist asking, "Hippocrates? You don't mean the famous doctor that died twenty-five hundred years ago?"

"Oh, no, not him," answered the god, catching himself. "No, this is Haralabos Hippocrates, better known as Harry Hippocrates. He had quite a reputation in Athens, pretty slick with the scope too, but sadly he has been deceased for quite a while."

"Anything you eat bring on these attacks?"

"Well, I love the traditional dishes of our civilization, spanakopita, moussaka, baklava, and of course ambrosia, always ambrosia.'

"Ambrosia? That dessert, with fruit, walnuts and all that whipped cream?"

"You betcha, just like that. The ambrosia that I eat is a special food for gods and contains honey and nectar, but you're on target, I like mine with lots of whipped cream."

"Gods?"

"You see I'm a very rich and powerful man in Greece. My ships travel all over the world, and yes, I'm often referred to as a lord, Lord Aristotle Yanakakis."

"How about stress, any stress in your life?" as Kugelman typed his history into the computer.

"That's another problem. I've had many concubines and you know, when you have this many female companions, things tend to backfire on you. It becomes difficult to mollify the jealousies of all these women. Sometimes I turn myself or my consort into an animal to throw my wife Hera off the scent, so to speak, and that sometimes causes my gut to feel like it's on fire."

"An animal?"

"Yes, I'm really an animal in bed, just ask any of my sexual partners," responded Zeus, nimbly ducking the question.

"I have only one wife and she ties my gut in a Gordian knot too, if you know what I mean," rejoined the gastroenterologist. "Anything else?"

"Well, my religion doesn't give me the comfort that it once did. It's on the decline which causes me considerable anguish."

"Religion, what religion?"

"Oh, I'm a pagan."

"A pagan eh, not too many pagans come in here as patients. We've had some Scientologists, Seventh Day Adventists, Jehovah's Witnesses, Druze, Bahai, and even a Zoroastrian, but I can't remember a pagan in the office."

"Being a pagan can be a challenge. There's lot of gods, temples, oracles and statues to pray to, but it's never boring, not like the one-god religions. I mean a solitary god can be pretty dull at times, but I'm sad to say, polytheism is on the decline. We haven't had a convert for quite some time." Zeus was about to say millennia.

"I see your point. I'm a Jew and those services can stretch out pretty long. All those laws and customs we need to observe can be pretty onerous. Do you ever feel depressed? This can aggravate your gut. As a matter of fact, we often use antidepressant medication for bowel problems."

"I've been diagnosed as bi-galactic but I never took any medication for it."

"You mean bipolar," corrected Kugelman. He quickly finished his history and performed the physical, including a rectal and prostate exam that had Zeus squirming; even gods don't like that finger in their butt massaging that sensitive gland. At the end of the interview, Kugelman asked "Have you ever had a colonoscopy?"

"No, never. Hippocrates had scheduled one but I cancelled at the last minute due to a business emergency. Then the unfortunate man passed away, so I think I'm overdue."

"O.K., we'll set one up for next week, and then I'll come up with some recommendations. You can pick up the instructions from my nurse. She'll go over everything with you. And you'll need a ride. You won't be able to drive after the procedure."

"Not a problem, my good man. I have a friend in Brooklyn, Mr. Georgopoulos, who can give me a lift. Thanks for your time. I'll see you next week."

Kugelman left the exam room with a bewildered expression on his countenance. *Geez the world is full of odd balls and odd bowels and now I think I've seen them all. A pagan with pain in his gut, and I've heard that name Georgopoulos before, but where? And why would such a rich man seek me out for a colonoscopy when he could have gone to any of the high profile gastroenterologists along Park Avenue?*

CHAPTER FIFTEEN

Zeus re-read the instructions for his colonoscopy prep which was scheduled for the following day. He hadn't comprehended the explanations of the nurse at Kugelman's office due to his suboptimal grasp of the English language, so he recruited George for assistance. He quizzed him about the clear liquid diet, wanting to know if wine or goat's milk was on the list, but George repeated the guidelines: broth, water, Seven Up, clear juice and Jell-O. He prepared the gelatinous mixture for the god, and Zeus sampled a morsel.

"This tastes just like the jelly I ingested after we dcfeated the Titans. My mother told me it was frog eggs but I later learned it was the brain of the Titan, Coeus, who was the most intelligent of those monsters, which isn't saying all that much." He pulled a pitcher of crimson juice from the refrigerator and took a sip, "I hope this isn't the bull's blood that King Midas drank to commit suicide before I reincarnated him."

"No that's cherry Kool-Aid, can't you tell the difference between that and blood?" sighed George.

"Of course I can, my good man. I was just testing you," Zeus backtracked. In reality he had never drank any blood.

About ten p.m., George handed the god the first quart of laxative with the interesting name of Movie Prep. Zeus bravely downed it with one large chug, but then he grimaced. "That stuff's awful! Reminds me of the time I when I was just starting out. You know, just after my mother hid me in the bushes to prevent my father from swallowing me. She took me down to the underworld to visit some Giants. The boat capsized after a sudden gale, and I fell into the Acheron, one of the five rivers in Hades. I almost drowned, took in quite a bit of water and it tasted just like that. No, this stuff is worse. Maybe I can take some of it back with me to Mt. Olympus. Remember Tantalus, the fellow who wants a drink but he never quite gets the cup to his lips? This will be perfect for him. I'll let him have a swig of this juice!" Zeus howled, and George shuddered a bit. *You've got to be kidding! This guy's a god? Maybe god of the buffoons. No wonder things are floundering with this joker at the helm.*

Soon Zeus sensed a gurgling in his gut. At first it was a slight tremor, but within minutes he felt a full blown earthquake racking his bowels followed by an overwhelming urge to defecate. He ran to the commode in the one bathroom apartment, almost colliding with George, who was exiting. The descendant of King

Eurystheus was having a flare of his prostatitis at an inopportune time, and was in frequent need of the toilet himself. One explosion led to another, and finally Zeus crawled out of his foxhole to grab a few hours of sleep. At five a.m., George knocked on the bedroom door with the second bottle of Movie Prep. Zeus turned green as he contemplated another taste of the sickening, sweet, salty concoction that even the lowest member of the animal kingdom would never drink for fear of extinction.

"I don't know if I can do this," whined the god.

"Just man up to it. If you don't get it down and Kugelman can't get a good look in there, he will need to repeat the procedure," responded George in a rather stern voice. "I have to treat him like a little kid," he muttered to himself.

Zeus plugged his nose with his thumb and fore finger and drank it down, gagging a few times. He lay back in the bed only to jump up quickly when the second bottle began its work, but by seven-thirty they were in the Mercury, on their way to New Jersey for the colonoscopy engagement.

After checking in, the Olympian hopped up on a stretcher, and was wheeled into a cubicle in the holding area. A very professional nurse, Katherine McKnight, started his IV. She had helped Kugelman remove the golden ball from the Midas esophagus. Recently Kugelman had hired her away from the hospital to work for him at the endoscopy center. Zeus immediately perked up at the sight of the attractive woman. He began chatting about his shipping business and the yacht that he owned, even suggesting that the two of them sneak away on his boat maybe to Nantucket or even the Bahamas where they could watch the sun set, drink a bottle of aged Bordeaux, and then descend below deck for further fun. Ms. McKnight strained to be polite, but gave a pleading look to the anesthesiologist as if to say "Get this dirty old man into the procedure room and put him to sleep."

Kugelman visited with the Greek before the colonoscopy, and was friendly but reserved. He didn't have time for small talk. The first colonoscopy of the day had been difficult and he was behind schedule. The shipping magnate wanted to tell him the joke about the mouse and the gastroenterologist, but Kugelman cut him short, stating that he had already heard that one when in fact he hadn't. Soon Zeus was fast asleep, dreaming of Ms. McKnight as a mermaid splashing provocatively in the Aegean Sea. The examination went smoothly. The divine colon appeared completely normal except for a tiny, benign-looking polyp that Kugelman removed with a forceps. The gastroenterologist made note of some small hemorrhoids which he attributed to his patient's intermittent problem with constipation.

Zeus awoke in his cubicle as if from a restful nap. After all his tribulations from the night before, he had needed the sleep. While Ms. McKnight was obtaining his post-procedure vital signs, Zeus inquired, "When will my colonoscopy begin?"

"It's already completed, Mr. Yanakakis. You're doing just fine. I'll bring Mr. Georgopoulos in to sit with you until the doctor gives you your results."

"I'm already done!" cried Zeus incredulously. "Wow! The miracles of modern medicine! I was swimming with a good looking fish, and the next thing I'm awake, and my colonoscopy is done. You weren't ever a mermaid,

Katy? I *can* call you Katy even though we just met. Just call me Zeus," forgetting his cover momentarily.

Due to the retrograde amnesia of the anesthetic, he again repeated the possibility of the two of them taking a cruise on his yacht. As she was completing his vital signs, he sat up and clumsily tried to put his arm around her waist, but as she pulled away, his hand inadvertently or on purpose made contact with Ms. McKnight's shapely behind. She curtly pulled the curtain across his stretcher and went looking for Kugelman. She discovered him in the break room pouring his second cup of coffee.

"Please come and talk to this jerk so we can get him out of here. The guy tried to grope me as I was taking his pulse. He thinks he's Zeus."

Kugelman printed up Yanakakis' report and parted the curtain where Zeus's stretcher was parked. He and George were having an animated discussion in Greek, and Kugelman interrupted.

"I have good news, Mr. Yanakakis. Your colonoscopy came out fine. I removed a small polyp which appears benign, but I want to see you again in three days. At that time I will have the biopsy report and then I'll give you some recommendations to help with your bowel problems." He gave the Greek a copy of his findings which included some images of his colon.

"I can't thank you enough" enthused Zeus. "The whole thing was a breeze and I want to compliment Nurse McKnight. She did an absolutely fantastic job. This is my friend, Mr. Demetrius Georgopoulos."

"Good to meet you doctor, I've heard a lot of about you," complimented George as he extended his hand.

"I hope nothing bad."

"Oh no, only good things, you have a great reputation."

Kugelman remarked, "Your name sounds familiar. Have we ever met?" He could have sworn that he had heard that voice before.

"No, not that I can recall" the Greek replied evasively. "I live in Brooklyn, don't get over here much."

Then Zeus interrupted, "Did I ever tell you the joke about the mouse and the gastroenterologist?" but Kugelman was already out of the cubicle and on to the next patient.

Meanwhile, Dr. Clepius had completed his hospital rounds and ran into Katherine in the break room. "You won't believe the kook that Kugelman just scoped. The guy is from Greece just like you. A Mr. Yannakakalis or something like that, but he wanted me to call him Zeus."

Asclepius froze for a moment when he heard that appellation. He wolfed down a chocolate donut, then walked over to the recovery area just as Ms. McKnight was pushing Zeus in a wheel chair toward the exit with a fellow trailing behind that Asclepius immediately recognized as George. Although the man in the wheel chair was in human disguise, he instinctively identified him as the real Zeus, surmising correctly that the top-god had come to Earth for a consultation about his unruly bowel, and he felt somewhat slighted that the deity had not looked him up when he arrived in the U.S. At the exit, their eyes met and Zeus blurted out, "Asclepius, good to see you. I was hoping to run into you today."

Sure you were contemplated the physician-god.

"I just had a colonoscopy by your illustrious partner. Everything came out O.K. except for a small polyp. I didn't feel a thing. By Jove, those colonoscopes are amazing. Do you want to see my pictures?"

"I'll just take your word for it," answered Clepius dryly. He didn't want to spend time chit-chatting with this bombastic blowhard any longer than he had to.

"I'm coming back in a few days. The great Kugelman will have some recommendations at that time. How are you getting along? I hope you're not resurrecting anyone from the dead?" Zeus roared at the presumed joke and Ms. McKnight smiled, but Clepius knew he wasn't kidding. Just the thought of those thunder bolts from years ago still frightened him.

"No, nothing like that. Everything's going according to plan. I enjoy working with Kugelman. I've shown him a thing or two about the practice of medicine," boasted Asclepius. He didn't want to let on that he wasn't the successful modern day doctor that he had once imagined, but he wasn't quite ready to concede on their bet. He yearned to return to the old mountain and mentally kicked himself for making such a stupid bargain with Zeus. He walked away and Zeus was wheeled out to the Mercury for the trip back to Brooklyn.

After his schedule of colonoscopies and endoscopies, it was close to two p.m. As Kugelman munched on his late lunch, a hummus and pickle sandwich that he had brought from home, he started to think about the Yanakakis fellow who called himself Zeus. He remembered that the Greek shipper had told him that Clepius had referred him, but strangely Cleppy had never discussed this fellow in all their conversations. Surely he would have mentioned a man so prominent in the Greek community who was coming to him as a patient.

Just then, he remembered to google the Academy of Colonoscopy in Athens. Despite finding ten search pages and numerous references to "Academy" and "Colonoscopy," he could not locate the two names linked together. He thought about the recruiter that had called him that day about Dr. Clepius. Then, abruptly, Kugelman remembered that Mr. Georgopoulos, the same Mr. Georgopoulos that he had seen today, had recommended Clepius for the job. The ugly awareness suddenly came over him that his associate was probably a fraud. Just out of interest, he started reading about the Greek physician-god Asclepius, with his snakes wrapped around his staff, and how he was hurled into the heavens by Zeus for resurrecting Hippolytus from the dead.

That night Clepius received a call from the emergency department. Hortense Polk had been brought in by ambulance. She was hemorrhaging from the colon. He hung up the phone, put on his tan Dockers pants that he had purchased at Macy's to replace his toga, buttoned up his Land's End multicolored checked shirt, slung his badly wrinkled lab coat—with Dr. A.S. Clepius embroidered above the front pocket--over his shoulder, and traversed the one mile walk to the hospital on foot (he had never learned to drive). Mrs. Polk had that pale xanthic complexion of someone who has lost several pints of blood. Her breathing was rapid, as her body pleaded for more oxygen than could be supplied by the nasal cannula in her nostrils, but she was still alert and pleased to see him. She had received two chemotherapy treatments, but it was obvious that the tumor, which had not been extirpated, had started to bleed profusely. After the ER physician discussed her case with Dr. Zuckerman, they agreed to admit Hortense for end of life care. Polly arrived soon after, and Clepius apprised her of the grave condition of her mother. The Greek tried to comfort the distraught daughter, but there was nothing much he could say in such a dire circumstance except to mumble, "We'll do the best we can and keep her as comfortable as possible," which is the same phrase that doctors have mumbled in the past and will mumble in the future. He wrote some orders for an IV and the transfusion of three units of packed red cells--concentrated blood--and went back to his apartment to get a few hours of sleep before morning.

Asclepius arose early the next day. The terminal state of Hortense Polk had greatly disturbed him, and he had tussled with the blankets in his bed until the faint light in the window indicated that dawn had arrived. He took his daily shower—Kugelman had instructed him that this was compulsory in America--grabbed the same scruffy lab coat off its hook, and headed to the hospital. Mrs. Polk was the first patient that he visited. Her vital signs had stabilized, and her color had improved after the transfusion, but her eyes had the sunken, glazed fixation of a person in the last days of her life. Clepius had seen many individuals die in the course of his career, but Hortense was a special patient.

Outside in the hallway he ran into Kugelman, who was making his morning rounds, and he apprised him of the terminal condition of Hortense Polk. Kugelman didn't seem to be listening. Instead, he motioned Clepius to accompany him into an empty consultation room. He quickly closed the door.

"Yesterday, I discovered something very disturbing about you," he started in a somber voice. "I tried to locate your place of training in Greece but when I looked for the Academy of Colonoscopy, I couldn't find it, and as a matter of fact, there is no Professor Chiron, Pontia Panacea or Hypsipyle Hygea to be found, plus Georgopoulos is not registered as a physician recruiter. He's the same guy that brought your buddy Yanakakis in for his colonoscopy. I need to examine your medical license and training certificates to see if they are legit. If not, you will be terminated from the practice immediately."

"You're right. I'm a fake, although not exactly the typical charlatan," replied Clepius in a quiet voice. "I had all my documents forged in order to practice with you. I am the ancient God, Asclepius. I made a bet with the chief god, Zeus, that I could practice medicine successfully in the twenty-first century and show you fellows a thing or two about how to treat patients. Zeus extolled your great skill in removing the golden sphere from King Midas' esophagus but I was skeptical of contemporary medicine and foolishly thought that I was far superior as a physician. But I want you to know that with all the healers that I have worked with, you are the best. Your compassion, your honesty, your knowledge and your skill are equal if not greater than the great Hippocrates himself, and I stand humbled before you."

Kugelman was taken aback by such an admission. *This whole thing is ludicrous.* Then he remembered the story of King Midas that Sally had relayed to him. *Were all these people whacko? Some kind of weird cult?* Instead, he responded, "That's the strangest story I've ever heard.

Maybe one day I'll know the truth, but thank you for the compliments and your respect. And whoever you are, I've become very fond of you, Cleppy, but I'm still going to ask you to leave. I can't have a fraudulent physician in the practice."

"I understand that," rejoined the physician-god. "I'll be out of here in twenty-four hours. Twenty-first century medicine is not for me. The large volume of patients, the paper work, the insurance companies, the threat of malpractice, and the computer entries were extremely stressful. The only aspects of the job that never changed were the gratefulness of the patients, and the same opportunity to help those who were sick and in most need of assistance. And of course, I loved operating the scopes and marveled every day at my journey through the human body, but I'm still deeply troubled by patients that I can't fix, just like you, sir. Unfortunately I'll be returning to Mt. Olympus and conceding to Zeus that I have lost the wager. I've been a complete failure here. I'll accept my fate and be banished to perdition."

"You're a compassionate doctor Cleppy, a real mensch, if you know what I mean. I disagree that you've been a failure. On the contrary you've been a real asset. But when you mention Zeus, you don't mean the real Zeus do you?" countered Kugelman. *Maybe it's me that's nuts and I'm buying into this goofy delusion. Am I losing my mind?*

"One and the same."

"And is that fellow, the pompous guy that I colonoscoped yesterday, your Zeus? The god who threw the thunderbolt at you, and propelled you into the firmament, is that him? He used you as a reference, still,

I wondered why you never mentioned him to me."

"Yep, that's him. After that episode, we never got along. He's not exactly my idea of a supreme god, but maybe you can help him. He's been bothered by that intestinal disorder for years except for the time that Hippocrates was alive. And before I leave, just one more thing, take good care of Hortense Polk. I've grown very fond of her, maybe the mother I never had. You know my real mama was killed at my birth by Apollo."

"Sadly, she won't be in this world for long. This will be a blow to Polly. They're very close."

"You might be surprised," reprised the Greek, "sometimes even terminally ill patients survive longer that any one would believe." Asclepius put out his hand, and Kugelman shook it. Then he put his arm around his former associate, while escorting him out of the room. He would never see him again.

Asclepius went back to his apartment and rummaged through the goat bladder until he found what he was searching for. Then he reconstituted the potion that he had used on Hippolytus so many millennia ago. He justified this action while cursing silently. *Damn Zeus, it's the last noble act left for me on this earth before I do my time in purgatory.* He returned to the hospital and had Hortense sip the concoction in a small paper cup.

The following morning, Kugelman made rounds at the hospital and visited Hortense, who was now on his list. To his disbelief, the bleeding had abated, and she was her usual chipper self. He telephoned Polly to tell her that her mother had stabilized and could be discharged home under outpatient hospice care. Polly requested a house call over the next few weeks which Norman readily agreed to do.

Kugelman arrived at his office and plowed through his usual day. During lunch he noticed a message on his cell phone that must have come through during one of his colonoscopies that morning. It was from Selma. Kugelman had moved back just a few weeks ago. The couple's therapy had commenced with Dr. Gregory while they both saw her individually, a total of three visits per week. Kugelman considered the money well spent if the marriage could be fixed, similar to a leaking basement or a hole in the screen door. Selma was busily planning a trip to China and that's all she talked about these days. But the message indicated that he needed to come home immediately after work instead of attending a drug company dinner to promote a new product for heartburn. Her voice had an icy tone that was often a predictor of bad karma; how bad, Kugelman was soon to find out.

Right after work, the obedient Kugelman *did not pass Go*, but went directly home. He turned his Lexus onto the familiar driveway, and into the immaculately appointed garage that he had spent the entire weekend cleaning, as one of his honey-dos from Selma. When he entered the house, Selma did not greet him. His inner antennae rose, alerting him to imminent danger and directing him to the bedroom. He saw her laying there in the dark, with her arms folded over her face, a posture that she often selected when her husband was in deep trouble. He bent over her to give her a kiss, but she turned her head away. In a gentle voice he timidly asked, "Is there something wrong sweetie? Do you have a headache? Can I get you something for it?"

Selma ignored his questions. "I had lunch with

Cynthia Levy today. She and Max spent several weeks in the Adirondacks this summer and I hadn't seen her for a few months."

"How's she doing? We need to get together with her and Max. I know we've been so busy with one thing and another..."

"You bastard!" Selma thundered. "You fucking, god damned bastard! Don't stand there looking innocent with your thumb up your ass, I know what you've been up to."

"I don't understand," offered Kugelman lamely, having no idea what crime he had committed, but fearful that whatever it was, it must have been a doozy.

"Of course you understand!" shrieked Selma, her fury rising, her eyes fixating on her poor schlub of a husband wringing his hands with that worried look on his countenance. "Don't play that innocent, *I don't know what's going on* act on me. You know goddamned well you were out with that Polk woman just before you moved back in. Cynthia saw you embracing her at the Starbucks. She didn't want to disclose her secret but I dragged it out of her. No sooner do I start hoping that our marriage will survive than you go back to that whoring nurse who's copulating with all the doctors at the hospital. And I know she's not the only one. I had a private detective follow you a few months ago when I contemplated filing for divorce. One evening he discovered your car parked in front of a house whose occupant is a woman named Sally Simpson-Midas. I have pictures of you kissing her in the living room and then accompanying her into another room, most likely the bedroom. I have a photo of you leaving her dwelling with a ridiculous grin on your face. It doesn't take a genius to know what you were doing over there. I didn't mention it to you, as I hoped you had reformed, but I was wrong. Wrong!"

"You don't know what you're talking about," Kugelman responded haplessly. "Those women are just good friends. As a matter of fact, Polly's mother was recently diagnosed with terminal cancer and she's having marital problems and she wanted to know the name of a therapist and I told her about Samantha, and Sally is an old co-worker from the hospital. You met her at a few Christmas parties. We went out for dinner a few times and had a few laughs, if you know what I mean. She gave me some advice as to how you and I could get back together, and it's not what you think, we never had sex..."

His voice trailed off. He was embarrassed at the fecklessness of his excuses even if they happened to be true. "I'm sorry if my actions disturbed you so much, and I promise that I will never see either one of them again." He spoke in the pleading tone of a prisoner about to be executed. He tried to hold her hand but she pulled it away as if the rash of leprosy had just appeared on his palm. His blubbering apologies and tepid renditions of "sorry" had only enraged Selma even more.

"You expect me to believe that bullshit! That fucking bullshit! Sure, stop seeing those sluts and you'll find another tramp at the hospital or in your office to fornicate with. I know you Norman. You can't fool me. This has been going on for years. Here I was, going to therapy with you, trying to make sense of your coldness, your lack of affection, your complete blindness to my needs while you sat there wondering what harlot you would be calling when you got back to the office, hoping for a quickie before coming home at eight o'clock and falling asleep on the couch."

And with that, she leaped off the bed and started kicking and pummeling him with her clenched fists. He held his arms over his face to protect his bifocals from injury and bent into his customary shell reserved for these physical attacks, but then he snapped. He became angry. Angrier than the time a kid in the third grade had thrown his baseball glove into the pond behind his house. Angrier than the time a senior fraternity brother had made him drink a beer which turned out to be urine. Angrier than the time when he was an intern, and the surgical resident forced him to stay until ten p.m. on his evening off to hold a retractor for an emergency gall bladder operation. Angrier than their quarrel after the golf outing, and angrier than the time when she scratched him in the shower. Kugelman locked his arms around her waist and started to squeeze as hard as he could, and then he heard her gasping, "Stop, stop, I can't catch my breath!" and they fell back on the bed entwined in a hater's embrace. Kugelman had the urge to grab her neck and squeeze until she turned blue, to put an end to all the shit that she had thrown in his face all these years, but then his inner voice took over. *Don't be an idiot Norman, don't be a complete idiot.* He relaxed his grip, and got up from the bed.

"This is it!" he bellowed. "I just can't take it anymore!" He rummaged through the walk-in closet, throwing socks, underwear, ties, dress shirts, and a few suits into a suitcase that he yanked down from the top shelf pulling with it some old shoe boxes and a seldom used brief case that bounced off the top of his balding head. Selma lay on the bed watching him pack his stuff and snarling,

"Get out of here you son of a bitch. I can't stand the sight of you with your whore friends. I've wasted my life with you. Howard Fishman told me I was the best Ophelia that he had ever directed! And you can bet I'll tell my lawyer about your abuse. I'll take every penny from you that you ever made!"

"I'm on my way. And do you know where I'm going from here? Do you? I'm going to screw every nurse in the hospital, every single one of them and I'm going to start as soon as I get out of here!"

As he clumsily exited from the dark bedroom, luggage in hand, silk cravats extruding from the edges, he experienced a rush of wind and then the plangent slam of the bedroom door. He lurched down the stairs banging the unwieldy suitcase at every step. At the bottom, he bumped into his son, and the frightened look on Adam's face disturbed him but he could only mutter, "Everything will be alright Adam, don't worry about it," but he knew everything wouldn't be all right. In fact, everything in the Kugelman household was downright lousy.

He checked back in to the Courtyard by Marriott and was greeted as an old friend by Pete, the night clerk.

"Things not working out with the missus again?" inquired the fellow.

"Nope," responded Kugelman, "this time it doesn't look like I'll be going back there."

"Oh, you never know," replied Pete, "I left my missus four times before we finally worked things out."

"Now that must be some kind of record."

"I don't know, maybe. You see, she found a lover, a fella about twenty years younger than me, and then she didn't care what I did or who I was with. I live down the basement, have my own room, and only come up for meals. I can bring all the girl friends I want down there. Like I said, we finally worked things out."

"I doubt my wife will agree with that arrangement," grunted Kugelman. When he got to his room, the same one he had stayed in for all those months, he numbly surfed through the television channels, and as the sleepless night wore on, it became apparent to him that despite his valiant efforts to steer the ship of marriage, it had hit a rock and sunk to the ocean depths.

He knew that the road ahead would be difficult; Selma wouldn't let him off easily. He would need to pay plenty for his freedom; the *Get out of Jail Card* wouldn't be free, and would cost a lot more than a blue $50 bill of Monopoly money. And that emerald brooch that he had purchased just a few short weeks ago, four thousand bucks in the toilet. The Beatles had it right, *Money can't buy me love, can't buy me love, no, no, no, no, no.* He thought about his son, who would be devastated by the news, well, no, he already knew that his parents couldn't get along. Perhaps he might view his father differently from now on, no longer the wimpy clown with his hat in his hands and a phony smile on his face, ready to perform the soft shoe according to his mother's command. They would spend every other weekend together, go hiking and to ball games. He fantasized about Polly Polk, but before they made love he fell asleep.

CHAPTER SIXTEEN

The following day, a stunned Norman Kugelman plowed through his case load of patients, but it didn't surprise him that he was still able to function as a physician, for he had learned long ago to compartmentalize the person Norman from the doctor Kugelman. The urge to kill his wife in that moment of rage had frightened him, and he never wanted to be in that position again. Now that his anger had spewed forth from the recesses of his psyche, he recognized that his malice toward Selma was as great as her malice toward him, maybe more so, and perhaps his forgetfulness and tardiness was a passive-aggressive shield to cover his discontent. Sometimes, two otherwise decent individuals just aren't meant to be man and wife; so be it. He no longer cared that Cynthia Levy and her friends envisaged him as a despicable adulterer and now a wife abuser. Let those people think of him anyway they pleased, he wouldn't be seeing them again. Besides, he could no longer afford the country club membership. They were Selma's friends, not his. With his long work hours and chores on the weekend, he hadn't the time to cultivate his own set of pals, and he'd lost track of all his buddies from high school and college except for his best friend, Howard, whom he hadn't seen for five years. He was pretty much on his own. The rabbi had advised him months ago to pack up and start over, but he had refused to take his advice. It crossed his tortured mind to make an appointment with Cohen for more counselling, but the notion of going back to the synagogue for more sessions didn't appeal to him, at least for the present. Anyway, now that the marriage was over what could a therapist tell him? *Nice try Norman, you picked a lemon in the basket of peaches but maybe you were an onion. I'm sorry you rolled snake eyes the first time around, go back to the crap table and hope for a seven. Why don't you wear a rabbit's foot in your lapel instead of a carnation if you ever walk down the aisle again?* No, he had been to therapy to fix his unfixable marriage and now he had no need for any of them.

He tried to fathom why his tenacious conscience and rigid ethics, things that had made him a good doctor, maybe even a great doctor in the words of Clepius, had not translated to success as a husband. Perhaps if he had been a bit more carefree, sewn a few wild oats in adolescence, played cards all day in the fraternity lounge or gone out every night for a few beers instead of studying in his room until midnight, he might have had a character more well-rounded, more frolicking, and with more pizazz. Perhaps if he hadn't married the first girl that ever looked at his large Semitic nose and seen a handsome Casanova underneath--he had to give Selma credit for that first attraction—and instead played the field and gained more experience, he would have been wiser as to how to be a loving husband. Perhaps another woman, more tolerant of his foibles, more willing to put up with his self-centered preoccupation, somebody less needy than Selma, might have loved him and he would still be happily married, but now he was unhappily married and soon he wouldn't be married at all. But then again, if he had lived a more libertine existence, he never would have entered into and exited out of medical school, survived the torment of internship and the rigors of practice. All these circular arguments rotated in Kugelman's brain as he bent the colonoscope around the corners of all of the colons that he entered that morning. It was time to start life over, put his failure in perspective. Begin again. Or could he?

During his coffee break, he called a divorce lawyer, the same one that his anesthesiologist colleague had employed. Norman knew that he would lose half of his net worth, and be required to pay alimony and child support. His living standards would drastically drop while those trips to Hawaii and Europe would be off the table. The card to get out of jail wouldn't be gratis for him, no siree. He knew Selma was no fool and would hire a smart Jewish guy to be her lawyer just like he had, and these fellows, probably the best of buddies outside of the court room, would know how to drag things out so they could maximize their fees, but that was just how the American system worked. If he was reincarnated in the next world, he would ask to be a divorce lawyer; what a piece of cake. But that was silly, listening to the child-like claptrap of "he said, she said, he did, she did," would not be for him; no, better to tend to the sick, the poor, the derelicts, and the dying, than to talk to a bunch of unhappy rich people who hated each other. Or perhaps he could come back as a Philosophy or English professor, lecturing to perky undergrad girls and testosterone overloaded boys about subjects that would help them cope with life or at least remind them that others before them had tried and failed to cope with life. He regretted that he knew so little of these disciplines, for he had taken mostly math and science courses in order to qualify for medical school; a C in Philosophy might have knocked him out of the running for the few spaces allotted. He wended his way through the last colon and headed to the lunch room. Despite his tribulations, he had not lost his taste for food.

Today's repast was supplied by the buxom lass with the expensive colitis drug. Kugelman had made a mental note to obtain more samples for Daniel Stewart. For the first time, he approached the comely rep as a single man. She was extremely helpful and promised to leave him a whole sack full of the stuff. Daniel would be placed on a compassionate list of patients to receive the medication through the mail. However, it was obvious that she had no physical attraction to the thin on top, mid-century, moderately overweight Jewish man with an overdeveloped proboscis. Kugelman wasn't surprised. He wasn't much of a catch anymore, and now his mountain of money would be more like a mound.

He worked through his office patients until he came to the last. He saw the chart of Aristotle Yanakakis on the door of the exam room and entered with some trepidation. He didn't look forward to another meeting with the boorish Greek, but maybe he could obtain more information about his recently departed associate. Kugelman immediately remembered that as of today, he was on his own and would be working twice as hard, but then again, he had nothing to go home to, so the extra work might be a blessing, at least for now.

The man-god was sitting there in the grey pinstriped suit with the green and silver tie, a concerned expression etched on his borrowed shepherd's face, as he anxiously awaited the words of the great physician. He wasn't concerned about the biopsy result. Kugelman had told him not to worry, and after all he was immortal, still, he feared that the gastroenterologist would tell him that his symptoms were incurable. This fact made him uncomfortable, that he, a chief of gods, should be under the power of a mere earthling.

"Good to see you again, Mr. Yanakakis, or can I call you Aristotle?"

"Actually, I prefer Zeus; most people call me that. It's a name that I acquired many years ago from my father when I was just a chubby baby, so cute that he wanted to eat me up."

"O.K. Zeus, I have good news. Your polyp was benign, as I suspected, although the tissue looked a bit unusual. Some of the cells were misshapen almost like an electrical current had passed through them. The pathologist attributed it to the effect of the cautery that I used to burn off the polyp, but in your case, I never used that method as the lesion was so small.

"Oh, well, maybe it was from the thunderbolts that

I shot off in my youth."

"Thunderbolts?"

"Well, not exactly that," Zeus replied, correcting his malapropism, "as a child, I played around electric wires and more than once, I received a severe shock."

"Well, anyway, everything came out benign, but getting back to your abdominal pain, I've made a tentative diagnosis."

"Bravo!" cheered the god. "Good to hear someone knows what ails me."

"I think you have irritable bowel syndrome and a food intolerance."

"Irritable bowel? I didn't know my bowel could be moody, but tell me, why do my intestines have a disposition to be cranky?"

"That's an excellent question; as a matter of fact, even the gods don't know," as Kugelman evinced a smile and Zeus nodded his head. "But there are things we can do to improve its behavior. I recorded on our first interview that most of your symptoms come on after a voracious meal, which you end with a generous helping of ambrosia."

'That would be true. It's been called the food that keeps the gods immortal."

"How much whipping cream do you add to this food for the gods?"

"I love a creamy texture. I always ask my cook to put in twice the amount indicated by the recipe, but it does increase my waistline," chuckled the Greek.

"Have you ever heard of lactose?"

"Lactose? No, not that I recall. In Greek mythology, there is a two-headed dog named Orthos who was thrashed by Hercules. Is there any relation?"

"Lactose is a substance found in dairy products similar to sucrose in sugar. Some people can't break it down in their small intestine where digestion takes place because of a missing enzyme called lactase. All these lactose molecules reach the colon where they are fermented by billions of bacteria. This process produces large amounts of gas and a sensation of bloating. In people with an irritable bowel, this gas becomes extremely uncomfortable, and leads to just the symptoms that you have described to me. The whipping cream in the ambrosia contains a large amount of this constituent, and if you are lactose intolerant, that would explain the severe symptoms after your meal. We can run a test to ascertain if you have the missing chemical in your gut or you can just cut down on the whipping cream and see if your abdominal pains improve."

"But my ambrosia," sighed the Greek, "it's what I love and I don't think I can live without it."

"In that case, before you devour this god-food, you can take a pill which contains lactase to break down the lactose, and you should do fine."

"By Jove! A pill, a pill will help me!" cried Zeus. "Why couldn't my other doctors make this diagnosis? I knew you were the best!" And with that, Zeus stood up, pumped the physician's hand, clapped him on the back, and abruptly left. Kugelman assumed that he was gone forever, but he was wrong.

The next day was Kugelman's day off. The gastroen-terologist was in the office cleaning up his paper work. He had some time to kill as his appointment with the di-vorce lawyer wasn't until four o'clock. There was a knock on his office door, and there stood Zeus with a wrapped package in his hand and a Hallmark card entitled The World's Greatest Doctor.

"I just wanted to get you a card and this small gift," announced Zeus. On the card were a few verses of boilerplate, expounding on the wonderfulness of his doctor and thanking him for the care, compassion etc.; one that Kugelman had seen many times in the past. But then the god handed him the wrapped gift. It was much heavier than Kugelman anticipated, and he almost dropped it on the floor. He tore through the paper and there it was, a gold ball, almost exactly like the one sitting on the shelf behind him. Kugelman gasped.

"Where did you get this?"

"From Midas, the man who had a great talent to turn stone into gold. Too bad he couldn't put this ability to greater use. He was a louse when he worshiped me, and sadly, he was even worse as a Christian." Kugelman went to the shelf and pulled down the golden sphere that Sally had given to him.

"This is the one that I pulled out of his gullet. His ex-wife told me that he had once been King Midas. He was sent back to the modern world by Zeus to proselytize for Greek paganism. He had lost the *Midas touch* and needed to manufacture the precious objects by putting the stones into his mouth. One of them lodged in his esophagus and I just happened to be the gastroenterologist on call that Sunday morning and I fished it out. Up until now, I didn't believe her story. I would trust that you're not Aristotle Yanakakis but the great Zeus himself, who has arrived on earth for a second opinion."

"Yep, correct on all counts, that's me."

"And Hercules, known as Herky Frum, who lifted that girder off the man's foot, was sent here by you to perform heroic tasks to gain favorable publicity for your religion. He owns a turkey processing plant and has a child named Uranus but they call him Uri. Your grandfather had that name and just for a joke, I used that word, which sounds just like 'your anus' to title my limited liability corporation, but it had nothing to do with my love of the Greek gods, to be honest with you."

"It didn't?"

"Sorry to say no, but tell me more about my former partner Dr. Clepius, whom I trust is the god Asclepius, with the snakes entwined about his staff and the ability to raise the dead. As a matter of fact, I just found out that he forged all his medical certificates. I fired him yesterday."

"I knew he'd be a failure. He thought he could return to earth and be a great doctor again. Told me all my symptoms were in my head. Can you believe that? What an idiot!"

"Well, as I told you on our first meeting, irritable bowel syndrome can be aggravated by depression, so Asclepius was partially correct. You might be helped by an antidepressant, and I believe that since Asclepius has been with us, he has more respect for modern pharmacology, although I have to admit I'm not sure if any of those medications will work for a god. But let me tell you a little bit about your fellow divinity. Once he learned the ways of modern medicine, he turned out to be a damned fine doctor. We parted with mutual admiration for each other. When he told me that he was returning to the mountain, I presume he meant Mt. Olympus. He should be back there any time now. In the future, listen to what he tells you, he knows the ancient and the modern ways, not a bad combination."

"You think he's a good doctor? I've been angry with him since he brought that fellow Hippolytus back to life, but if you tell me he's an accomplished physician then I'll take your word for it. Sally told me the same thing a few days ago."

"Sally? Sally Simpson-Midas, you know her too?"

"Yes, that Sally. George and I visited with her before my colonoscopy. I offered an apology after the deceitful way she was treated by the conniving king. It was the least I could do. After all, it was my idea that he revisit earth, but how did I know he would become a Christian preacher and a dishonest one at that? That Sally's a great gal, and funny, you wouldn't believe. I invited her to come with me to Nova Scotia but she turned me down. I think she's a little too old for me anyway, but maybe you should give her a call."

"If you're out of her life maybe I've still got a chance with her." Kugelman laughed but then he became serious. "While I have you here, can I ask you a few questions about myself? It's not often that one gets to speak directly to a god, if you know what I mean."

"Sure, my good man, anything you want but I already know the questions. I'm not a god for nothing although some say I'm a good for nothing god." Zeus heehawed at his own joke.

"O.K., tell me why I'm a success at preserving life but a failure at living. Tell me why the patients, employees and nurses admire me, but my wife, soon to be my ex-wife, loathes me. I once thought I was a religious man, now I'm not sure that I have faith in god anymore, at least not my god…"

"Yahweh," interrupted Zeus.

"Yes, Yahweh, you know him?"

"You betcha, I know him. We're in the same profession. He's a powerful immortal, but he doesn't have much of a following these days, not many Jews in the world. I'm on good terms with Yahweh's employee, the under angel Morris, the seraph you met when you were in that severe car accident."

"You know about that? Looking back, I was never sure if it wasn't just a dream."

"I checked you out with Moe before I came down for my appointment. He affirmed that you were a superior soul but not as devout as you could be. When he allowed you to eat pork, he didn't proclaim that you chuck the whole religion."

"More religion? You think that might help?"

"No, not exactly. I have a different take on your problem. You see, in every organized society from ants, bees, termites, to humans, there are two countervailing forces: the obedient force that allows the species to work together and make their ant hill, beehive, community or nation to compete with their rivals, and individualistic forces which enables man to make discoveries and become entrepreneurs and advance civilization. Every creature has both in their makeup in different proportions and unfortunately Dr. Kugelman, can I call you Norman?"

"Sure."

"Unfortunately Norman, you have a large amount of the *working together for society gene*; you humans call it a conscience. Our fellow Socrates called it the *inner voice*.

I know that voice, sometimes it drives me crazy," offered Kugelman.

"As I said, you have a surfeit of guilt, even though most mortals have too little, and some none at all, like Midas. That's why you obsessed over the pork. You couldn't just say to yourself *Oh what the hell, if I enjoy a few strips of bacon or a slice of ham, I'm going to eat it.* You had to follow the dictates of Judaism, and if Yahweh tells you it's a sin then by god it's a sin."

"You may be right there. I've always found it strange that when Morris told me I could eat all the pork that I wanted, then for some reason the obsession went away. Maybe if I hadn't been so fixated with my marriage working, maybe it would have worked, or at least I wouldn't have tried and failed at it so many times. I guess that fixing a marriage isn't like repairing a hole in a fence, paving a crack in a sidewalk, or treating a patient with a bellyache. You know, I became so incensed last night that I almost strangled my wife."

"Now we Greek gods give man a choice. If you can't get along with your wife--just look at my relationship with Hera--a desire for a dalliance isn't such a strange compunction for a human. But if you don't like my style, maybe you'll find the chaste and brilliant Athena more fulfilling, the alluring Aphrodite more mesmerizing, or the musical Apollo more comforting, and yes, even Asclepius can be your deity if you need some healing. For some people, the monotheistic god is stern and demanding, a multitude of rules and regulations, and for many humans, that's what they need. Take my son Hercules for example. In the loose laissez faire society on Mt Olympus there were too many temptations, too much sinning, too many nubile maidens, too much wine. He didn't have the will power to resist these attractions, but now he's a devout and pious Christian, a Catholic no less. The father, the son, and the Holy Ghost have shown him a different way to live his life. Some might call it the straight and narrow. He's much happier, so I guess there's a religion or a creed for every man, but sorrowfully in the twenty-first century it's not paganism," and Zeus sighed while his piercing eyes became a little moist. "I'm willing to concede that Greek mythology requires a makeover but all I'm telling you, Norman, is to find your own god, something or someone that gives you comfort and solace and maybe allows you to enjoy life beyond your demanding profession. Could a little carousing, imbibing or a loving woman be so harmful?"

The Jewish physician leaned back in his leather chair, removed his glasses and rubbed his chin, taking in the profundities of the Greek god. Nobody had ever spelled out his problem quite as succinctly as this god or man or whoever he was. Suddenly, it came to him why the prayer books didn't comfort his inner psyche. *They weren't meant for him.* They were meant for the sinner and the only sins he committed were against himself, and there was no section in the prayer book for the *too righteous.* He needed somebody to tell him that a few misdeeds here and there were acceptable and maybe Yahweh himself made a mistake or two or three. Zeus had it right: he longed for a pat on the back, not a kick in the butt. All at once, he felt sorry for the weepy creature sitting in front of him.

"You've given me some insight into my shortcomings. I thank you for that. And I agree that we humans have a longing for god-like spirits to help us with living. Naturally, when we contemplate death, we'd like to believe there's a being in the afterlife to take care of us, but I guess if there's no one there at the end, it really won't matter. The French writer, Voltaire, once wrote, 'If god did not exist, it would be necessary to invent him.' Someday, man or woman might re-embrace polytheism. Heck, we're only in the twenty-first century, and as you said, not one size fits all. In another epoch, multitudes might flock to your temples again. Hades will fill up with all the dead, and that rower Charon, on the river Styx, will need a power boat to ferry all of the people over to the underworld, and new condominiums will be built in the Elysian Fields and that dog…"

"Cerberus--"

"Yes, that dog Cerberus, the one with the three heads will need to mate with Lassie and have some energetic offspring to keep order down there."

Zeus perked up when he heard these pronouncements. He imagined new marble fixtures, a new roof, and a luxury toilet with a heated seat. Maybe a university for nymphs where he would be the headmaster… He caught himself thinking these lewd thoughts in front of the august Kugelman, whom he compared to the venerable Hippocrates.

"Thanks for the encouragement. It could be there's still hope, possibly in the twenty-second century or the two millionth century," declared Zeus, and a grin lit up his visage.

"And I bet your irritable bowel syndrome would improve if you stopped being so preoccupied with your popularity. Worry more about being a loving father to your one hundred and three children, and four hundred odd grandchildren, starting with Uri right here in New Jersey."

Then it was time for his conference with the lawyer. Kugelman arose, came over to the god, and firmly shook his hand, then patted the deity on the back. He directed him to the waiting room where the faithful George was patiently waiting to chauffer him back to Brooklyn, but Zeus instructed him to drive to Hoboken so he could see his son and grandson one last time.

CHAPTER SEVENTEEN

A few weeks later, Kugelman made his house call to the Polk-Dredge residence where Hortense was residing under the care of hospice. It was a long trek from the office but the gastroenterologist never wanted to miss an opportunity to visit with Polly. He had been extremely busy in the practice after the departure of Dr. Clepius, as well as the frequent meetings with his lawyer regarding the divorce. Selma had called him once, and her voice had been desperate. In a sobbing soliloquy she begged Norman to come back and give the marriage another chance. Kugelman almost fell into his old rut, particularly when Selma told him that she was seeing yet another therapist and finally had some understanding of her anger. She was willing to concede that she had resented Norman for his success and her lack of it. But for Norman, the memory of that last ferocious fight was still vivid. For once, he told her that the marriage was unsalvageable and he was not interested in reconciliation, then he hung up the phone. Kugelman moved into a sparse apartment near his office. The only ornaments adorning the place were the golden stones that he placed on the second hand coffee table.

The sprawling dwelling was located in one of the wealthiest suburbs in the state. He parked his car, walked up the immaculately laid tiles of the driveway and pressed the gold encased doorbell. To his amazement, the previously moribund Hortense Polk answered the door. Her unruly hair was coiffed into short curls tinted to a darker shade of grey, and she wore a heavy coating of scarlet lipstick. She had gained some weight, and the color in her cheeks had returned, indicating to Kugelman that she was no longer anemic. In an energetic voice she asked. "What can I do for you, Dr. Kugelman?"

"As a matter of fact, I've come to check on you. I presumed that you would have difficulty coming to the office, but you look fabulous. Are you still in hospice?"

"Yes, they come by every day. They marvel at the progress that I've made. I really don't think I need them anymore."

"I can believe that. I hadn't heard from them, but I guess they report to your primary physician, Dr. Zuckerman. By the way, is Polly around?"

"Come on in, she's making dinner." Just then Polly came out of the kitchen. Even wearing an apron, she looked as desirable as ever. Kugelman embraced her, *nothing to lose at this point,* and Polly gave him an unexpected kiss on the cheek.

"Well, our patient looks terrific," he remarked.

"Yes, it's just incredible" answered Polly. "After Mom left the hospital she continued to improve. The bleeding stopped and her appetite picked up. We visited the oncologist last week and he ran another CT scan. You won't believe this, but the cancer in her abdominal cavity has completely melted away. Dr. Montgomery was dumbfounded. He's never seen just two doses of chemotherapy work so well. Usually it takes six to eight weeks of treatment and then only a marginal remission. He told us it's almost a miracle. He wants Dr. Clepius to perform another colonoscopy to see if the tumor inside her colon has regressed as well."

"Yes, occasionally the chemotherapy has a dramatic effect. Dr. Montgomery should be proud of himself."

"No, it was Dr. Clepius," piped up Hortense. "He gave me some bitter tasting medicine one morning in the hospital and ever since then I've never felt better."

"Hush, mother, that just doesn't make any sense. She keeps talking about some concoction that she received. She must have been delirious that day."

That struck Kugelman like an Olympian thunderbolt. He remembered Asclepius telling him that Hortense might survive longer than anyone believed. Now he understood that she must have been given the elixir that the physician god had employed eons ago, but he knew Polly would never believe him so instead he responded, "Probably so, and by the way, Dr. Clepius has relocated to Greece so I'm looking for another associate."

"I'm awfully sorry to hear that," replied Hortense, "but if you're done with me I don't want to miss the PBS NewsHour. It starts at six." She bustled off to the living room to turn on the TV.

"Your mother's progress is astonishing. She won't need me for anymore house calls. I guess I'll be one my way; my nurse will call you to set up another colonoscopy."

"I'm sorry I put you out by making you come here, but you and I need to talk."

"Talk?"

"Percy and I aren't making much progress," and that beautiful face took on a dispirited expression. "He says that Dr. Gregory is a lousy therapist, and he can reform on his own if I would just stop nagging him. He blames me for having a repeat affair with his former tech. He claims he did it out of anger. He's probably right. I'm looking for another counsellor, at least for myself. But it gets worse. We just received a call from a Medicare fraud agency last week. It seems that the office manager that Percy fired for incompetence has notified the Center for Medicare and Medicaid Services. Now they're sending an inspector to investigate. I told him so many times to be more careful with his billing. He just wouldn't listen. Now I'm fearful that we'll be indicted for intentionally over charging the patients which I found out is a criminal offence. But Percy informs me he was just doing what the other doctors do all the time."

"We?"

"After his office manager quit, I took over. We were having so many marital problems that I just went along with his old billing practices. Our relationship was bad enough without more arguments, and yes, I knew what was going on but I just couldn't stop him. I even contemplated a trial separation to let things cool off, but now with the Medicare investigation, I just keep thinking of you."

"Why would you be thinking of me?" queried Kugelman, his heart pounding with excitement.

"Percy really respects you, always telling me 'that Kugelman is an honest guy, he runs a tight ship in his practice.' I was praying that you might get involved, talk to him, and help us through this," as she batted those magnificent blue peepers slowly filling with tears.

The scent of her lavender perfume wafted over him. He glanced at her generous breasts, heaving with the rhythm of her burgeoning sobs. His first impulse was to obey the wishes of this woman who filled his dreams. He would agree to meet with Dredge and give him some guidance on the business end of medical practice, while letting him know that he had a gorgeous and caring wife. It would be the honorable thing to do. Someday Polly would see the light and break up with Dredge and then maybe, just maybe, he'd have a chance. But then Zeus's words came back to him and instead he offered, "I'll give you some counsel. Leave the son of a bitch right now. He'll never be any good. He'll never change his ways and he'll cheat on you every chance he gets. He's a rotten bastard. Everyone but you is aware that he's banged or tried to bang every available female at every hospital that he's ever worked at and even some where he didn't work. He's performed unnecessary procedures to rake in as much money as his grubby hands can possibly grasp, and no, *all the other doctors* don't do this *all the time*, only swindlers that prey on innocent people, and bilk the government for as much as they can. It's vermin like him that contaminate the medical profession, and I'll tell you another thing. Testify against him. Take the government's side; admit you made a mistake, and the feds will probably go easy on you. You'll need a lawyer and I can help you with that. Let's get together at my place tomorrow evening. In the meantime, I'll work on finding you some legal advice. Don't make the mistake that I did, and spend years trying to salvage a marriage that can't be saved." Then he paused and added, "You know, I've wanted to make love to you ever since you were my nurse after the car accident."

Polly looked at him incredulously. "You mean leave Percy now and turn against him? You must be joking! How can I leave him in such a crisis? A man who has taken care of me and my mother, put us up in this fabulous home, bought me the best jewelry, taken me on so many trips, and whose two kids are closer to me than their own mother. You know, he loves me so much. How dare you suggest I divorce him?" Her voice rose to a shout. "I'll be taking my mother to Dr. Katz for her next colonoscopy, and I wouldn't screw you if you were the last fucking man on this earth!" The sobbing became crying. The large limpid tears increased in number and overflowed the now stony blue eyes, smearing her mascara. They travelled down her cheeks producing small rivulets in her makeup. Kugelman back tracked through the hallway to the front door. When he reached the porch, she slammed the door. He felt the rush of wind as the door closed behind him, and he appreciated that her door slamming was just as vehement as Selma's ever was.

When Kugelman got back to his apartment, it was past seven p.m. He dialed the number of Sally Simpson, and her honeyed voice came on the line.

"Hello."

"It's Norman."

"Oh hi Norman, I haven't heard from you for a while, how are you getting along?"

"You were right."

"Right about what?"

"Right about everything. Right about me and Selma and my marriage, and now I believe that King Midas was your husband and he produced the golden stones in his mouth. And you were right. Asclepius was the Greek god of physicians. He faked his medical credentials, and he brought Hortense Polk back from the dead. I met with Zeus himself and helped him with his irritable bowel syndrome. He gave me some advice about gods and men, and he told me to call you. Now I'm giving you a call to tell you that you were right about everything and I agree with Zeus. You are a great gal. I'm sorry that I ever doubted you."

"Well, that's O.K. You know you're a great doctor but maybe not so great about living life for yourself."

"Isn't that the truth? Can I come over tonight and talk more about this?"

"I'm just sitting at home with Elmo so of course you can stop by."

"That's great, I feared that maybe you found someone else and then you wouldn't want to see me."

"Nope, you're still in luck. I'm just simple Sally sitting at home on a summer evening."

"And one more thing, I wondered if I might bring an overnight bag and maybe my toothbrush and some dental floss as well."

"Sure bring it all. I'll open a bottle of wine." After Kugelman hung up the phone, he picked up the golden spheres from the coffee table and gave each one a little kiss. Then he jumped in his Lexus and gunned it over to Sally's house as fast as he could.

Zeus was soaking in the bathtub in the regal quarters, when the timorous Asclepius came calling. Since his reentry to Mt. Olympus, Zeus had taken his lactase tablets faithfully before gorging on the ambrosia, and had not suffered any attacks of the gripe. The Supreme Being had given up on the idea of reintroducing Greek mythology to the human race, at least for now. After knocking nervously on the bathroom door, Asclepius heard the booming voice of his boss.

"Come on in and close the door, there's a draft out there."

"I guess you heard what happened down on earth, sire," offered the physician-god contritely, prepared to endure the wrath of the Preeminent One.

"Heard what?"

"That Kugelman fired me, and I didn't exactly wow anyone with my knowledge of medicine. I had a lot to learn about doctoring in this millennium. And then I brought that woman, Hortense Polk, back from the dead. Well, she was almost dead."

"You betcha, I know about all of that. I keep track of every god's performance including you. Are you interested in seeing my spreadsheet?"

"So you're not angry, and no thunderbolts?"

"If I wanted to throw an electric missile your way, you would already have one on your kisser and you wouldn't be coming here with that frightened look on your face. You'd be up in Orion or the Big Dipper or knocking on the International Space Station for some cold compresses for your puss." Zeus hadn't lost any of his boastfulness.

"I lost the bet and I'm prepared to take the trip to Tartarus and spend the rest of my days in Hell. I'm willing to replace Sisyphus if that's my punishment."

"On the contrary, you did good things down there, my boy. Kugelman told me you were one hell of a healer. So you didn't lose the bet, I did. I'm sorry. I guess I underestimated you for all those ages. From now on you're my doctor, and I want you living here in the palace where I can get medical advice immediately." Zeus emerged from the soapy water, dried himself off, stepped into a clean ivory tunic with gold embroidery and slipped into a pair of royal sandals with the help of Castro, his new bathroom attendant, whom he had promoted to keep his salacious impulses in check.

"Let's go for a walk," suggested Zeus. Then the two of them sauntered into the woods near the palace until they came to an anthill, and Zeus began, "See these insects. When I kick the nest with my foot, the female soldier ants come out to attack me. They want to protect the queen. There's a whole civilization in there. You know it's just possible that in another million or two million years these critters will take over the earth and replace men. When that happens they will need some gods to help them live and die just like humans do today. Then, my boy, we'll get another chance. Let's not blow it the next time around. My era has come and gone. I'm not sure I can ever mend my ways but I'm willing to give it my best shot. Nevertheless, I think we need a fresh god to help with the operation, a new CEO so to speak, and I'm appointing you and not just because you won the wager. You're the kind of righteous, straight-laced deity that we need, someone to come in and clean house, so to speak. Sure you're a bit humorless, but that's not a trait that people generally look for in a god. I'm going to step back, become more like the chairman of the board without the day to day duties of running the place. Do something else with my eternal existence. I'll stop chasing after all the nymphs in the galaxy and settle down with Hera. I've never been much of a husband as I'm sure you can attest. I'll visit all my grandchildren, watch them grow, and I'll study the Greek scientists, philosophers, playwrights, and poets; some of the most brilliant minds that ever walked the face of earth. He pulled out the last page of Athena's treatise, which concerned the writings of Aristotle and he began to read:

Suppose there were men who always lived underground, in good and well-lighted dwellings, adorned with statues and pictures, and furnished with everything in which those who are thought happy abound. Suppose, however, that they have never gone above ground, but had learned by report and hearsay that there was a divine spirit and power. Suppose that then, at some time, the jaws of the earth opened, and they were able to escape and make their way from those hidden realms into those regions that we inhabit. When they suddenly saw earth and seas and skies, when they learned the grandeur of clouds and the power of winds, when they saw the sun and realized not only its grandeur and beauty but also its power, by which it fills the sky with light and makes the day; when, again, night darkened the lands and they saw the whole sky picked out and adorned with stars, and the varying light of the moon as it waxes and wanes, and the risings and settings of all these bodies, and their courses settled and immutable to all eternity; when they saw those things, most certainly would they have judged both that there are gods, and that these great works are the works of gods.

ABOUT THE AUTHOR

David Margolis retired from the practice of gastro-enterology in 2013. His stories have appeared in several medical journals, humor sites, and literary publications. His first book, *Looking Behind: The Gaseous Life of a Gastroenterologist*, a collection of biographical and humorous short stories, was released in 2013. He resides in St. Louis, Missouri with his wife, a dog, and a set of golf clubs.